MURDER
in
FIRST CLASS

BOOKS BY HELENA DIXON

HELENA DIXON

MURDER
in
FIRST CLASS

bookouture

Published by Bookouture in 2022

An imprint of Storyfire Ltd.
Carmelite House
50 Victoria Embankment
London EC4Y 0DZ

www.bookouture.com

ISBN: 978-1-80019-545-5
eBook ISBN: 978-1-80019-544-8

This book is a work of fiction. Names, characters, businesses, organizations, places and events other than those clearly in the public domain, are either the product of the author's imagination or are used fictitiously. Any resemblance to actual persons, living or dead, events or locales is entirely coincidental.

This book is dedicated to all of the unsung heroes and heroines of the railways. The steam enthusiasts who give up weekends and evenings to fundraise, manage and run the trains for us all to enjoy. Thank you.

PROLOGUE

Torbay Herald – June 1934

Caught at Last!

Inspector Pinch of Exeter Police has confirmed that Ezekiel Hammett, wanted for the murder of his half-brother, Denzil Hammett, in the city last September is finally behind bars. Hammett is also suspected of murdering Mrs Elowed Underhay in Exeter in June 1916, along with a series of serious offences including attempted murder of a police officer in Brixham in January, assault, smuggling, arson and other charges.

After evading capture for several months Hammett was finally captured after information was given to the police leading them to his whereabouts in a cellar in the city. Hammett is currently being held at Exeter Gaol.

Sensational Evidence at Tower Hill Trial

The trial continues at the Old Bailey in London of the men arrested for the robbery at the world-famous Tower Hill jewellery establishment. Some of the jewellery and silver taken *during the violent robbery, in which the shop assistant, Arthur Perks, was brutally assaulted, has still not been recovered.*

The men behind the robbery are suspected of being members of a notorious underworld criminal gang and may have been responsible for several other high-profile violent robberies in the capital.

Evidence was given today by a key witness in the trial. Mr Simon Travers, a civil servant, delivered a dramatic eyewitness testimony identifying the accused as having been involved in the robbery at the jewellers.

It is expected that a verdict on the various charges faced by the defendants will be delivered in the next few days. Tower Hill Jewellers are offering a substantial reward for information leading to the recovery of the missing items of jewellery and silver.

ONE

Kitty Underhay frowned at her newly acquired fiancé, Captain Matthew Bryant.

'I cannot believe the lengths I must go to in order to secure an interview with Ezekiel Hammett. Even if permission is granted Inspector Greville says that there is no guarantee that Hammett will agree to see me. I have applied to the Home Office, the governor of the gaol and now I have resorted to Hammett himself.'

She replaced the cap on her fountain pen and set it down on the open leaf of the writing bureau. They were taking morning tea in her grandmother's spacious salon at the Dolphin Hotel in Dartmouth. Bright summer sun shone through the large leaded panes of the bay window, which afforded a fine view of the embankment and the River Dart.

Her emerald and diamond engagement ring caught the light as she picked up the envelope to seal it, sending sparks of refracted light glittering onto the plain plastered ceiling.

Her fiancé gave her a sympathetic smile. 'Hammett is a dangerous man. It's taken months for the police to capture him.

The trial is to be held in London due to the severity of the charges and to try and prevent an escape bid.'

Kitty sighed. She knew Matt was right but even so she desperately wanted to finally confront the man who she believed had been responsible for the death of her mother all those years ago.

Since their arrival back in Dartmouth from Yorkshire a couple of days previously she had been feeling oddly out of sorts. The hotel was busy, but she was still on holiday, her grandmother assuring her that she could be spared for a few more days.

'Lucy and Rupert must be in France by now,' Kitty changed the subject. She had recently been bridesmaid for her cousin, Lucy, at her marriage to Rupert, Lord Woodcomb. She and Matt had become engaged themselves during their stay and had curtailed their visit when Inspector Greville had sent word of Hammett's capture.

'Do you think you would care to travel abroad for our honeymoon?' Matt asked, his eyes twinkling with amusement at Kitty's ready blush.

'I'm ashamed to say I haven't given it any thought yet. Everything has happened so swiftly we haven't even discussed when the wedding should take place.' It was true, all pleasure in Matt's proposal of marriage had been overshadowed by the news about Hammett.

Her grandmother had been delighted to learn of their engagement when they had returned from Thurscomb Castle. Together with her friend, and Kitty's least favourite person, Mrs Craven, they had already attempted to embroil her in discussions about lace, orange blossom and wedding invitations.

Before Matt could respond, the black Bakelite telephone next to Kitty gave a short ring, signifying a call had been transferred from the reception desk downstairs.

Kitty picked up the receiver and listened to Mary, her

receptionist. 'I see, thank you.' She looked over at Matt who had moved from the sofa to stand in front of the window gazing out at the busy river scene below. 'Matt, it's a call for you.'

He crossed the room in a couple of long, loping strides and accepted the receiver from her. Kitty removed herself to take his place at the window. She didn't wish to be thought nosy, but she wondered who could be telephoning Matt at the hotel. If it had been Inspector Greville or Doctor Carter, the police doctor, then Mary would have said, but her receptionist had said the call was from London.

She affected an interest in rearranging the vase of peony blossoms that stood on the table in the centre of the bay while she listened in discreetly on Matt's conversation.

———

Mary transferred the call from the internal line to the external one. Matt flinched and held the receiver a little further away as the familiar bellow of his former employer barked into his ear.

'Matthew my boy, taken my staff all morning to get a hold of you. Understand congratulations are in order, eh what?' Brigadier Remmington-Blythe always conducted his conversations on the telephone at high volume. Matt suspected that the brigadier believed he would not be heard unless he shouted.

'Yes, sir. Thank you.' He also knew that a man in the brigadier's position deep in the secret service was unlikely to be calling merely to offer congratulations on his engagement to Kitty.

'Splendid, splendid. Got a small favour to ask of you, my boy.'

Matt braced himself for the meat of the brigadier's call. He glanced over to where Kitty was fiddling around with a vase of flowers, conscious that she was listening to the call. He winked at her, causing her to blush and smile back at him.

'Certainly, sir, how can I be of assistance?' He knew there would be no point in trying to wriggle out of anything the brigadier requested. He wasn't a man accustomed to being refused. He also conveniently tended to forget that Matt no longer worked for him, having set up his own private investigation business in Torquay over a year ago.

'You'll have seen the newspapers, no doubt? This trial that's on at the Old Bailey? The Tower Hill robbery?'

'Yes, sir.' Matt's interest was piqued. The capture of the gang of notorious jewel thieves had filled the pages of the papers now for several days.

The brigadier harrumphed and cleared his throat before continuing. 'Yes, well, fact of the matter is we have a problem with the chief witness in the case, Travers.'

'Simon Travers?' Matt had seen the name in the press.

'He's a member of our department. Been working undercover on a few operations. Now, we think there is a credible threat against his life from several quarters. There are also a few other concerns about him. You may have seen in the papers that some of the items stolen in the robbery have not been recovered?'

Matt could believe this would be the case about Travers's safety given the publicity about the trial. He didn't see where the brigadier thought *he* might fit into the scheme of things though.

'So, to get to the nitty-gritty, I'm worried, Bryant. I think there may be problems internally with the department. Nothing I can put my finger on, but enough to make me think that Travers can't be placed in the usual safe houses. I'm sure you can appreciate why I'm unable to be more specific. Security clearances, don't you know.' The brigadier coughed again, and Matt saw Kitty's delicately arched eyebrows rise slightly as she heard this statement.

'Hmm, quite a problem, sir.' Matt had an inkling of what was coming but decided to let the brigadier spit it out.

'Need to get him out of London for a bit. Can't go too far in case he has to go back and give more evidence. Or, not that it's likely, but in case anyone shady tries to get in touch with him, or he with them for that matter. Keeps dodgy company. Somewhere safe, quiet, where he can blend in with a crowd. Then it came to me. Thought of you.' The brigadier sounded quite pleased with himself.

'Sir?'

'Yes, Torquay, seaside what, capital. A stranger won't stand out amongst the day trippers and holidaymakers, eh. Need you to put him up for a couple of days. Keep a friendly eye on him. Shouldn't cause you any bother. The department will pay, of course. We'll pop him on the train at Paddington at lunchtime and you can collect him from Dawlish at three-fifty. Better for him to get off there, throw anyone watching off the scent, eh.' The brigadier chortled at his ingenuity.

'But, sir...' Matt didn't even know why he was trying to protest. It seemed he would be entertaining an unexpected house guest for a few days.

'Capital, tell people he's your cousin or an old school chum or something. Oh, and by the way, he'll have his dog with him.'

The call ended before Matt could protest any further.

Matt replaced the handset and heaved an exasperated sigh.

'The nerve of that man. I take it you heard all that?' He turned to see Kitty trying to conceal a smirk.

'Would you like me to drive you to the station at Dawlish this afternoon?' Her grin widened.

'I had thought I'd left all this nonsense behind when I left the department. Let us hope there is no trouble during his stay.'

'Will the brigadier let the local police know Mr Travers will be staying with you?' Kitty asked.

'I'm not sure. He may telephone Inspector Greville I

suppose.' Matt drummed his fingers on the polished wooden top of the bureau.

'Will there be any danger to you?' Kitty asked. A look of concern flitted across her elfin features. 'I mean, if someone does discover this man's whereabouts then they may make an attempt on his life, or yours.'

'I doubt anyone will find him. The plan seems to be that in just over an hour he'll be seen discreetly onto the train accompanied by his dog and then we shall meet him at the station in Dawlish.' Matt glanced down at his wristwatch. 'I'd better telephone the house and ask my housekeeper to prepare the guest room.'

Matt owned a small cottage in Churston, near the golf course, on the other side of the river from Dartmouth.

'I would offer a room here, but the Dolphin is fully booked at the moment.' Kitty slipped her arm around his waist. He could see that she was still concerned.

'Thank you, but I rather think the brigadier wants me to keep a close watch on him. I'm sure it will all be fine. If this Travers fellow is in danger, then there will be precious little time for anyone to act. By the time anyone discovers where he's gone it will be time for him to return and then he'll be the brigadier's headache again.' He gave her a reassuring hug.

'At least you will be able to recognise him.' Kitty shook her head as she picked up a folded copy of the *Torbay Herald*. A grainy black-and-white image of Simon Travers was placed prominently below the article about the trial on the centre of the front page.

'I suppose so. I think the dog may be a giveaway too.' Matt grinned at his fiancée.

Kitty laughed. 'Very true. It's a good thing you like dogs. You said you wanted to get one yourself.'

'Indeed. I had made some enquiries about some Labrador puppies before we went to Yorkshire. We have a little time before we need to set off to collect Travers. Come to lunch with me and I'll tell you about them.'

Kitty collected the letter she had been writing before the telephone call. 'Very well, let me go and collect my things. I can post this on the way and after lunch we'll motor down to Dawlish and meet the train.'

She reached up to kiss his cheek and darted from the room. Matt watched her leave before allowing the smile to slip from his face. He had been quick to reassure Kitty, but the brigadier's request had troubled him.

He knew his former superior well and there had been definite coded warnings during their telephone conversation. There was every likelihood that, despite the precautions that had been taken, someone would try to find Travers during the next few days. Not that it would affect the outcome of the trial. The evidence had already been given. No, if any harm were to befall the man, it would be a revenge attack.

He couldn't help wondering about the other reasons the brigadier wished him to observe Travers. The papers had indeed reported that a quantity of jewellery and silver was still missing. Did the brigadier really think that Travers might know something about it? The remark about the kind of company the man kept had been a clear hint. It was all very mysterious.

TWO

Kitty had folded back the roof on her little red Morris Tourer. The car had been a gift from Matt at Christmas, and she was proud of her newly developed skills as a motorist. Matt usually preferred to travel around on his Sunbeam motorcycle. His experiences in the trenches during the Great War had left him with a strong dislike for enclosed spaces.

The sun was still shining brightly as they bowled along the country lane leading out of Torquay and on towards Dawlish, a small neighbouring coastal town.

'I'm glad I used plenty of pins to secure my hat,' Kitty remarked as a sudden gust blew in from the sea to tug at the narrow-brimmed straw confection perched on top of her short blonde curls.

Matt glanced at her, a smile curving his lips. 'Then I'm glad too, or I suppose I would have been deputised to retrieve it from whichever tree or cliff face it may have landed on.'

They had enjoyed a leisurely early lunch at one of the tea rooms in Dartmouth. This had been followed by a walk along the embankment beside the river, before collecting Kitty's car from its shed and setting off to retrieve Matt's house guest.

To Kitty's relief their conversation had been mostly about the trial in London and speculation about Mr Travers's involvement in the case. Then they had discussed Matt's intention of acquiring a dog. Neither of them had brought up the subject of a wedding date. It wasn't that she didn't wish to be married to Matt but talk of a wedding so soon after becoming engaged somehow made her uneasy.

Matt's first marriage had ended tragically several years ago when his wife and baby daughter had been killed in a bombing raid on London. It had taken him a long time to come to terms with those events and Kitty didn't want there to be any pressure or hurry to plan their own nuptials.

There was a lot to consider. Where they should live, for instance. Matt had his own house in Churston, and Kitty lived-in at the Dolphin, so she was easily at hand to assist her grandmother with running the hotel. Her grandmother was not getting any younger and Kitty was concerned about how this could all be managed once she and Matt were married.

She pulled her car to a halt outside the small stone-built station that was situated right on the seafront, near where the river flowed out onto the beach.

'I can see why the brigadier felt it better that your man alight here instead of Torquay. There are a lot more day trippers here and there is a lot of commercial traffic too.' Kitty looked around at the horse-drawn wagons and carts mingling with the motor cars and lorries.

Matt pulled back the cuff of his light summer jacket to check the time on his watch. 'The train is due in at any moment. We had better hurry.' He jumped out and crossed around the bonnet of the car to open Kitty's door for her to get out.

Together they hurried inside the station to wait for the arrival of the London train. The waiting room was busy with passengers waiting to board and others, like themselves, waiting to greet those leaving the train at the stop.

Kitty wished she had a few of Matt's inches as she struggled to see through the press of people. The air was filled with cigarette smoke mingling with the heady scent of violets from the perfume that was made and sold in the town. It was now a sought-after commodity amongst visitors all keen to acquire a souvenir of their visit.

Presently over the noise of chatter she heard the sound of the train approaching and the smell of smoky steam replaced the previous scents as the train wheezed to a halt at the platform.

Those boarding moved forward, and Kitty managed to obtain a view of the locomotive. She was about to ask Matt if he could see Mr Travers when a piercing scream rang down the platform cutting through the hubbub.

Kitty clutched at the sleeve of Matt's jacket and tried to see where the sound had come from. To her dismay she spotted a familiar summer hat adorned with artificial blue flowers popping out of the window of one of the first-class carriages.

'Help. Police. Murder!'

'Isn't that...?' Matt started to ask.

'... Mrs Craven,' Kitty replied. 'Yes, it is, and I have a horrid feeling that your Mr Travers may have met an unfortunate end.' She hurried alongside Matt to where Mrs Craven was busy preventing her fellow passengers from exiting the carriage.

'What's a goin' on then?' The portly stationmaster had also hastened to the spot, along with a small group of interested onlookers.

Mrs Craven peered around, a look of relief dawning on her pale face when she spied Matt and Kitty's approach.

'Matthew, Captain Bryant, you must summon Inspector Greville. There has been a murder and one of these people must have committed it.' She was forced to withdraw her head back inside the carriage at the end of her statement and Kitty could hear a number of voices vociferously denying any such thing.

Mrs Craven's place at the window was swiftly taken by a young man of a similar age to Kitty. His good-looking face was flushed with annoyance, and he spoke with a distinct cockney accent.

'Ain't nobody 'ere killed no one, but the old bird is right, the geezer's dead.'

The stationmaster was galvanised into action by the man's confirmation that there had indeed been a death aboard the train. He promptly ordered everyone on board to disembark, except the occupants of the affected carriage.

'Keep watch for a moment, Kitty. Do not allow anyone to leave and observe the window in case anyone attempts to dispose of anything,' Matt murmured his instructions in her ear before boarding the carriage to see the victim for himself.

He was back in a trice, a sombre expression on his face. 'It's our man, Travers, all right. Stabbed through the heart. This is a bad business.'

Matt dispatched a porter to inform the local police, while the rest of the station staff dealt with the other passengers and saw to the uncoupling of the carriage so it could be shunted to a siding. Kitty, chafing that she had not yet been permitted to see the victim, waited impatiently for the police to arrive.

Mrs Craven and the other passengers from the carriage were escorted from the train and seated in a small room just off the waiting room under the watchful gaze of the station's tea-room lady, who hastened to supply them with refreshments.

Mrs Craven was accompanied by two younger women. The first was a blonde-haired young lady, smartly dressed in couture apparel and carrying a cream patent leather handbag that stirred envy in Kitty's heart as she strode past. The other woman was of a similar age, with dark continental good looks, but her clothing was not of such good quality, and she was heavily made up for such a fine summer's day.

The young man who had called out of the carriage window trailed behind them and gave Kitty a cheeky wink as he strolled by. Finally, bringing up the rear was a tall thin man with stooped shoulders, dressed in the dusty black garb of a clergyman as he supported a rail-thin elderly woman. Beneath the nut-brown tan that spoke of long exposure to the sun, she looked frail and tired, seemingly glad of the support of her clerical companion's arm.

A ruddy cheeked and slightly breathless constable arrived on the platform wheeling his bicycle. Kitty apprised him of events and left him to take over from the tea lady in watching the carriage occupants while she went to find Matt.

She found him with the stationmaster at the siding where the carriage containing the body of Mr Travers had been shunted.

'The constable has arrived and is in the waiting area with Mrs Craven and her companions. He told me that the inspector is coming from Torquay and his sergeant is also on the way here.'

'Good work, Kitty.' He offered her his hand so she could hop up inside the carriage.

'Here, don't you be doing that, miss. The police is coming and 'tisn't fitting as a lady should be going in there.' The stationmaster stepped forward as if to prevent her from gaining access to the carriage, but Kitty was too swift and stepped smartly inside.

'Miss Underhay has assisted me in many cases. Rest assured, we will touch nothing. Inspector Greville will vouch for us when he arrives.' Matt followed Kitty inside the carriage, closing the carriage door on the indignant stationmaster.

Kitty drew a breath and looked around the carriage compartment. It was one of the older first-class carriages in which each compartment seated eight people in two rows of four upon plush upholstered luxury, facing each other. There was no corridor to link to other carriages.

The murdered man sat still upright in his seat at the opposite end of the compartment. His newspaper lay open on his lap. She wondered who had been sitting opposite him. The passengers had taken their personal belongings from the overhead luggage racks, and she presumed that any bulkier items were in the guard's van.

Travers was older than Matt. In his mid-forties, Kitty guessed from his hair, which was greying at his temples. He was dressed for travelling in a light grey summer-weight suit and a white shirt with navy tie.

To the casual observer it would have appeared as if he were asleep. However there was no mistaking the handle of the knife protruding from his chest. It was small, with a fancifully carved handle and it appeared almost like an ornate silver shirt stud, until one noticed the dark red stain that was still slowly spreading across the white front of his shirt.

Kitty grimaced. 'Whoever killed him seems to have taken him by surprise.' The boldness of the enterprise quite took her breath away.

'Yes, there is no indication of a struggle and whoever did this must have acted swiftly.' Matt glanced around the carriage. 'They would have been in view of the others if anyone had happened to glance in this direction.'

Kitty frowned. 'I will be astonished if no one saw anything. He must not even have cried out, or surely one of the others would have heard him.' She glanced at the dead man's features. It was definitely Simon Travers, she recognised him instantly from the image she had seen in the press.

'I suspect whoever did this hoped that the murder would not be discovered until everyone had alighted at their stops. His jacket and the newspaper would have covered the knife. Mrs

Craven alerting everyone here at Dawlish certainly would not have been part of the plan. I expect that the murderer would have assumed Travers was continuing on to Torquay or even as far as Paignton,' Matt said, his tone thoughtful.

The sound of male voices outside the carriage caused Kitty to glance through the window.

'Inspector Greville is here with the sergeant. They have arrived surprisingly swiftly.'

She followed Matt off the train, accepting his hand to step down onto the platform. The stationmaster glared disapprovingly at her.

'Miss Underhay, Captain Bryant.' The inspector raised his hat. 'I saw your little red motor car parked outside.'

'I'm not certain if you have had any communication from London, sir?' Matt asked.

The inspector's moustache twitched. 'Ah, from the brigadier? Yes, he telephoned me at lunchtime. I take it that you know the victim?'

Matt nodded. 'I'm afraid so, sir. It was the gentleman I had come to meet.'

'Oh dear.' The inspector's moustache drooped. 'That puts a pretty pickle on things. Doctor Carter is on his way here. Once he has examined the victim one of us must let the brigadier know what has happened. Perhaps you wouldn't mind accompanying me back inside the compartment?' He looked at Matt for a reply before he turned to Kitty, adding. 'Miss Underhay, I believe Mrs Craven alerted everyone to the murder. Perhaps you might be so good as to wait with her and the others in the waiting room with the constable. Sergeant, could you perhaps be on hand to support the stationmaster and ensure the public do not enter the station for now?'

The sergeant nodded and set about his business. Kitty was keen to learn more about the other occupants of the carriage so made no objection to the inspector's instruction.

She was about to cross the platform to the waiting room when the guard from the train appeared. His thin face was flushed with indignation. In his one hand he held a brown leather leash. Attached to the other end of the leash was a rather doleful looking black and grey cocker spaniel.

'Here, what's got to happen with this one? I can't be keeping him in the van. Been howlin' all the way from London, he has.'

'Oh dear, he must be poor Mr Travers's dog.' The leash was thrust into her hand by the guard.

'According to his collar, he answers to Bertie. Best as you have him, lady. I can't keep him in the wagon no longer and he was supposed to be put off 'ere.'

'But...' Kitty started automatically to protest.

'Sorry, lady, got to get the train out.' With that, the man hurried away leaving Kitty with the dog.

THREE

Matt did his best to hide a smile at Kitty's expression at being left with the dog as he followed Inspector Greville inside the compartment.

'Hmm, whoever murdered him was certainly chancing their arm. Let us hope Doctor Carter can shed some light on when he might have been killed. That may assist us in determining who the culprit might be, that is, if none of the others in here saw or heard anything.' The inspector glanced around the compartment.

'If everyone stayed in their seats, then we can assume it must have been someone seated either opposite or next to him.' Matt peered at the ornate handle of the dagger. 'It doesn't look as if he was struck at an angle.'

'He could have been killed as they boarded or when the train passed through a tunnel, I suppose. It would have been the work of seconds to accomplish.' The inspector's moustache appeared increasingly depressed as he considered the possibilities.

'Quite a risk though, sir. Surely it speaks of someone either desperate or a committed gambler to take such a chance,' Matt said.

'Quite, and presumably with some medical knowledge to know where to attack. We had better go and ascertain who the passengers sharing this compartment were and if any of them are connected to the dead man or the trial.'

Matt exchanged a look with the inspector. 'I take it we can exclude Mrs Craven from suspicion?'

'I believe so. I would not dare suspect that lady of anything untoward.'

The polished wooden and glass door to the compartment opened and the plump, cherubically cheerful face of Doctor Carter peered inside.

'Good afternoon. Captain Bryant, our paths cross again. I understand, Inspector Greville, you have a body for me?'

'I'm afraid so, sir.' Matt exited the compartment to allow the doctor to enter and carry out his preliminary observations under the inspector's watchful gaze.

———

Kitty was certain she had detected a smirk on Matt's face as he had followed the inspector back inside the compartment.

She huffed out a sigh and tugged gently at the dog's leash. 'Come along, Bertie. I'm afraid you will be sadly missing your master tonight.'

The dog trotted at her heels as they approached the waiting room. Even before she entered the sound of voices raised in argument reached her. She paused for a moment and her newly acquired dog took the opportunity to relieve himself on the wheel of one of the porter's luggage carts.

Bertie appeared unrepentant as she glared at him. Kitty pushed open the waiting-room door and entered into the midst of chaos. The constable appeared to be attempting to restore some kind of order, while the passengers from the train were all talking at once and appearing to be arguing with each other.

'Kitty, thank heavens. Where is Inspector Greville? I saw him go past the window; I really did think he would have at least called in here first. And what on earth are you doing with a dog?' Mrs Craven swooped down on Kitty.

'Madam, please resume your seat. The inspector will be here shortly.' The constable gave Kitty a pleading glance.

'The inspector is with Matt. Doctor Carter has arrived.' Kitty looked at the other passengers. 'Whatever is going on here?'

'Ask Mrs Hoity-Toity there. Throwing her accusations about and us all respectable people.' The young man from earlier glared at Mrs Craven.

The two younger women who had been bickering with each other and the reverend all looked in Kitty's direction. The older woman, she noticed, had her eyes closed and was resting her head against the cream painted wall of the waiting room.

'The inspector will be joining you shortly. Perhaps it might expedite matters if you could all co-operate with the constable,' Kitty suggested.

She took Mrs Craven's arm and drew her aside to sit on one of the wooden chairs arranged around the edges of the room. Bertie settled across her feet with a heavy sigh.

'Yes, thank you, miss. Like I was saying, name please, miss?' The constable addressed the well-dressed blonde-haired young woman.

'Lady Meribel Jacques of Cockington Manor.' The woman produced an ebony cigarette holder from her handbag and inserted a cigarette.

The young man who had winked at Kitty earlier promptly took out a lighter and lit it for her.

'Sir?' The constable looked at him.

'William Ford, Esquire. Salesman for the Little Home-maker Brush Company.'

'Humph, they must pay him awfully well if he travels first class,' Mrs Craven remarked to Kitty in a loud stage whisper.

The constable frowned and carried on to the other young woman. 'Miss?'

'Carlotta Dubois. I'm on my way to Torquay where I have a singing engagement at the Pavilion Theatre.'

Kitty had seen posters in the town advertising the concert. Miss Dubois sang light opera, if she recalled the flyers correctly.

'And you, sir?' The constable turned to the clergyman.

'Reverend Greenslade of St Mark's Church. I am on my way to Paignton for a rest cure. Surely you cannot suspect a man of my standing to be associated with such a heinous crime as murder?' Beads of sweat were dotted along the reverend's brow, and he mopped them away with a rather grubby cotton handkerchief.

Another ripple of protest ran around the waiting room at the clergyman's words but were swiftly silenced by the constable.

'And you, madam, might I have your details?' he asked the older woman who had opened her eyes at the sounds of protest.

'Miss Xanthe Briggs. I returned recently from missionary work in India and am on my way to stay with my sister in Torquay.'

Kitty guessed that accounted for the darker tones of the woman's skin if she had been abroad for a length of time. It also seemed unlikely that she would have a motive for murdering Simon Travers. In fact, all of them appeared to have no motive, and yet one of them must have killed him.

'This is insupportable. Are we to be detained here for much longer? The most likely person to have murdered this man is her. She was sitting next to him.' Carlotta Dubois stood and pointed a dramatic finger at Mrs Craven. 'And she is accusing us to put the police off the scent.'

'How dare you. My late husband was Mayor of Dartmouth. I can assure you, young lady, that I am a well-known and very respected figure in Torbay.' Mrs Craven fixed her accuser with a rapier glare, which saw Miss Dubois subsiding back down onto her chair.

The door of the waiting room opened once more, and Kitty was relieved to see Inspector Greville enter, with Matt following behind him. The constable stepped back, relief showing on his face at the arrival of his superior.

'Ladies and gentlemen, I apologise for the necessity of requesting that you all remain here for now. As you are aware the other passenger occupying your compartment has unfortunately been murdered.'

Another ripple of protest rang out and the inspector held up his hand to quell the complaints.

'I must now ask you all if any of you knew the gentleman who has been killed. If any of you may have, perhaps, recognised him from the press, for instance?'

Kitty looked around at a sea of blank faces at the inspector's question.

'I have only been in England for a few weeks, Inspector. I certainly did not know the man. I know very few people in England,' Miss Briggs said.

'I barely even noticed him. He was in his seat reading his paper when I boarded the train. I'm not sure I even saw his face until... well, afterwards.' Lady Jacques gave a disinterested sniff and blew a thin stream of blue smoke into the air from her cigarette.

The inspector looked at Mr Ford.

'Search me, governor. I ain't got no clue who he was. Like her ladyship there said, he was behind his paper.'

Reverend Greenslade shook his head. 'I doubt that he was one of my flock, Inspector. I must confess I did not take much notice of him. Like Lady Jacques said, he was behind his newspaper when I too boarded.'

Carlotta Dubois burst out angrily. 'Pah, why would I know this person? I was at the far end away from him. Like I said before ask her, the old woman. She was sitting beside him.' She cast a spiteful look at Mrs Craven, clearly pleased to have scored a point against her rival.

'I most certainly did not know him. He was seated when I boarded. I spoke to him briefly when I reached up to place my things on the rack above his head. He barely even acknowledged me, and I thought it rather rude that he did not offer any assistance. Clearly he was not a gentleman.' Mrs Craven huffed and adjusted her light-linen coat around her shoulders.

'And no one entered or left the carriage at any point during any of the station stops on the journey to Dawlish?' Inspector Greville asked.

There was a general shaking of heads.

The inspector looked around the room. 'Thank you. I will ask that you all give the addresses where you will be staying to the constable. Also your seat position within the compartment and your addresses in London. I request that you all stay at the local addresses you provide and inform the police station if you intend to travel elsewhere.'

''Ere how am I supposed to make a living doing that? I got appointments to keep. A bloke has to earn his livin'.' Mr Ford held up a compact, burgundy leatherette covered case, which Kitty surmised must contain samples of his brushes.

'Then let us all hope that we solve this case quickly. If any of you saw or heard anything during the journey, then I would be glad if you could also pass that information to the constable. Anyone standing up, moving around, or going near the murdered man either whilst moving or when stopped at a station.'

Kitty noticed that the inspector was careful not to name Mr Travers directly, perhaps hoping that an expression on one of the passengers' faces might betray some prior knowledge of his identity. Matt slipped out of the waiting room and Kitty wondered if he had gone to make use of the stationmaster's telephone. The brigadier would have to be informed, and swiftly, because if news of the murder reached the press, she supposed it might influence the trial findings in London. It would certainly be a sensation in the newspapers.

The constable began to circulate around the group once more, scribbling assiduously into his notebook. Bertie sighed and shifted on Kitty's feet reminding her that she had somehow been landed with the responsibility for Simon Travers's dog.

Matt reappeared and addressed Inspector Greville. 'I've telephoned London, sir.'

'Thank you. Mrs Craven have you provided the constable with your information?' The policeman turned to Kitty's companion.

'Indeed I have. Unlike some people here, I know my civic duty. I presume, Inspector, that I have your permission to leave?'

'By all means. Perhaps, Miss Underhay, you might be so good as to give Mrs Craven a ride back to Dartmouth?' The inspector's tone was bland, but Kitty suspected from the twitch of his moustache that he was gaining some small amusement from this suggestion.

'I'd be delighted, Inspector, but what about Bertie?' Kitty indicated the dog that was now regarding them both with large liquid brown eyes.

'Ah, um, yes, I asked our friend in London about the dog. It seems the dead man had no family,' Matt said.

'So, we are stuck with him?' Kitty asked.

Bertie raised a paw and rested it on her knee. She made the fatal mistake of meeting the dog's woeful gaze. 'Oh, very well.'

The look of dismay on Mrs Craven's face when she discovered the dog would be accompanying them back to Dartmouth was worth the dawning realisation that Bertie might well become a permanent addition.

FOUR

Mrs Craven was installed with some difficulty on the front passenger seat of Kitty's little red car. Bertie was secured upon the back seat beside Matt, who somehow managed to fold his long legs into the available space.

'I suggest you ensure your delightful hat is well secured, Mrs C. It gets a little breezy on the approach back into Torquay,' Matt suggested.

Kitty met his gaze in the driver's mirror and saw him smile.

'This is very kind of you, Kitty, but I really feel perhaps it may be better if Matthew drove.' Mrs Craven clutched at the parcels on her ample lap.

Kitty gritted her teeth and concentrated on reversing out of her parking space.

'I haven't driven a motor car for years, Mrs C. Last time was about four years ago, I think, in Istanbul. I doubt I'd even remember how to change gear,' Matt said cheerfully. 'I think the chauffeuring is best left to Kitty.'

Mrs Craven continued to look concerned as Kitty negotiated her way out of Dawlish and back along the coast road. One of the gusts of wind that Matt had warned her about tugged at the brim of her hat causing her to squeak and place a hand on top of the crown, flattening a sprig of the blue flowers.

'I gather that you were seated next to the man who was killed, Mrs Craven?' Kitty said chattily as she overtook a horse and cart on one of the level stretches of the narrow road.

'Yes, indeed. I cannot believe the man was stabbed right beside me and I saw and heard nothing. It was such a shock. I had risen from my seat to start to get my parcels off the overhead luggage rack and asked Mr Travers for help. When he didn't answer I nudged him, thinking that he had dozed off, and saw that there was blood on his shirt where I had disturbed his jacket.'

Kitty glanced across and saw Mrs Craven's lip tremble. It seemed that the shock of what she had just witnessed was starting to make itself felt.

'Who was seated opposite him?' Matt asked, leaning forward in his seat so he could make himself heard above the road noise.

'That brush salesman. Mr Ford, a most impertinent young fellow. And what was he doing in first class, that's what I would like to know?' Mrs Craven's indignation at Mr Ford sharing a first-class compartment at least restored a little colour to her cheeks.

'Where were the others seated?' Kitty asked.

'That rude young woman, the opera singer, was on my other side with the reverend at the end of the row. The missionary woman was seated beside Mr Ford and Lady Jacques was last in the carriage. I must admit I was most annoyed that it was an eight-seater compartment and not a six.' Mrs Craven huffed as she considered the temerity of the train company at failing to provide a better carriage.

'Did anyone else speak to the man or go near him during the journey?' Kitty asked as she slowed up behind a bottle-green grocer's van.

'Miss Dubois was put out that my parcels were occupying the luggage rack, so she stowed some of her things on the opposite rack. I think she rose a few times to get things from her luggage.' Mrs Craven considered Kitty's question. 'I think that impudent brush salesman may have said something to the murdered man about the sport on the back of his newspaper. Oh, and Lady Jacques also rather rudely moved some of my parcels to place some things of hers on the rack. I don't recall the others moving much or saying anything to the dead man.'

'That's most helpful, Mrs C,' Matt said.

'Who was the man that was killed? Clearly you two seemed to know him, as did the inspector, and that was a strange comment about seeing him in the press. Was he well known? Or notorious?' Mrs Craven turned her head to look at Kitty.

'Um.' Kitty was unsure how to answer her.

'This obviously has to be kept quiet for now, but I know that we can trust your discretion, Mrs Craven. The murdered man was Simon Travers, the key witness in the Tower Hill jewel robbery trial. I was expecting him to stay with me for a short visit,' Matt said. 'I must emphasise the confidentiality of this information.'

'Oh absolutely. You know that I shall not breathe a word of his identity.' Mrs Craven looked positively smug at having been entrusted with such a secret.

Kitty wondered how the older woman would manage to restrain herself from sharing this inside knowledge. Especially when she was regaling the gals – her long-time group of friends, of whom Kitty's grandmother was also a member – with the story of her discovery of the body.

Before long they were driving towards Churston, where Matt's house was situated near the common.

'May I invite you ladies in for tea? My housekeeper has made scones, I believe, in the expectation of Mr Travers's arrival. It would be a pity to waste them,' Matt asked as they passed the old stone tollhouse before the turn to the common.

'Mrs Craven?' Kitty deferred to the older woman, although she dearly longed to stop for scones and a chance to quiz Matt on what Doctor Carter may have said.

'Well, a cup of tea would be most refreshing, and the chance to stretch my legs for a moment or two. My journeys today have been most traumatic. Thank you, Matthew, a most thoughtful invitation.'

Bertie gave a short bark as if adding his agreement and so Kitty parked her car at the side of Matt's house, behind his beloved motorcycle.

The house was a modest white-painted square affair in the modern style. It was conveniently placed for the golf course and afforded some very nice views of the sea from all of the floors.

Kitty jumped out so that Matt and Bertie could exit the rear seats. Matt handed Bertie's leash to Kitty and went to open the car door for Mrs Craven. He placed her parcels on the back seat and offered her his arm for the short walk to his front door.

Matt installed Mrs Craven in the seat of honour in his pleasant, sunny sitting room with its view of the garden and glimpse of the sea. Kitty took a seat on the sofa while Matt went off to prepare a tea tray, Bertie trotting happily at his heels as if he had always lived in the house.

Mrs Craven drew off her white cotton gloves and looked around the room. Matt had furnished the house in a modern minimalist style. The suite was black leather and chrome, and he had a few carefully chosen ornaments. Kitty approved of the comfortable, uncluttered style of the house and always enjoyed spending time there. She supposed it would be her house too when they married.

'Well, this is very nice, I must say, Kitty. I'm sure you will improve the decor with a few feminine touches when you and

Matthew marry.' Mrs Craven nodded her head, the sprays of flowers in her hat bobbing in approval.

'I rather like Matt's taste in furnishings, and we have not decided where we shall live, or even a date for the wedding just yet,' Kitty remarked and hoped her irritation at the woman's presumption did not show in her tone. It was as if the woman had read her mind.

Mrs Craven waved her hand dismissively. 'Yes, you really must set a date, Kitty dear. I presume you will wish to marry sooner rather than later? After all you have no reason to delay.' She beamed at Kitty.

Kitty wished Matt would hurry up with the tea tray. If Mrs Craven continued her interrogation at this rate, she would require a stronger beverage than tea. Perhaps a large cocktail might be more in order.

'There is a lot to consider, Mrs Craven. My position at the hotel, for example.' Her grandmother was not getting any younger and managing the hotel was a full-time job. The Dolphin had been in her family's hands for many years. She had realised long ago that she would inevitably be handed the task of continuing the business.

'Oh, but, my dear, surely you do not intend to continue working? Or at least not so many hours. After all you will have other calls on your time. A home to manage and, perhaps shortly, a family?' Mrs Craven gave her a coy smile.

The sitting room door opened, and Matt entered carrying a fully laden tea tray. Bertie once more followed behind him.

'Do let me help you with that.' Kitty leapt to her feet to assist Matt in placing the tray down on a low occasional table in front of the sofa.

'I was just saying to Kitty, you really need to set the date for your wedding soon. I know Kitty's grandmother is very much looking forward to it. I expect your parents are pleased to see you settled again, too, Matthew?' Mrs Craven accepted a delicate porcelain cup and saucer from Kitty and helped herself to sugar for her tea from the matching bowl.

'Yes, I'm sure my parents are delighted.' Matt took the tea Kitty offered and gave her a small smile.

Kitty was not so certain that delighted would have been Matt's parents' reaction at news of their engagement. They had disapproved of his first marriage and, when they had visited Dartmouth before Christmas, they had not been overly enamoured of Kitty. This was despite his parents being old friends of her grandmother.

'An autumn wedding might be quite pleasant. Such lovely colours and not too cold.' Mrs Craven was not to be deflected.

'It would also depend on when my father is able to organise his affairs.' Kitty helped herself to a scone and sliced it neatly in two.

'My dear, surely your father is easily able to make time to attend his own daughter's wedding.' Mrs Craven dismissed the suggestion as of no consequence.

Kitty's father had been estranged from her for many years and had only recently come back into her life. He resided mainly in America, however. Kitty was unsure what he actually did there and judged it better not to make too close an enquiry. He did not have the best of reputations on either side of the Atlantic.

'Kitty is right, there is a lot for us to discuss before we are able to agree upon a date.' Matt helped himself to a scone. 'You may be assured, Mrs C, that your name will be at the top of our list when sending out the invitations.' Matt winked at Kitty when Mrs Craven wasn't looking.

'Also, I have quite enough to keep me busy for now,' Kitty said. 'I have sent another letter today to try to obtain permission to see Ezekiel Hammett at Exeter Gaol before he is moved to London.' She added jam to the cream on her scone.

Mrs Craven's face froze in horror. 'Kitty, you surely do not intend to try entering the prison to see that man?'

'I want to talk to him. To see him face to face and try to discover how my mother came to be murdered and placed in the cellar of that public house in Exeter. He is the only person who might be able to tell me anything.' Kitty lifted her chin mutinously.

She was well aware of how dangerous Hammett and his sister, Esther, were. There had been an attempt on her own life a few months ago when the Hammetts had decided she posed a threat to their criminal empire.

'But, Kitty dear, a prison!' Mrs Craven shuddered.

'It is in the hands of the Home Office at present to grant permission for a visit and that of the governor of the gaol. Hammett is refusing to speak to anyone at all, not even his own defence solicitor,' Matt said. 'So unfortunately, at the moment, it is all rather moot.'

The look he gave Mrs Craven was enough to silence even that lady on the subject, although Kitty could tell she had a lot she clearly wished to add. Kitty wanted more than anything to look Hammett in the eyes and ask the questions that had plagued her all her life. She had been a small child when her mother had disappeared in June 1916. It had taken years to finally uncover what had befallen her and someone had to be held to account for her death.

FIVE

Kitty woke later than her usual time the following day. She decided that being a lady of leisure did not suit her constitution as she had a headache. Although whether that was due to the later hour or that Mrs Craven had talked of nothing but weddings all the way back to Dartmouth yesterday, she was not quite certain.

A rap at her bedroom door announced the arrival of Alice, one of the hotel maids and Kitty's particular friend. Alice often acted as Kitty's personal maid when visiting Kitty's family and had accompanied her on many of her previous adventures.

'I thought as you might like a cup of tea, miss. I heard about what happened in Dawlish on the train yesterday.' Alice set the tea tray down on Kitty's small rosewood bedside cabinet.

Kitty pushed herself up into a sitting position and propped herself up with pillows ready to receive her tea. 'How?'

It never failed to amaze Kitty that news in small towns and servants' halls seemed to travel faster than a galloping horse. At Kitty's invitation Alice perched herself on the edge of Kitty's bed and helped herself to tea in the extra cup that she had happened to bring along.

'Mrs Craven's maid, Annie, run across our Dolly this morning on her way here and told her that her mistress had found a body on the train at Dawlish yesterday. She said as you and Captain Bryant was there,' Alice said.

Kitty took a reviving sip of tea. Dolly was Alice's younger sister and had recently started to work at the Dolphin assisting her grandmother with various administration tasks. Alice was the eldest of eight children and invariably knew everything that was happening in Dartmouth and beyond.

'Yes, I'm afraid it's true. A man was murdered in one of the first-class compartments yesterday afternoon. Mrs Craven found him and raised the alarm. I suspect it shook her up rather more than she let on.' Kitty had wondered if that had been partly why Mrs Craven had been badgering her about the wedding yesterday. Perhaps to deflect thinking that she had been in a confined space with both a murderer and his or her victim.

'And how come as you and Captain Bryant was there, miss?' Alice asked, eyeing her curiously over the brim of her cup.

'You must keep this to yourself, Alice.' Kitty knew she could trust her friend implicitly, so told her the identity of the dead man and why she and Matt had been waiting to meet him from the train.

The younger girl's eyes widened. 'I've read all about that trial, miss. Our Dolly and me has been following it in the papers. I said to her as I thought as they would be making a film of it once the trial was over. It would make a good movie, what with all the jewels that was stolen and them desperate crooks.'

Kitty smiled. Alice loved going to the pictures and avidly followed all her favourite film and radio stars in the press and magazines. 'It certainly has the makings of a good film,' she agreed.

The maid picked at the seam on the edge of her starched white apron. 'But if it were one of them carriages with no corridor, miss, then one of the people travelling in the compartment must have done it, mustn't they?'

Kitty drained her cup and placed it back on the saucer. 'Yes. There is no other explanation possible. No one entered or left the carriage during the journey. I think we can rule out Mrs Craven though, so that leaves the other five people.'

Alice's brows rose as she considered this. 'That would have been difficult, miss. I mean how could they manage it? Unless I suppose as they was going through a tunnel or something. It would be dark then, wouldn't it?'

'I think this is the problem Inspector Greville will have to unravel. There must be some kind of connection or motive with one or more of the passengers. Something that connects them to the dead man.' Kitty had been giving the matter some thought, and it had occurred to her that two people could have been working together in order to pull the murder off successfully. The motive must be something to do with the trial. If it wasn't and it was something connected with Mr Travers's job, then Matt might now be in jeopardy too.

'Our Dolly said as Annie told her as Mrs Craven stood up to start to get her parcels off the luggage rack and she asked that Mr Travers to help her. When he didn't answer she nudged him, thinking he had dozed off like, and that's when his coat fell open and she looked down and saw the blood.' A shiver ran through Alice's thin frame.

'Yes, that's what she told us and the constable. She said she didn't see or hear anything even though she was seated right beside him.'

'Cor, that's a proper mystery. In a film he would have been drugged first so as he didn't cry out, but there weren't no restaurant service was there? So that can't be it. I suppose as you and Captain Bryant will be investigating as well as Inspector Greville? I mean, seeing as you said as the captain was having

Mr Travers stop with him for a few days?' Alice rose and set her empty cup and saucer back on the tray.

Kitty grinned. 'I think so, after all when one's house guests are murdered it seems the very least we can do.'

Alice smiled back, a stray lock of her auburn hair escaping from under her cap. 'I thought as much, miss. Just don't go putting yourself in any danger this time.'

Her comment made Kitty laugh out loud. 'I assure you, Alice, I never intend to place myself at risk. It just seems to happen somehow. I swear I have become a magnet for murder.'

Her friend collected up the tray. 'I'd best get back to it. Mrs Homer will have my guts for garters if she thinks I'm slacking. If you wants my help with anything though, miss...?'

'I shall come and rescue you from my housekeeper,' Kitty promised as Alice whisked out of the room and back to her chores in the hotel.

———

Matt arrived at the Dolphin at the same time as Inspector Greville. He had been forced to leave his beloved Sunbeam at home and had travelled to Dartmouth by bus, since he was accompanied by Bertie.

'Good morning, Captain Bryant. I see you still have the dog then?' the inspector greeted Matt inside the wood panelled lobby of the hotel.

'Yes, I had to bring him with me. He seems to be missing his master and my housekeeper objected to him remaining at home as he howls when I'm out of sight.' Matt looked at Bertie who had flopped down at his feet and was pretending not to chew the end of Matt's shoelace.

Mary, the hotel receptionist, had alerted Kitty to their arrival, and she strolled down the broad oak staircase to greet them. Matt's spirits rose at the sight of her trim figure in a blue flower-sprigged dress.

'Inspector Greville, Matt.' She smiled at the inspector and stretched up to kiss Matt's cheek. 'And, Bertie.' She looked at the spaniel. 'Please come up to the salon. Mary will arrange for refreshments to be sent up.' She looked at her receptionist who immediately picked up the telephone to contact the kitchen.

Matt saw the inspector's eyes brighten at the mention of refreshments. Inspector Greville was fond of his food and Matt and Kitty knew that, at home, Mrs Greville was determined that her husband should watch his weight.

Kitty's grandmother had placed the salon in her quarters at her disposal as she herself was busy working in Kitty's office downstairs. Kitty had telephoned Matt after dinner the previous evening to tell him that her grandmother had been dismayed to learn about the murder. She had also been equally concerned that Kitty was once again intending to investigate the death.

'Do please take a seat, Inspector.' Kitty took the armchair beside the fireplace and Matt sat opposite her. Bertie sprawled at his feet and resumed his nibbling of Matt's shoelace.

Inspector Greville took his place on the sofa. 'I thought it would be useful, given your involvement with Mr Travers, if you were to work alongside the police on this case. The brigadier is very keen that it is resolved swiftly so that he can manage the press. As you can imagine when this gets out the place will be crawling with journalists.'

Matt saw Kitty nod her agreement at this. They paused for a moment as there was a knock at the door and Alice appeared, smart in her black-and-white uniform. She wheeled in a trolley containing a large silver jug of coffee, crockery and a plate laden with small cakes and biscuits.

She parked the trolley next to Kitty and left them to help themselves. Once the door had closed behind her, Kitty served the coffee and offered the inspector the plate of cakes. Matt did his best to hide a smile as the inspector cheerfully piled up a selection of treats on the white linen napkin that rested across his lap.

'I take it you have been busy, sir, making enquiries about Mr Travers's fellow passengers and any potential links with our victim?' Matt asked.

'Indeed.' The inspector paused to brush some errant crumbs from the front of his shirt. 'The brigadier has also been using his own channels. Discreetly, of course, as he is keen to keep Travers's identity as the murder victim under wraps from the press for the time being.'

Matt exchanged a glance with Kitty.

'And what have you learned so far, sir?' Kitty asked.

'I confess that I was a little surprised yesterday that Mrs Craven did not know Lady Meribel Jacques. Mrs Craven always appears to know everyone who is anyone in Torbay society.' The inspector paused to nibble at his last remaining cake.

'Isn't Lady Jacques new to the area though, sir?' Kitty asked. 'I seem to recall that Cockington Manor was sold a few months back for use as a holiday home. I'm sure that was the name connected to the sale.'

'Indeed, Miss Underhay.' The inspector waved his cake around in agreement, scattering more crumbs. 'Lady Jacques's parents apparently wanted a summer house near the sea and settled on Cockington.'

'Do you know if she has any connection with Mr Travers?' Matt asked.

Inspector Greville frowned at the empty cake plate on the trolley. 'Not that we have uncovered as yet. However, she is in a considerable amount of debt. She is rather fond of cards and not too good at them. Her parents have refused to bail her out of this last lot of trouble and she owes money all over London.'

'Hmm, so a gambler and possibly open to blackmail or pressure. But is that enough to murder a stranger?' Kitty mused.

'What of the opera singer, Miss Dubois? She was very keen to try to place blame on Mrs C?' Matt asked.

'Another shady character. She's a genuine performer all right and apparently a good singer, but she keeps some very unsavoury company. Often the case, I believe, with theatrical people. We think there may be a link between her and one or more of the defendants, but we're waiting for confirmation on exactly what that might be. The brigadier thought she had attended the trial in the public gallery. He has had men watching who attends hoping to discover anything that might lead them to the missing goods.'

'She lied then, about not knowing who Travers was. And that rather forward gentleman? William Ford, the brush salesman? Mrs Craven was most surprised he was in a first-class compartment,' Kitty asked.

'Yes, well. His ticket wasn't for first class, that's for sure, although with no corridor on the train I reckon he thought as he could get away with a free upgrade.' The inspector's moustache was stiff with disapproval.

'Interesting. Do we know why he chose that compartment, sir? Is there a connection between him and Travers?' Matt asked.

'We have contacted the Little Homemaker Brush Company but have not yet received a reply to our enquiry. The London address he gave was that of a hostel. So, safe to say, we're looking closely at Mr Ford.' The inspector dabbed the corners of his mouth with his napkin. He placed the linen on the trolley with an air of regret.

'I suppose that leaves Reverend Greenslade and Miss Briggs, the missionary,' Kitty said thoughtfully.

'Now they are an interesting pair. Reverend Greenslade's church, St Mark's, is opposite Tower Hill Jewellers where the

robbery took place. According to Mr Travers's witness statement he saw the men who have been charged with the theft and
overheard their conversation in the same churchyard.' Inspector
Greville looked at Kitty.

'And some of the proceeds of the robbery are still missing
you said?' The frown on Kitty's brow deepened.

'Some valuable silver, a diamond necklace and matching
earrings. Several gold sovereigns and some gold rings,' Matt
said. 'At least that is what has been reported in the press.' He
looked to the inspector for confirmation.

Greville nodded. 'Yes. There is a theory at the Yard that the
loot was divided, and the missing articles are all the smaller,
more portable items. Cigarette cases, snuff boxes and pins.
They would be easy to conceal and disperse.'

Matt could see how that would work. Small items could be
melted down and broken down into their component pieces. It
would be easier to dispose of such items if you had the right
contacts.

'Hmm, and Miss Briggs, she said she had recently arrived
from India. She has been a missionary.' Kitty added her
crockery to the trolley. 'Does she know the Reverend
Greenslade? Before arriving in England, I mean. We know he
assisted her whilst she was on the train.'

'We believe she may have attended services at the church
since her arrival in London. She was staying at a hostel for
Christian Ladies, which is very close to St Mark's. We have not
yet confirmed it, but we think the church supported her
mission. Also of note is the fact that Miss Briggs is unwell and
has been undergoing tests at one of the large teaching hospitals.'

Kitty nodded her head at the inspector's reply. 'Mr
Travers's murder could have been carried out by two people
working together,' she suggested. 'Do we know yet, sir, if any of
the other passengers knew one another before boarding the
train, apart from Reverend Greenslade and Miss Briggs?'

Matt was surprised by Kitty's theory, but he supposed two people working together could carry out such a crime if one covered for the other.

Inspector Greville stroked his moustache thoughtfully. 'I'm not sure. As I said, Miss Briggs obviously knew Reverend Greenslade. As for the others, I will ask our London colleagues if they have any knowledge on the matter. None of them admitted anything yesterday.'

'And Travers himself, sir, what do we know of him?' All Matt had been told was that the man had been a civil servant employed in some capacity by the brigadier's department. He hadn't recognised either the man's name or his appearance from his time there, so presumably Travers had joined after he had left.

The inspector shuffled uncomfortably on the armchair. 'I tried asking the brigadier. Travers had been with the department for about two years. Apparently, he was based in Tangier, but something occurred out there that necessitated a move back to London.'

Matt's brows lifted at this. He recognised his former employer's coded speak for 'major diplomatic incident'.

'There have been some issues, I believe, with Mr Travers. The brigadier believed he might be a "wrong 'un", but he was a slippery character and there was no proof.'

Matt caught Kitty's eye and he knew her thoughts were running along the same lines as his own. It seemed there might be plenty of people with a desire to murder Simon Travers.

SIX

Matt accompanied the inspector downstairs, leaving Kitty in the salon. She crossed to the window and watched the policeman walk away along the embankment towards the waiting black police car. Inspector Greville had promised to keep them informed of any further information he received from Scotland Yard.

In the meantime, he had said that he intended to carry out further in-depth interviews with each of the passengers. Kitty wished she or Matt could have been present for those. Instead, however, the inspector had suggested that she and Matt carry out a low-level unofficial investigation.

She knew this was because the powers that be did not wish to draw attention to Simon Travers's real role in the department. She suspected it was also because they hoped she and Matt might learn more about the connections, if there were any, between the travellers. And, possibly, where the rest of the missing jewellery and silver had gone. It also avoided causing any ripples in the police force about the use of private investigators in a murder inquiry.

When Matt returned to the salon, he was not alone. Kitty's

spirits dipped as the stout familiar figure of Mrs Craven bustled into the room ahead of her fiancé. She guessed that Mrs Craven had no doubt been closeted in the office downstairs, taking tea and gossiping with Kitty's grandmother.

Matt mouthed, 'Sorry,' to Kitty behind Mrs Craven's back as the older lady seated herself on the chair recently vacated by the inspector.

'Kitty my dear, I was just visiting with your grandmother when I saw the inspector leaving. Do you have any news? Has he made an arrest yet? I expect it's that impertinent brush salesman or the upstart singer.' Mrs Craven settled back in her seat, drew off her cream cotton gloves and looked expectantly at Kitty.

'Good morning, Mrs Craven. No, I'm afraid there is no news of an arrest just yet. The inspector is continuing to make enquiries about poor Mr Travers's death.' As Kitty spoke, Bertie, who had been recumbent beside the sofa, lifted his head to gaze mournfully in her direction.

'Typical. There were only five other people in the compart-ment, surely it can't be so difficult to determine who the culprit might be.' Mrs Craven shook her head making the blue sprays of artificial flowers adorning her hat waggle.

'But you yourself said that you didn't hear or see anything when Travers was killed?' Matt suggested.

Kitty noted the wry smile tugging at the corners of his mouth as he reminded their guest of her own words. 'Perhaps we could go over the events of the journey again?' she suggested.

Mrs Craven huffed. 'Very well, if you think it will help, but there really is not much more to tell.'

'You said Mr Travers was already seated when you boarded the train?' Matt prompted.

'Yes. He was in the far corner reading his newspaper. That impudent young brush salesman was in the seat opposite to him. He had a small leatherette case on the rack above his head. Mr Travers appeared to be travelling without luggage. I expect he must have placed it in the guard's van along with the dog.' Mrs Craven's brow furrowed as she concentrated.

'You placed your parcels on the overhead rack, you said?' Kitty queried as Bertie lumbered to his feet to stagger over and flop down on top of Kitty's shoes with a deep sigh.

'Yes, I had some difficulty and I considered it most ungentlemanly that neither of them offered me any assistance. The summer sales had been very tempting, and I had acquired quite a few new items. I had to stretch over Mr Travers and I did remark to him that I hoped I would not drop one of the boxes on his head. He didn't take the hint, however, and merely continued to read. That brush salesman just smirked and said something to Mr Travers about the horse racing on the back page of his paper.' Mrs Craven looked affronted. 'Such bad manners.'

'Did you hear Mr Travers respond to Mr Ford?' Kitty asked. She wondered if Travers might already have been dead when the others had boarded, in which case perhaps none of them would have been responsible.

Mrs Craven frowned. 'Yes, I think so.' Her expression cleared. 'Ford asked about the winner of one of the races. It was a morning edition paper so I presume the races must have been the previous day. Yes, he muttered something about that he wasn't a gambling man. That was it.'

Kitty sighed. That, at least, however, proved that Travers had been alive when the others had boarded.

'What happened next?' Matt asked.

'Miss Dubois, that so-called opera singer arrived. She too had quite a few things that she wished to place on the overhead racks. She chose to sit beside me. I assumed it was because she did not wish to sit next to Mr Ford. He kept leering at her.

Although he was quick enough to offer her assistance with placing her things on the racks.'

'Did she speak to Mr Travers at all?' Kitty asked. She could picture the scene in the compartment with Mrs Craven's indignation that Miss Dubois had received help while she hadn't.

Mrs Craven thought for a moment. 'Yes, she apologised to him as I believe she stood on his foot while putting her things away. Not that she offered me an apology when she knocked my hat sideways.' Mrs Craven placed a hand lovingly on the straw brim of her hat as if to reassure herself that it was undamaged by the encounter.

'Did Mr Travers reply to her?' Matt beat Kitty to the punch.

'Yes, he assured her he was unhurt and moved his foot.'

It seemed clear to Kitty that Travers had not seemed to recognise either Miss Dubois or Mr Ford. He had spoken with them both and Mrs Craven had not appeared to detect any signs of a prior acquaintance.

'Reverend Greenslade and Miss Briggs arrived together,' Mrs Craven continued. 'The reverend was assisting Miss Briggs, who I must say appeared quite unwell. She took the place beside Mr Ford. I think because there was more room on that side of the compartment, and she appeared in need of space. She had a very small carpet bag, which the reverend put on the rack for her. He then took a seat beside Miss Dubois and took out a book to read.'

'And did either of them speak to Mr Travers?' Kitty asked.

Mrs Craven shook her head. 'No, not at all. It was almost time to depart. Indeed, I rather thought our compartment was full when the door was flung open and Lady Jacques arrived, all out of breath and flustered. She took her seat beside Miss Briggs then the whistle went, and the train set off. Silly girl had cut it rather fine. She told us all she had been having coffee with a friend in the refreshment rooms and hadn't realised the time.' Mrs Craven gave a disparaging sniff. 'The reverend helped

Lady Jacques to place her bag on the rack. There was just enough room. Miss Dubois was most put out as the reverend rearranged a couple of her things.'

'And Lady Jacques did not appear to recognise or acknowledge any of the other passengers?' Kitty frowned as she posed her question.

'No, she addressed the entire compartment as if she expected us all to sympathise with her for almost missing the train. Other than that, no, there was nothing out of the ordinary. Mr Ford made some vaguely lewd response, Miss Dubois tutted, and Miss Briggs had her eyes closed.' Mrs Craven gave a small shrug.

'And Mr Travers?' Kitty asked.

'He rustled his paper and muttered some kind of response.' Mrs Craven adjusted her pearls around her neck as if growing bored with the questions.

'Did anyone move during the journey? Stand up to access the luggage racks or to open or close a window, perhaps? It was a very warm day.' The more they learned, the more impossible it seemed that someone could have murdered Mr Travers and not have been noticed. Kitty was starting to lose hope that they would glean anything new from this conversation.

'Reverend Green let down the window part way, but he was seated next to it. Of course, he was at the opposite end to Mr Travers. It was fortunate that we were far enough away from the engine not to have the smoke and smut coming in. The window beside Mr Travers and Mr Ford remained closed. Of course, there was no corridor, so it was quite warm. Fortunately, I always carry a small fan in my handbag.' Mrs Craven beamed at them as if proud of her forethought on the matter.

Matt glanced at Kitty. 'Did anyone else move or stand up? Perhaps as you approached a tunnel?' He tried the question again.

'A couple of times when we were stopped at a station

people stood to retrieve items. Miss Dubois kept getting things from her bags. She really is quite vain, you know. A shocking fault in a young woman. First her mirror and compact, then her lipstick and then some fashion magazine or other.'

'Did she approach Mr Travers?' Kitty could see now why Miss Dubois had developed a dislike for Mrs Craven.

'I must confess I was resting my eyes for part of the journey. The heat, you know. She did have to try and reach over for various items. I rather think Mr Ford offered her some assistance at one point.' Mrs Craven's tone was rather nettled by the abruptness of Kitty's question.

'This is terribly helpful, Mrs C. You really are painting a picture for us,' Matt soothed the older woman's injured feelings and winked at Kitty when Mrs Craven wasn't looking.

'Yes, well, I pride myself on being a great observer of people as you know.' Mrs Craven adjusted the edges of her lightweight knitted jacket. 'Miss Briggs stood at one point as she wished to get some medication from her bag, but the train jolted on a bend, and she almost fell. Reverend Greenslade caught her in time and helped her to sit down again.'

'So, all attention would have been on Miss Briggs. When did this occur?' Matt asked.

'Shortly before we reached Exeter. Well, yes, we were a little concerned. Poor Miss Briggs did appear very pale.'

This was exactly the kind of moment when the crime could have been committed, Kitty thought. A diversion when everyone's attention had been elsewhere.

'Was Mr Travers one of the people who aided Miss Briggs?' she asked.

Mrs Craven screwed up her face as she considered the question. 'No, I don't believe so. I think he was asleep. We had all been dozing off and on, I think.' She stopped speaking and a dawning look of realisation spread across her face. 'Oh, yes, I see. I suppose Mr Travers could have been attacked then. I was fanning Miss Briggs with my fan. Lady Jacques offered her a sip of some kind of liquor from a silver hip flask. Miss Dubois produced a vial of smelling salts and even Mr Ford attempted to be useful.'

'Hmm, well, thank you, Mrs Craven, that has been most helpful. I believe the inspector will be very interested in your report of the journey.' Matt smiled at the older woman.

Mrs Craven visibly preened under his approbation. 'Thank you, Matthew. One tries one's best.'

Kitty was thinking about the inspector's comment from earlier about Mrs Craven not knowing Lady Jacques.

'I rather gather that Lady Jacques is a recent arrival in Cockington?'

Mrs Craven's delicately arched brows raised. 'Yes. I know her parents vaguely. Her mother is a delicate little thing, old family. Her father is some years older. I vaguely recall that Meribel was adopted when she was young. Her and her brother, oh dear, what was his name, Valentine, that's it, Valentine. Not that they are related at all really, different parents so I was told. He is something in the City, I believe, rather staid fellow. Lady Meribel is a bit of a gadabout, so I've heard. Just rumours, of course. Yesterday was the first time I'd actually met her. I rather think she is attending a cocktail party at the Royal Torbay Yacht Club this evening. It's to raise funds for something or other. Why don't you both come? I'm sure I can arrange it.'

Kitty frowned. 'I didn't think ladies were allowed at the club?'

Mrs Craven gave a girlish laugh. 'Oh, not in all of the premises, obviously, my dear, but a few selected rooms by invitation on occasions such as these.'

Kitty scowled. 'You mean when they wish to raise money and require the ladies to do all the work?'

Mrs Craven heaved herself to her feet and drew on her gloves. 'There is no need to take that attitude, Kitty.'

Matt immediately leapt up. 'We would love to attend. Thank you, Mrs Craven, it's most kind of you to offer.'

'Yes, well, seven thirty. White tie and formal wear. I shall arrange for your names to be at the door.' She fixed Kitty with a glare and said her farewells.

SEVEN

Matt returned from escorting Mrs Craven out to find Kitty mutinously drumming her fingers on the arm of the chair.

'Cheer up, darling. It seems we now have our evening plans taken care of, and you'll have the opportunity to quiz Lady Jacques.' He dropped a kiss on top of her short blonde curls.

'There was a lot to unpick from the information Mrs Craven gave us. Do you think the incident she described with Miss Briggs is when poor Travers was killed?' She jumped up from her seat and paced about the room, much to Bertie's annoyance.

'It's certainly a possibility. Or it may have been one of the times when the train was standing at a station. Although I think that would be unlikely as there would be a greater chance of discovery. It will be interesting to learn if the other passengers' statements tie in with Mrs C's recollection of events.' Matt patted Bertie's head and hoped his new canine companion was not about to commence howling again.

'And if anyone else spoke to Travers or saw him alive after the incident with Miss Briggs,' Kitty said.

'Come, let's take Bertie here for a walk and get some air.

Then we can work out how and when we can get to see the other passengers to hear their stories.' Matt picked up the end of Bertie's lead as the dog had sprung up, ears and tail alert at the mention of a walk.

Matt waited while Kitty collected her hat and handbag before they set off down the broad polished oak staircase leading to the lobby, Bertie charging ahead of them on the stairs.

'Is there any post for me today, Mary?' Kitty stopped at the reception desk and Matt guessed she was probably hoping for some news of when, or if, she could see Hammett at the prison.

'Just a postcard, Miss Kitty.' The receptionist collected the card from the pigeonhole and passed it over the counter.

'It's from Lucy and Rupert. Goodness, she must have scarcely arrived in France when she sent this.' Kitty smiled as she looked at the image on the front of the card and read her cousin's scribbled note.

'I expect as honeymooners they wished to get the cards out of the way so they would be free to enjoy their holiday.' Matt grinned at her and received a playful smack on his arm as his fiancée took in his meaning.

Kitty dropped the card inside her bag to show her grandmother later and took Matt's arm to step out into the sunshine.

By mutual consent they walked out of the town towards Warfleet Creek and up towards the ancient castle that kept watch over the river estuary. Bertie trotted happily ahead of them, nose to the ground and tail held high.

'He's a very handsome dog,' Kitty said.

'Indeed. It seems likely that I shall end up keeping him, but I hope the habit he has of howling at everything stops soon.' They had reached the castle tea rooms and Kitty paused, looking for a seat at a shaded table.

'Shall we stop for lunch before walking back down?' Kitty asked.

'Will it make you feel more as if you are on holiday, despite becoming embroiled in a murder?' Matt grinned at her as he led the way to an empty table with a view of the river.

'Of course. I have just under a week of freedom before I must go back to the accounts and invoices.' Kitty took a seat under the shade of a tree and sighed as she took in the sight of the water sparkling a deep blue green in the estuary below. Small pleasure craft laden with day trippers ploughed their way up and down the waterway.

A waitress emerged from the tea room dressed in a smart black uniform with white apron and frilled cap. Matt ordered a pot of tea and sandwiches, along with a dish of cold water for Bertie.

The dog found his way under the table to nestle at their feet. 'I take it you won't now be going to see those Labrador puppies?' Kitty asked Matt as the girl returned bearing their lunch.

'Hmm, I rather think Bertie will be quite enough to look after for now.' Matt frowned as the dog raised his head to sniff the air appreciatively at the arrival of their potted meat sandwiches. Spying his chance, a sausage roll was quickly snaffled before Matt could prevent him.

Kitty giggled. 'I rather think Bertie might give Muffy a run for her money.' Her cousin Lucy's dog was a notorious thief and a glutton.

Matt shook his head and moved the plates into the middle of the table. 'I rather fear you may be right.'

They continued to eat their lunch amicably, talking on this and that, when Matt suddenly paused and touched Kitty's arm. 'Look towards the path leading from St Petroc's. Isn't that Reverend Greenslade?'

Kitty glanced across. The tall, stooped figure of the reverend stood uncertainly near the entrance to the tea room. A small dark green canvas knapsack was on his back, and he was mopping his brow with a large spotted handkerchief.

'Reverend Greenslade, would you care to share our table?' Kitty was on her feet and making the offer before Matt could prevent her.

He did his best to hide a smile as Kitty steered her quarry back to the vacant seat at their table.

'Oh my goodness, I had not realised it would be so warm.' The priest took a seat, an expression of relief on his pleasant middle-aged face. 'I took the bus and then the ferry, before using one of the water taxis to visit St Petroc's Church there. Most interesting, most interesting indeed, but I fear I have underestimated the strength of the sun.'

He flagged down the waitress and ordered a pot of tea and scones with cream. 'After those terrible events yesterday, I needed to clear my head and seek some spiritual solace. St Petroc's was recommended to me by my host.'

He tucked his hanky inside the breast pocket of his jacket and blinked at them.

'Yes, indeed. It was such a shock to everyone yesterday,' Kitty said as she slipped a titbit to Bertie, who had started to sniff the reverend's trousers rather too enthusiastically.

'Forgive me, Miss Underhay, Captain Bryant, but I think the inspector mentioned that you knew the unfortunate gentleman that was killed?' Reverend Greenslade pulled off his Panama hat and used it to fan his face.

'An acquaintance of mine from some years ago. He had written to me saying he intended to visit the area for a few days and wished to meet. Naturally I invited him to stay. He wasn't a person I knew terribly well, so I was surprised to hear from him.' Matt tried to steer a line between a lie and the truth.

'Oh, dear me, how dreadful. I see you still have the poor man's dog.' The reverend twitched the leg of his trousers away from Bertie's inquisitive nose.

Kitty smiled. 'Yes, the police said that Simon had no family, and the poor thing was simply handed over to us by the station staff. I don't think they quite knew what to do with Bertie.' She bent to fuss the top of the dog's head.

The waitress deposited Reverend Greenslade's tea and scones.

'I hope Miss Briggs has recovered from yesterday's events?' Kitty asked as the waitress left their table. 'The poor woman looked most unwell.'

'Yes, indeed. She had to return from her missionary work in India because of her health. She has been seeing a specialist in London.' The priest poured his tea and started to apply jam and clotted cream to his scone.

'Do you know her well? I thought I might call on her to make sure she has recovered. I was most concerned about her. Mrs Craven said she had been unwell during the journey too.'

Matt pressed his lips together to keep from smiling as Kitty turned on the charm for Reverend Greenslade's benefit.

'That is such a kind thought, Miss Underhay. I had some correspondence from Miss Briggs before her return to England. My church has been one of the sponsors of her mission in India. Naturally I have endeavoured to support her as she has been residing close to my church and when she said she intended to stay with her sister here in Devon, it happened to coincide with my own plans.' Reverend Greenslade's hand trembled slightly as he cut his scone into four neat quarters.

'The air in the bay is reputed to be very beneficial for one's health,' Kitty mused, and Matt knew that she too had noted the tremor.

'Indeed so. My own health has been an issue this past few months so the bishop has kindly granted me some time away from the parish to recuperate.'

A loud bang came from the direction of the tea-room kitchen as the waitress dropped one of the trays on the stone floor. Reverend Greenslade started and looked around wildly, before settling down again to continue eating.

'Gracious, that made me jump.'

'Forgive me for asking, sir, but I too am a veteran of the Great War. I take it that you saw active service?' Matt's tone was gentle. He recognised all too well the signs of a man who had been exposed to shellfire.

'Yes, I was in Belgium. My ministry took me to the front.' Reverend Greenslade straightened in his chair and his eyes took on a troubled expression.

'I understand, sir. The effects of that terrible conflict are difficult, if not impossible, to forget,' Matt sympathised with the man. He knew from his own experiences about the dreadful lingering after-effects of that awful war.

Matt called the waitress across so they could pay for their lunch. They made their farewells and left the reverend to continue enjoying his scones. The impromptu meeting with him had proved quite useful.

———

Kitty slipped her hand into the crook of Matt's arm as they set off back down the hill towards Dartmouth. Bertie once more trotted ahead, seemingly content to explore his new surroundings.

'That was an interesting conversation,' Kitty said as they strolled leisurely along the road.

'Indeed. I take it that you intend visiting Miss Briggs tomorrow?' Matt's eyes twinkled and the dimple in his cheek flashed as he looked at her.

'I think it would be a very Christian thing to do,' Kitty responded primly, and Matt laughed aloud. She knew that he knew her all too well.

'We are tackling Lady Jacques this evening at the yacht club, so that leaves Miss Dubois and Mr Ford,' Matt mused.

'I wonder if Miss Dubois will be at the Pavilion this afternoon. No doubt she will wish to have a rehearsal before her performance. Shall we take a drive into Torquay?' Kitty asked.

They were near the shed where she stored her car.

'Why not? It's a pleasant day to go motoring,' Matt agreed.

Bertie was secured on the back seat of the car as Kitty reversed carefully out of the garage. She was proud of her driving skills and considered she had done well to master them since her first lessons in the New Year with Robert Potter. Robert was the son of their regular taxi driver and was walking out with her friend, Alice.

Her grandmother and Mrs Craven were still dubious about lady motorists in general and Kitty had already had one near squeak when the brakes on her car had been tampered with a few months earlier. However the freedom of the open road and the delight of being mistress of her own destiny had overcome any worries the accident might have inspired in her.

She took a moment to add an extra couple of bobby pins to secure her hat before setting off to cross the Dart. She had no desire to lose her favourite summer hat in the middle of the ferry crossing.

The breeze on the river was a welcome relief as they landed at Kingswear on the opposite bank. Soon they were heading along the lane in the shade of the trees and the green leafy hedgerows that brushed the side of the car. Wildflowers spilled out from the verges; white daisies with yellow centres and pink and red poppies attracted butterflies from the yellowing fields of corn on either side of the road.

Kitty's heart thumped a little faster as they followed the coast road down into Torquay. The previous year had seen her battling to save Matt from the noose when he had been wrongly suspected of murder. The culprit had finally been caught at the iconic white theatre on the seafront. Ever since then, although she had attended the occasional concert there, it had not been her favourite place to visit.

The fine weather had attracted a number of visitors and it took her a while to find a suitable space to park her car.

'Gosh, it's terribly busy. Let's hope our luck is in,' Kitty remarked as she looked around at the bustling promenade and the groups of people sitting in the pleasure garden.

Matt rescued Bertie from the back seat of the car, setting him down on the pavement. Kitty strolled over to a nearby board displaying a poster advertising the concert.

'Miss Dubois is high on the playlist, so she is clearly a talented singer,' Kitty observed.

'Let's go and try the playhouse and see if any of the cast or staff are there,' Matt suggested as Bertie sat down for a good scratch.

Kitty took Matt's arm once more and they set off along the front. Overhead the seagulls wheeled and screamed, and the air smelt of ozone and salt. The palm trees waved in the gentle breeze and the red sandy beach was crowded with people.

They were almost at the entrance to the theatre when Kitty halted, tugging on Matt's jacket sleeve. 'Look.' She nodded her head towards the rear of the playhouse. Miss Dubois, elegantly clad in a form-fitting pale blue chiffon dress, was clearly taking a break, smoking a cigarette in a small black holder.

More surprisingly the person accompanying her appeared to be Mr Ford.

'Hmm, it certainly seems as if those two know each other,' Kitty said. 'Let's see if we can get closer before they see us.'

EIGHT

The crowded promenade made it easier to draw nearer without attracting either Miss Dubois or William Ford's attention. They certainly appeared to be engrossed in conversation, with Miss Dubois's neatly coiffured dark head next to Mr Ford's.

As they got nearer Kitty caught a snatch of William Ford's comments.

'I'm telling you it was a hit. I don't know who ordered it. We need to find out where the stuff's gone though. Someone has had it away.'

Miss Dubois extracted the remains of her cigarette from the holder and dropped it on the floor, extinguishing it with the toe of her shiny black patent shoe. Whatever her response may have been to Mr Ford's comment was lost as she lifted her gaze and spotted Kitty and Matt approaching.

At first Kitty thought William Ford was going to attempt to sidle away to avoid speaking to them. However, he appeared to realise that they had seen him so instead decided to stay and brazen it out.

'Lovely day today, isn't it?' Matt raised his hat politely to Miss Dubois and nodded at Mr Ford.

'It certainly seems to be. I must admit I haven't seen much of it. Your policeman friend was interviewing me before lunch and then I have been rehearsing all afternoon. This is my first break.' Carlotta Dubois looked bored by the conversation.

'What a surprise to see you here too, Mr Ford. I didn't realise you and Miss Dubois were acquainted?' Kitty did her best to look innocent and wide-eyed as she asked her question.

'Only since yesterday, Miss...?' Mr Ford looked at her.

'Underhay, Kitty Underhay. I forgot we all met in such strange circumstances yesterday that none of us were properly introduced. This is my fiancé, Captain Matthew Bryant.' She smiled back at Matt who nodded his head to acknowledge the introduction.

'Yes, you were both there with the police. What's your interest in the fellow that was murdered?' Carlotta Dubois cut straight to the point, her dark-eyed gaze darting suspiciously between Matt and Kitty.

William Ford had folded his arms and was also clearly waiting for a response.

'The man that was killed was an old acquaintance of mine. I hadn't seen him for many years when he got in touch and said he was visiting the area for a few days and wished to catch up. Naturally I suggested he stay with me. My fiancée and I went to meet him at the station. I work as a private investigator here in the bay so, of course, I know some of the police here. When I saw what had happened, I offered my assistance,' Matt explained with a slight shrug of his shoulders.

Miss Dubois shot a quick glance at William Ford. 'You know he was involved in that big case at the Old Bailey? The jewel robbery? I recognised him afterwards from pictures in the paper.'

'We have been in Yorkshire for Kitty's cousin's wedding so haven't paid much attention to the news. Simon did tell me that he wished to get out of London but as it's summer, with the heat, I didn't think anything more of it. No doubt he would have told me more when he arrived.'

Kitty admired Matt's casual handling of Miss Dubois's questions.

'Did you recognise Mr Travers too?' She decided to take a leaf out of Carlotta Dubois's book and aimed her question at William Ford.

Ford had lost the air of laddish banter and flirtatiousness from the previous day. His eyes were as sharp as flint and just as cold as he answered her question.

'Yes, I knew on the train. Got his picture all over the front of that paper he was reading, hadn't he? I asked him about the race results on the back and when he lowered it a bit to answer me, I clocked as it was him.' His tone was belligerent.

Kitty wondered why Mr Ford had seen fit to keep that information from the inspector yesterday. It seemed Miss Dubois was not the only dishonest person in the carriage.

'Did either of you notice anything odd at all during the journey? Any possible moments when people stood or moved around the compartment when Simon Travers could have been killed?' Matt asked.

'You working with the police now?' Ford asked.

'No, just trying to find out who may have killed the man I was expecting as my house guest.' Matt's tone was still casual, but Kitty could tell his shoulders had tensed.

'I already told that policeman, what's his name? Greville. I didn't notice anything. I was reading my magazine and stood up a few times to get things from my bags. That Craven woman had hogged all the room on the luggage rack. I think I must have closed my eyes for a moment, then Miss Briggs was standing up. I think to get medication and she staggered and almost fell. Reverend Greenslade caught her, and we all tried to assist her.' Miss Dubois's brow puckered.

'Did Mr Travers help?' Kitty asked.

Carlotta shrugged. 'No, I think he was asleep. It was very warm in the compartment.'

'Mr Ford?' Kitty turned to William.

He attempted a smile that she noted didn't reach his eyes. 'Nothing. Like Miss Dubois 'ere just told you. I was pretty tired myself, so I'd been dozing until that missionary woman started staggering about. Almost landed in me lap she did.'

The stage door at the rear of the playhouse opened and a young man popped his head out.

'Carla, they're waiting for you.'

Miss Dubois turned to leave. 'I must get back to work.'

'Thank you for talking to us. I hope we have the pleasure of hearing you sing,' Matt said.

Miss Dubois turned her head and gave him a swift assessing glance that Kitty did not care for. 'I'll have some tickets left for you at the front for tomorrow night.'

She sauntered back into the theatre and the door clicked shut behind her.

'She never offered me no tickets,' William Ford muttered.

'Perhaps she thought you might be too busy to attend. You know, selling brushes?' Kitty couldn't resist probing a little.

She would have thought that Mr Ford would have had a full diary of business appointments. It was odd that he was dressed in a linen jacket, with a navy cravat at his neck as if he were on holiday. It was also clear to her that he and Carlotta had known each other before their meeting on the train.

'I had to rearrange my plans, thanks to that friend of yours getting himself killed. Then that policeman come poking about after lunch asking questions. This has been the first chance I've had to come down here and take in the sights.' Ford leered at Kitty and winked at two pretty girls as they walked past where they were standing.

Matt felt in his coat pocket and produced his silver card

case. He flicked it open and took out a card, passing it over to Mr Ford.

'Please take my card. I'm not the police. If you think of anything, recall anything from that journey, however small, please contact me.'

Kitty half-expected the man to reject the proffered slip of card but instead Ford tucked it in his pocket.

'I've told you all I know.'

'Thank you.' Kitty slipped her hand back onto the crook of Matt's arm and they moved away. Bertie trotting obediently alongside them.

'Did you think he was hiding something?' Kitty asked once she was certain they were out of earshot.

'Definitely. And so was Miss Dubois. Those two clearly know one another and they both knew who Travers was.' Matt frowned.

'It will be interesting to see if Inspector Greville receives any more information from London about them.' She couldn't help but wonder if her thoughts about two people working together to murder Simon Travers were true. If so, then Miss Dubois and Mr Ford would be likely culprits.

'Yes, let's see what we can find out tonight at the yacht club and then we'll go and see Inspector Greville tomorrow and pool our findings. Right now, Miss Dubois and Mr Ford have certainly moved up the list of suspects,' Matt agreed.

They had reached Kitty's car and she opened her handbag to retrieve the key. Bertie jumped onto the back seat as soon as she opened the door.

'He has soon made himself at home,' she remarked as Matt secured him.

'He certainly has. I'd better take him back to the house. I expect he will want something to eat, and we now have an evening engagement to look forward to.' Matt slid into the passenger seat.

Kitty pulled a face. She knew many of the members of the yacht club as they attended various functions at the Dolphin. Individually most were quite pleasant, but en masse in the stuffy male preserve of their club, she suspected the evening would not really be to her tastes.

————

Matt arranged for Mr Potter's taxi to collect Kitty and to call for him on the way to the yacht club. Kitty had offered to drive but Matt said he wished her to enjoy herself and, as the roads near the club were narrow and would be busy with other vehicles dropping off and collecting the members, she had reluctantly agreed.

She had selected a pale green crepe de chine evening gown that she had bought for her stay in Yorkshire. To give herself courage, she attached the small woman's suffrage brooch that her mother had always worn onto the silver chain Alice had given her at Christmas. With it secured around her neck and discreetly tucked below the neckline of her dress she felt prepared to face the yacht club.

'Oh, you look lovely, darling. Those jewelled clips in your hair really set off your gown.' Her grandmother approved of her outfit when she made her way to the salon to say where she was going.

Kitty draped a fine knitted silver evening shawl over her arm and checked inside her matching silver fringed bag to ensure she had her comb, compact and handkerchief. 'Thank you, Grams. I don't suppose I shall be too late getting back.'

'Nonsense, my dear, go and enjoy yourself. It's about time you and Matthew went out and simply relaxed instead of always working on one of those dreadful murder cases. A spot of dancing and supper sounds just the ticket.'

Kitty felt slightly awkward at deceiving her grandmother.

She guessed that she hadn't made the connection between the body her friend had found on the train and this sudden invitation to the yacht club.

The telephone rang and her grandmother answered.

'Mr Potter is downstairs, Kitty. Now have a lovely evening.' Her grandmother kissed her cheek and Kitty smelled the faint scent of lavender from her perfume.

'We shall.'

As she hurried down the stairs to her waiting taxi she hoped that the evening would be just dancing and supper.

Matt was ready when they called at his house. Kitty's heart always speeded up when she saw Matt dressed in evening wear. His dashing good looks always seemed set off by formal wear.

'All set?' he asked as he entered the taxi to sit beside her.

'I think so, what have you done with Bertie?' she asked.

'My housekeeper's grandson is staying in the house with him. I dare not leave him unattended or the poor thing will howl all the time I'm out.' Matt kissed her cheek and made her blush as he took her hand in his.

Mr Potter stopped as close as he could to the entrance of the club. The street was busy with chauffeur-driven motor cars dropping off couples dressed in evening wear. The foyer was a blaze of electric light spilling out onto the darkening street as the sun slipped down beyond the sea, lighting the sky with streaks of pink and gold.

Mrs Craven had been as good as her word and there were two tickets for the evening marked with their names at the door. The entrance hall was busy as Matt steered her through the crowds of people towards the function room where the fundraiser was being held.

'What was this in aid of again?' Matt murmured in her ear as they entered the room.

'I have no idea.' Kitty noticed Mrs Craven deep in conversation with a small group of people near the space that had been cleared for dancing at the end of the room.

A long table covered with a white cloth was set against the side wall. Kitty guessed the various bottles and other items must be raffle prizes, since a large brown teddy bear sporting a red ribbon around its neck appeared to be presiding over the selection.

'Would you care for a drink?' Matt asked, looking at the bar.

'Yes, please.' Kitty had not yet managed to locate Lady Jacques.

'Cocktail?'

Kitty smiled and nodded, her attention drawn to a large and somewhat noisy group of men and women of around her own age who had just entered the room.

Matt disappeared into the crowd around the bar and Kitty moved to the side, her target in sight.

NINE

With all of her attention fixed on Lady Jacques, Kitty was startled when a familiar voice remarked, 'Miss Underhay, this is a most delightful surprise to find you here this evening.'

She turned to see Doctor Carter's cherubic face beaming at her.

'Doctor Carter, I didn't know you were coming tonight. Matt has just gone to the bar to get us both a drink. Are you a member here?' She wouldn't have been surprised if he had said he was, although the doctor's love was for cars rather than boats, and the faster the motor car the better.

'No, not at all. I was invited along by one of the members. Is Captain Bryant a member? I hadn't put him down as a nautical type.' The doctor grinned happily at her.

'No, he isn't. Mrs Craven kindly invited us.' Kitty inclined her head to where Mrs Craven, resplendent in peacock blue, could just be glimpsed still holding court.

'Ah, I see, then won't you come and join us, my dear, there is room at our table for both of you.'

Kitty followed the doctor over to one of the circular tables dressed with a white linen cloth and fresh flower centrepiece.

To her surprise Inspector Greville was already seated there, alongside a cheery looking lady in a fussy grey gown, who the doctor introduced as his wife.

'Is Mrs Greville not here this evening?' Kitty said, once she had been formally introduced to Mrs Carter and had taken a seat.

'One of the boys has toothache so she was forced to stay at home.' The inspector didn't appear to be unduly put out by his wife's absence.

Matt came to join them, presenting Kitty with a drink. 'I'm afraid gin and orange was the best the bar could do.' He shook hands with the men and was introduced to Mrs Carter, who appeared a pleasant, sensible woman.

'Mrs Craven said Lady Jacques was expected to attend this evening,' Matt remarked as he took a sip of his whisky. 'Have you had the opportunity to speak to her yet, Inspector?'

Kitty tasted her gin and shuddered. It was not the nicest drink she had ever had. If it had been produced by one of her staff, they would have swiftly been looking for other employment.

'Not as yet, no. I telephoned her this afternoon, but her maid informed me that her mistress was out.' The inspector frowned.

'She's here this evening. I just saw her come in with that rather loud gay crowd over there. She's wearing a silver lamé dress.' Kitty indicated the noisy group of young people laughing and chattering a few tables away.

'Is she indeed?' the inspector mused as he eyed up the group.

Lady Jacques certainly seemed to be enjoying herself, leaning on the arm of a tall foppish young man in evening attire and quaffing from a large glass of champagne. Kitty thought that Meribel, and most of her party, were already slightly squiffy.

The music commenced, provided by a small six-piece band

with a female vocalist. Kitty had hired them before to play at the Dolphin and knew them to be a reliable group who knew all of the popular dance tunes.

Lady Jacques promptly set down her champagne and tugged her escort onto the pocket-sized dance floor. She was swiftly followed by several other couples from her group. Kitty watched for a moment contemplating how best to approach Lady Jacques, while Matt discreetly informed Inspector Greville of the results of their investigation earlier in the day.

Inspector Greville's moustache twitched when Matt informed him of Miss Dubois and Mr Ford's apparent connection.

'I've been told to expect more information on those two tomorrow.' He frowned at the half pint of bitter he had sitting in front of him.

'Inspector Greville! How goes the investigation? Are you here to make an arrest?' Mrs Craven perched herself down on the empty seat at their table and leaned forward to make herself heard over the music and chatter in the room.

'Mrs Craven, no, this is pleasure, not business. I was invited to attend this function by a club member.' The inspector kept his voice low.

Mrs Craven rolled her eyes. 'I wouldn't have thought you would have been able to spare the time for social gadding about with an unsolved murder on your hands. With so few suspects I thought you must have cracked the case by now.' Her bosom heaved with indignation under her sparkling blue chiffon evening frock. 'I do hope you will solve it quickly. I have my reputation to think of and, as one of the persons in the compartment, I do not wish to have any suspicion attaching itself to me.'

Kitty suppressed a sigh and wondered why the murderer hadn't ended Mrs Craven at the same time as Mr Travers.

'I am sure that no one who knows you could possibly think

you had a hand in Mr Travers's death, Mrs Craven,' Inspector Greville soothed.

'No one who knows me personally, but when this reaches the press and my name is mentioned, well mud sticks, Inspector. I am a very influential person. I sit on many committees and bear a great deal of responsibility. People look to me for leadership. I cannot afford to have that jeopardised.'

Mrs Craven had obviously been mulling about the murder and its possible consequences to herself all afternoon.

'I'm sure the inspector will have the culprit under lock and key very soon, Mrs C,' Matt made an attempt to reassure her.

'Well, I hope you're right, Matthew. I do have connections, you know. The chief constable's wife is a dear friend of mine.' Mrs Craven swept away, leaving her parting remark hanging in the air.

'Oh dear,' Mrs Carter observed.

'Oh dear, indeed,' Kitty agreed. She knew all too well of Mrs Craven's fondness for writing to the chief constable. Indeed, her grandmother was also on friendly terms with the chief constable's wife. She felt quite sorry for the inspector.

'Doctor Carter, forgive me for asking this but the weapon that was used to kill Mr Travers, was there anything of significance there?' Kitty asked, glancing apologetically at the doctor's wife as she made the enquiry.

She knew that the doctor would have extracted the weapon as part of his examination of the body when it reached the morgue. No doubt it was now tagged and labelled as evidence for a future trial once the killer was captured.

'Small knife, narrow blade, stiletto type. Went in like a hot knife through butter. Perfect for the job, went right between the ribs, straight into his heart.' Doctor Carter smiled happily.

'My dear.' His wife placed a hand on his arm.

'Oh yes, um, it's the sort of thing that could be acquired

easily I imagine. Inspector, I think you had some information on it.' He patted his wife's hand and looked at Inspector Greville.

'Yes, we had the London boys make some enquiries. The handle was slightly unusual, more decorative than you would expect. It seems that particular knife is sold from a market stall in Camden. The stallholder imports them from abroad. A constable made enquiries, but the stallholder was no help in identifying a possible suspect. High volume of sales apparently.' The inspector's moustache sagged in disappointment.

Kitty had noticed the unusual swirls and decorative elements on the silver handle of the knife when she had entered the compartment. It was annoying that the stallholder couldn't recall anything useful.

There was a break in the music and an announcement was made that the buffet was open and raffle tickets could be acquired from the ladies committee who would circulate around the tables.

Inspector Greville's face brightened at the mention of food. Kitty watched as Lady Jacques and her giggling friends returned to their table. The band paused for their rest and a pianist took over to provide background music while the guests ate, drank and refreshed themselves.

When she saw Lady Jacques detach herself from her group, presumably to visit the powder room, Kitty signalled to Matt and left the table to follow her. A small cloakroom had been designated for use by the ladies and Kitty was pleased to discover the room was empty as everyone else had obviously gone to the buffet.

She stood at the marble topped counter in front of the mirror with her lipstick in her hand and waited for Lady Jacques to emerge. Kitty moved aside so Lady Jacques could wash her hands, and applied a fresh coat of lipstick.

'Oh, it's Lady Jacques, isn't it? What a surprise to meet you here. Kitty Underhay, we met yesterday. That ghastly business at the station in Dawlish.' Kitty smiled brightly at Meribel.

The woman paused as she dried her hands on the dark green towel that matched the tiles surrounding the marble countertop. Recognition spread slowly across her face.

'Oh, yes, I remember. You were with that tall good-looking chap. Captain somebody or other.' Meribel blinked and frowned.

Kitty wondered how much she had had to drink. She was glad Matt wasn't present to hear himself described as good-looking. He would have developed a swollen head.

'Such an awful business. My fiancé and I were there to meet him, you know. The dead man.' Kitty kept her voice low aware that someone could walk in at any moment.

'I can't believe that he was killed under our noses. I mean I was at the opposite end of the compartment. I almost missed the train.' She giggled. 'Typical of my rotten luck. Just in time to get on board and I land up in a compartment with a murderer. I mean, what are the odds?' She swayed on her heels and grabbed at the counter to steady herself.

'I know,' Kitty sympathised. 'Did you know any of the others who were in the compartment?'

Meribel blinked her large blue eyes. 'Never seen any of them before in my life. The chap that was killed did seem frightfully familiar though.' She leaned forward and peered at her complexion in the mirror. 'I say, you don't happen to have a comb I could use for a moment, do you?'

Kitty dug inside her evening purse and obliged her with a comb. 'Did you see anyone stand up or move around the compartment? It seems incredible that anyone could do such a thing with five people all sitting right there.'

Lady Jacques tidied her hair and patted her blonde curls into place. 'I must admit I dozed off for a while. I'd had a hectic evening the night before and frankly, darling, I was wrecked. I think I woke up when that older lady had a turn, fainting or something.' She passed Kitty's comb back to her.

Kitty tucked her comb back inside her bag. 'Who do you think was most likely to have done it?' she asked curiously.

The other girl paused in the act of straightening the shoulder straps of her gown. Her gaze met Kitty's in the mirror.

'I don't know. I suppose that man, the salesman. He was sitting opposite him and well, this is silly, but I got the feeling he was watching him. On purpose, I mean. Like a cat watching a mouse hole.' She gave a delicate shiver. 'Ugh, I hope the police solve this soon.'

The door to the powder room opened and two older ladies came in talking and laughing, so Kitty slipped away leaving Meribel to find her way back to her friends.

'Did you learn anything?' Matt asked on her return to the table.

The inspector and the Carters were missing, and Kitty assumed they must have gone to the buffet.

'She didn't know the others, saw and heard nothing, but thinks Mr Ford was the most likely culprit. She feels he was watching Mr Travers.' Kitty picked up her drink and took a tiny sip. It still tasted foul.

She noticed that Matt, in common with the others at the table, had a small pile of raffle tickets in front of them. 'Oh dear, have I missed the ticket sales?'

Matt grinned. 'Don't worry, I got some for you. I don't want Mrs C to think we aren't contributing to the cause.'

She couldn't help smiling back. She knew he had no desire for any of the prizes on the table, any more than she did. Inspector Greville arrived back bearing a plate piled high with sandwiches and slices of pork pie.

'Better go and get a plate before all the food goes,' he remarked brightly to Kitty and Matt as he resumed his seat and began to tuck in.

Kitty accompanied Matt to the side room where a long table had been set out with a selection of cold foods. Doctor and Mrs Carter were on their way back to the table as Kitty and Matt joined the end of the queue.

Mrs Craven sidled up next to Kitty.

'Well?' she asked in a stage whisper. 'I saw you follow Lady Jacques. Did she have any information?'

Kitty glanced around to make sure no one was standing too close. 'Nothing interesting.'

Mrs Craven's face fell. 'How very disappointing. Is there anyone else you need to talk to?'

'I think we've spoken to all the other passengers now, except Miss Briggs, and Kitty hopes to call on her tomorrow,' Matt said as they shuffled forward in the line for the food.

'Well surely she is not a suspect. If the murderer took advantage of her faint to stab Mr Travers then it could not have been her wielding the knife.' Mrs Craven looked pleased with her deduction.

'She may have seen or heard something, or she may have been working with someone to provide the distraction,' Kitty said.

Secretly though, Kitty felt it was unlikely that Miss Briggs could have been in collusion with one of the other passengers. She had only recently returned to the country and there was no obvious motive that she could think of. Still, it couldn't be ruled out.

Mrs Craven seemed dissatisfied with Kitty's reasoning. 'Well, I'm sure Matthew will guide you on the line of questioning.' She paused and her expression brightened. 'Better still, Kitty dear, I shall accompany you myself. Miss Briggs would no doubt welcome a visit from a person closer to her own age with some standing in the community.'

Kitty's mouth dropped open and she looked at Matt hoping

he would step in. Annoyingly he nodded his agreement with Mrs Craven's suggestion.

'That's very thoughtful of you, Mrs C. I'm sure Kitty would welcome your support.'

'Splendid. I shall ascertain Miss Briggs's address from the inspector and call for you tomorrow morning, Kitty. I shall get some fruit and chocolate to take with us. The poor woman is clearly very unwell, and no doubt will welcome a little attention.' Mrs Craven swept away.

Kitty struggled to restrain herself from aiming a kick at Matt's ankle. 'What on earth are you doing?'

They had reached the buffet table and Matt collected a plate and handed one to Kitty.

'Mrs Craven will not be satisfied until she feels she has contributed to the investigation and at least it keeps her out of the inspector's way.' He helped himself to sandwiches and a sausage roll.

Kitty scowled. 'Yes, by putting her in my way.' She picked up a scotch egg and a vol-au-vent.

'Miss Briggs may well be better with two of you talking to her. She could hold a key to what happened if our hypothesis is correct that the murderer may have used her collapse as the moment to strike.' Matt fell into step beside Kitty as they moved away from the buffet to walk back to their seats.

'Well, Travers was the only one who didn't respond to Miss Briggs's collapse, so he could well have been dead at that point,' Kitty mused.

'No one recalls him speaking or moving afterwards either,' Matt agreed.

'Everyone seemed to think he was asleep.' Kitty looked at Matt. 'It will be interesting to hear from Miss Briggs, even if Mrs Craven is accompanying me.'

TEN

Matt was woken the following morning by the sound of Bertie howling downstairs. He rose, pulled on his dressing gown and went to investigate. He had left the dog fast asleep in his newly acquired basket in a corner of the kitchen when he had retired for the night.

He entered the room now to a scene of utter carnage. The wicker edge of the basket was chewed and shredded. The tartan blanket Matt had used to line it was in holes with clumps of chewed up wool scattered around the floor. The waste bin was overturned, and fragments of the previous days newspaper and some old eggshells were added to the mess.

Bertie sat in the midst of the chaos, his brown eyes large and remorseful. A strand of red wool dangled incriminatingly from the corner of his mouth. As soon as he saw Matt his tail began to beat happily on the quarry tiled floor as Matt surveyed the damage.

'Oh, Bertie, whatever have you done?'

The dog rose and came forward to greet him while Matt shook his head in despair, glad that his housekeeper was not due to arrive for another hour. He had scarcely finished cleaning up the debris when the telephone rang in the sitting room, and he went to answer it.

He flinched and moved the receiver further from his ear as the brigadier's stentorian tones reached him.

'Ha! Bryant my boy. Been trying to get hold of that inspector. Not at his desk yet apparently.' Matt suppressed a groan as he glanced at the clock on his mantelpiece. It was still only eight in the morning.

'Anyway, wanted to check how things were progressing. Jolly bad show Travers being killed like that. Makes a mockery of us all,' the brigadier continued.

'Yes, sir,' Matt managed to squeeze in a reply.

'Well then, man, give me a report on where you are with it all. Need to get this wrapped up smartish before the press get on the case. Can only hold the beggars off for so long you know.'

Matt delivered a concise report of their discoveries to date.

There was a brief moment of silence when he finished speaking.

'Hmm, this supports the information we've gathered at our end. I need to speak to this Greville fellow, but I think he should be rounding up the singer and, more particularly, that Ford chappie. Bad eggs, both of them.'

'Sir?' Matt waited for the brigadier to elucidate. He didn't care for Mr Ford or for Miss Dubois. He didn't think Kitty did either, but apart from a feeling that they were hiding something he had no direct cause to believe one of them had stabbed Travers.

'The woman is involved with one of the men on trial for the robbery. According to intelligence they were cohabiting in a rented apartment up until the arrest was made for the jewel heist. It's also thought that she is related to one of the other men standing trial. There was nothing to implicate her in the caper, so she was allowed to remain at liberty.'

'Go on, sir.' Matt could picture the brigadier sitting in a fug of cigar smoke, his moustache bristling as he imparted this information.

'Dubois is her professional name, but she is known under another couple of monikers and that's why it took a few hours to confirm it was the same blessed woman. Then there is that Ford fellow. Be on your guard with that one. Do warn Miss Underhay too as he's fond of the ladies. I know she's quite on the ball but even so.' The brigadier broke off into a coughing fit.

Matt knew Kitty was unlikely to fall for William Ford's dubious charms.

'What have you learned about Ford, sir?' Matt asked when the coughing on the other end of the line died down.

'Very nasty piece of work. Used to work at Billingsgate Fish Market as a porter. Hence his nickname, Billy the Fish. Got that partly because of the job and his slippery nature, but also his use of a blade. Nothing that the police this end could fix on him but he's a knife man with contacts in the various gangs here.'

Matt could see where this was leading, and he didn't like the sound of it. 'A knife man, eh, that would make him a prime suspect for having stabbed Travers. He knows Carlotta Dubois so he could have been hired for the murder.'

'There is also the matter of the missing jewels. This Dubois woman may know where they are stashed. She could be hiding them for the gang.' The brigadier gave another cough.

'Or she could have used some of them to pay Ford to kill Travers, hoping the case would collapse and the accused men would be freed.' Matt was thinking out loud.

'The case against them is pretty sound and Travers's evidence will stand. No, revenge is a more likely motive. Anyway, I'll inform Greville and you get to the police station, then together you can go and round these Johnnies up,' the brigadier instructed.

Matt barely had time to respond before the line went dead and his former employer rang off.

———

Mrs Craven arrived at the Dolphin promptly at ten o'clock to collect Kitty for their promised visit to Miss Briggs. Much to her annoyance, the older woman had firmly vetoed Kitty's offer to drive and had commandeered Mr Potter's taxi services instead.

The rear seat of the motor was already almost filled by Mrs Craven, a large basket of fruit and a bunch of flowers. Kitty had a job to squeeze in without sitting on anything.

'Do be careful, Kitty,' Mrs Craven admonished as Kitty balanced her cream leather handbag on her lap to avoid knocking the heads off a bunch of pink carnations.

'Is Miss Briggs expecting us?' Kitty asked as the taxi slid away from the kerb.

'I telephoned this morning and spoke to Miss Briggs's sister, a Mrs Pace. She suggested we keep our visit fairly short as Miss Briggs tires easily.' Mrs Craven adjusted the collar on her neat navy jacket as she settled back for the drive. The diamond brooch on her lapel sparkled in the sunlight streaming in through the taxi window.

'It seems Miss Briggs's illness is serious then. She certainly appeared very unwell after the murder when we were at the station.' Kitty would have much preferred to have seen Miss Briggs by herself. She couldn't help wondering if Mrs Craven in full flood might prove rather much for a lady in poor health.

'Mrs Pace did not say so directly, but I rather fear that Miss Briggs may not have much time left on this earth,' Mrs Craven confirmed.

The ferry was busy with traffic, and they had to wait for a while for the various horse and carts and vans to be loaded before they were waved aboard to cross the river. The roads continued to be busy all the way into Torquay. Kitty could only assume that there was an increase in the numbers of holiday-makers, as well as the usual business traffic. The fine weather always drew people to the coast.

Mrs Pace had a small lodging house in one of the back streets on the far side of the town. It appeared to be a respectable area with neat, terraced houses interspersed with small villas. Mrs Pace's house was on the end of a row. The walls were freshly whitewashed, and the blue painted front door and scrubbed step oozed respectability. A sign in the window read 'No Vacancies'.

Mrs Craven instructed Mr Potter to return for them in an hour, before turning to rap firmly with a gloved hand on the front door of the house. Kitty followed in her wake, having been instructed to carry the various gifts that Mrs Craven had brought for Miss Briggs.

The door was opened by a plumper, less tanned version of Miss Briggs wrapped in a pink floral overall.

'Mrs Pace, I presume? We spoke on the telephone this morning. I am Mrs Craven, and this is Miss Underhay.'

Kitty guessed that Mrs Pace had probably had a telephone installed to assist in attracting visitors to her boarding house.

'Come on through, Mrs Craven, Miss Underhay. My sister is expecting you. She's in my private sitting room at the back of the house.' Mrs Pace had a soft Devon accent.

She led the way along a narrow hall, past a room that Kitty assumed was for the use of the lodgers, and into another smaller parlour at the rear of the house. She assumed the kitchen and scullery were beyond the parlour.

Despite the heat of the day a small fire burned in the grate. Miss Briggs was reclined on the sofa with a paisley patterned shawl in the Kashmiri style spread over her legs.

'Please take a seat. I'll go and make some tea.' Mrs Pace looked anxiously at her sister and left the room.

Mrs Craven perched herself on an armchair and Kitty took the other seat. The heat in the small room was stifling and Kitty wished she could open the window and let in some fresh air.

'It was very good of you both to call. Please forgive the heat. Since my return to England, I'm afraid I have been unable to get warm.' Miss Briggs's voice was weak.

'We brought you a few things. We were most concerned that the strain of the journey and the shock of that poor man being murdered under our very noses may have worsened your condition.' Mrs Craven presented Miss Briggs with the flowers and Kitty placed the fruit basket on the low table beside the sofa.

'That really is too kind of you.' Miss Briggs gave a wan smile and Kitty could see that under her tan her complexion held a greyish hue.

'Has Inspector Greville called to see you?' Kitty asked.

'Yes, he came yesterday just before tea. A very nice man and most appreciative of Daphne's baking.' Miss Briggs smiled.

Kitty could imagine.

Mrs Pace nudged the door to the room open with a tray and Kitty leapt up to assist her.

'May I ask you to help yourselves?' She looked apologetically at her sister. 'It's just that I have new guests arriving later and there is so much to prepare.'

'Of course,' Kitty reassured her. 'I am in the hotel trade myself so I know how busy you must be.'

Mrs Pace gave her a grateful smile and hurried away. Kitty set to pouring tea for them all into the thick white pottery teacups.

'My sister has been very good to me. She runs this place alone since she lost her husband a few years ago.' Miss Briggs pushed herself further up her cushions and accepted a cup of tea from Kitty.

'It's always good to have a supportive family. Did you never marry, Miss Briggs?' Mrs Craven asked as she stirred sugar into her tea.

Kitty detected a blush on Miss Briggs's cheeks.

'No, unfortunately that never happened for me. However, I had the work of the Lord to do, and my calling sent me to India to the missions.'

'I'm sure you were most valued,' Mrs Craven said.

'I do hope so. I was sad to leave but my health as you can see is very poor and I hoped that I might get some treatment back in London.' The smile slipped from her lips. 'Alas it is not to be, and my time is short. My sister insisted I come to her, as the air is considered beneficial to one's health here. There are a few loose ends to my affairs that I wish to tie up and... I wanted to be with family.'

'Of course.' Kitty felt deeply sorry for this poor woman whose life was ebbing away. To have been caught up in a murder during her final days seemed to be making everything worse in Kitty's eyes.

'It was so fortunate that Reverend Greenslade was able to escort you during the journey.' Mrs Craven selected a short-bread finger from the tray and nibbled daintily.

'Yes, he has been most kind to me. His church, St Mark's, was one of those sponsoring the orphanage where I was work-ing, and the Christian Ladies' Hostel is just around the corner in the next street.' Miss Briggs waved away the biscuit plate when Kitty offered it to her.

'Isn't that near where that jewel robbery took place recently? It has been the talk of London, I believe,' Kitty asked.

Miss Briggs's gaze seemed to sharpen. 'I don't know. I think I saw something on the billboards about a trial when I was having tests at the hospital in town, but I'm really not sure.'

Kitty got the distinct impression that Miss Briggs was not being entirely honest. There was something about her gaze and the way she had looked when she had replied.

'Oh, my dear, it has been the most dreadful thing. The papers have been full of it. That poor man who was in our compartment was involved with the trial, you know.' Mrs Craven nodded her head sagely at Miss Briggs.

Kitty suppressed a groan. Mrs Craven appeared to have forgotten that she was not supposed to mention Simon Travers's role in the trial.

Miss Briggs gasped. 'Oh dear, do you think then that a member of this gang of thieves may have been amongst us in the compartment?'

Mrs Craven leaned in conspiratorially. 'My money is on that dreadful Mr Ford. I mean, a brush salesman in first class? And he was seated right opposite Mr Travers.'

'Goodness gracious, how dreadful. Such a good-looking young man. Impudent, I grant you, but still, one never likes to think ill of one's fellow man.' Miss Briggs shook her head.

Kitty was thinking very ill of Mrs Craven at that moment.

'You and your young man were there to meet the man that was killed, were you not, Miss Underhay?' Miss Briggs asked.

'Yes, he was an old acquaintance of Captain Bryant's. He contacted him unexpectedly to say he was in the area for a few days. Matt had no idea he was involved in the Tower Hill jewellery trial. We have been away in Yorkshire for my cousin's wedding so have rather lost touch with current affairs,' Kitty said.

'Captain Bryant is a private investigator so has good connections with the local police. Kitty assists him with some of his cases. I myself have also helped them out on a few occasions,' Mrs Craven added smugly.

Kitty decided that between the heat in the overcrowded,

stuffy parlour and Mrs Craven's idea of helpfulness, she was starting to feel quite unwell.

'Mrs Craven, I wonder if you might do me a small favour? These flowers are so lovely, and I fear the heat is starting to affect them. Could I trouble you to take them to the scullery and my sister will arrange them in a vase for me later. It's cooler there.' Miss Briggs passed the flowers over to Mrs Craven.

'Oh yes, of course.' Mrs Craven looked a little put out by the request, no doubt thinking that Kitty should have been the one to take the blooms to the scullery.

Once Mrs Craven had left the room, Miss Briggs turned her attention to Kitty.

'Miss Underhay, does your fiancé ever look for missing people?' The urgency in her tone and the unexpected request took Kitty by surprise.

'Yes, he does. Is there something we could assist you with?' She wondered what or who it could be.

'It is highly personal and obviously urgent. Do you think you could persuade him to call upon me to discuss the matter?'

Kitty could see from Miss Briggs's expression that this was something that mattered deeply to her. 'Of course, would tomorrow morning suit you?' She knew Matt would attend if she asked him.

Miss Briggs sank back on her pillows. 'Yes, thank you, my dear.'

Mrs Craven returned to the room. Her trip to the scullery had obviously allowed her to cool off a little and her complexion had lost some of its ruddy hue.

'I have placed the flowers in a bucket of water until your sister has time to arrange them.' She looked at her watch. 'I rather think that Mr Potter will be here in a moment to collect us, Kitty.' She gathered her gloves and bag.

'Thank you both for calling on me. I do appreciate your great kindness.' Miss Briggs looked quite weary.

Kitty patted her hand gently. 'Do rest, Miss Briggs. I shall attend to the other matter.' She added the last part in a low voice so Mrs Craven would not hear her.

Kitty thought that it would be very interesting to return tomorrow to discover who the missing person was that Miss Briggs wished Matt to find.

ELEVEN

Kitty was relieved when Mr Potter finally delivered her back to the Dolphin Hotel. Mrs Craven had not stopped talking all the way back to Dartmouth and Kitty's head was reeling. She bade her unwanted companion farewell and heaved a sigh of relief as she entered the cool, quietness of the lobby.

To her astonishment the first thing she saw was Bertie lying quietly next to the reception desk under Mary's watchful gaze.

'Oh, Miss Kitty, I'm so glad as you've come back. Captain Bryant asked me to watch his dog for him for a moment until you returned.' The receptionist's relief at her return to take charge of the dog was clear.

'Where on earth is Captain Bryant?' Kitty asked. She frowned at Bertie who sat up at her approach, his tail waving like a flag.

'He was here a short while ago, miss, with the police inspector, but then they had to go out rather sharpish like, so he left the dog here. I hope it's all right, miss?' Mary bit her lip anxiously.

Kitty wondered that her grandmother hadn't noticed that Bertie had been left in the lobby and said something to her receptionist. Dogs were always welcomed at the hotel, but it was generally expected that their owners look after them and not Kitty's staff.

'Did they say where they were going or how long they would be?' Kitty untied Bertie's leash from the back of the desk.

'No, miss.'

'I see, well, thank you, Mary. Come along, Bertie.' Kitty led the dog upstairs to her grandmother's salon. There seemed little she could do until Matt returned to the hotel and she could find out what on earth was going on. She wondered if the inspector had gone to make an arrest, but then why would Matt be with him and have Bertie on hand? It was all most peculiar.

She hadn't been in the drawing room for long when there was a knock at the door and Matt entered, closely followed by Inspector Greville. Bertie leapt to his feet and trotted happily over to Matt for him to fuss his head.

'Kitty, I'm so sorry I had to leave Bertie downstairs with Mary. I had forgotten that you had gone with Mrs Craven to visit Miss Briggs.' Matt kissed her cheek and apologised.

'Yes, well, perhaps you had both better take a seat. What has happened?' She noted the grave expression on the inspector's face and hoped that no one else had been murdered.

The inspector took off his hat and sank down gratefully onto one of the armchairs. 'Our apologies, Miss Underhay. Captain Bryant and myself both received telephone calls this morning from Brigadier Remmington-Blythe. He passed on information that he considered vital to the murder of Simon Travers. This necessitated urgently locating and questioning Miss Dubois and Mr Ford.'

'Has there been an arrest?' Kitty asked, glancing between the inspector and her fiancé. She still couldn't see why Bertie had ended up in Mary's care, or why they were in Dartmouth.

Matt looked glum. 'Not as yet. Miss Dubois was not at her lodgings, and we were informed that she had come to Dartmouth this morning. I volunteered to try and locate her while the inspector went in search of Mr Ford.' Bertie rested his chin lovingly on Matt's knee.

The frown on Kitty's forehead deepened. 'Did you manage to find them? And why is Bertie here?'

Matt exchanged a sheepish look with the inspector. 'I cannot leave Bertie unattended in the house. He has a some-what destructive streak, and my housekeeper finds his howling a distraction whilst she is working. I took him with me on the bus to the police station for my meeting with the inspector. Then he accompanied me back here while I enquired at the ferry compa-nies for any sign of Miss Dubois.'

'Her companions at the lodging house had said she intended taking a river cruise with some members of the compa-ny,' the inspector interjected.

Kitty could feel her brows rising as the two men continued with their story.

'I had no luck locating Miss Dubois. I had just returned here to wait for you when the inspector arrived,' Matt said.

'Mr Ford is missing from his lodging house, and no one seemed to know where he might be, so I came to find Captain Bryant, hoping that in the meantime he had located Miss Dubois.' The inspector's moustache drooped.

'We had scarcely set foot in the lobby when we received a message from one of the local constables to say Miss Dubois's party were on a private hire boat and expected to return at any moment.' Matt picked up the story.

'And so you left Bertie here in Mary's care, and went to find her?' Kitty guessed.

'Yes, except that when the party returned to the quay, Miss Dubois was not among them. She and a couple of others had decided to stay in Dittisham for lunch it seems.'

The inspector sighed. 'A constable has been sent to look for her return and another is on watch near Ford's lodgings.' He drummed his fingers on the arm of the chair. 'The whole matter is most unsatisfactory.'

Matt told Kitty the gist of the information they had received from the brigadier. In return she shared what little they had learned from Miss Briggs and also informed him of Miss Briggs's desire to engage his services.

'Hmm, interesting, I wonder who she is searching for?' Matt asked.

Kitty's stomach growled. With all the excitement of the morning she had forgotten that it was now after lunchtime.

'Inspector Greville, would you care to join us for lunch? I can request some sandwiches from the kitchen?'

The inspector's expression immediately lit-up at the mention of food, so Kitty telephoned and ordered lunch and a dish of water and some cold meat for Bertie.

The arrival of food lifted everyone's mood and Kitty was relieved to see that Bertie behaved himself, especially when Matt told her what had happened in the kitchen.

'I take it that you wish to question Miss Dubois further?' Kitty asked as the inspector pushed away his empty plate and dabbed the corners of his mouth with a napkin.

'Yes, I think we need to establish if she is working with Ford, or if it is merely a coincidence that she ended up in the same compartment as Travers.' The inspector placed the linen cloth down on the table.

'There was only one first class compartment in operation that day on the service. Most unusual, but the stationmaster told me that the railway company had been having problems with the carriages,' Matt said.

'Do you think this man Ford is the murderer, sir? I take it that he is expected back at his lodgings? You don't fear he may have attempted to disappear?' Kitty asked.

This had been playing on her mind throughout lunch. If

this Billy the Fish character thought he was suspected of the murder then surely he might try to evade capture.

'It is a possibility, but my feeling is that he thinks he is not under suspicion as yet.' The inspector looked at the clock on the mantelpiece to check the time. 'I would hope that Miss Dubois will be returning from Dittisham soon.'

The telephone rang as they were finishing their drinks. Kitty answered and called the inspector over to take the call.

'It is your sergeant in Torquay. He wishes to speak to you urgently.' She handed him the receiver and resumed her seat wondering if the call was connected with their case.

The inspector's face was grim as he listened intently to whatever the sergeant was telling him.

'Certainly, we shall come at once, and telephone Doctor Carter.' He replaced the receiver and turned to Matt and Kitty. 'A man's body has been fetched out of the harbour in Torquay. It sounds from the description as if Mr Ford has been found.'

Inspector Greville's car was downstairs, and Matt joined him in the front passenger seat, whilst Kitty and Bertie sat in the back as they set off at pace for Torquay and the harbour.

'My sergeant says he had a head injury. Whether that was the cause of his falling in the water or if it occurred after death, we shall need Doctor Carter to tell us.' Inspector Greville hunched forward over the steering wheel as he coaxed the police car up the hill at Kingswear.

'This puts a different complexion on the case, doesn't it, sir?' Matt asked. 'Could Billy have killed Travers as a hit and then been killed himself by someone who didn't wish to pay?'

'Or did he see whoever did kill Travers and try a spot of blackmail?' Kitty suggested.

'Or has there been a falling out amongst villains. Especially if one of them happens to know where the rest of the proceeds from that robbery might be hidden.' Greville swung the car down the coast road towards Torquay.

It occurred to Kitty that there was another, darker possibility. That someone else entirely had killed both Travers and Billy, and if so, then that person must have been one of the people in the carriage.

They drove past the Pavilion Theatre and reached the harbour in a few more minutes. The inspector parked his car near where a small knot of people were being kept at bay by a youthful uniformed constable. His cheeks were puffed out with the importance of his task as he tried to look imposing.

Kitty recognised Doctor Carter's sporty motor car also parked nearby and guessed he must have already been in town when the police had managed to contact him. Bertie trailed at her heels, sniffing the slightly fishy air as they approached the scene.

The inspector was allowed through with Matt at his side, but Kitty found her path blocked by the zealous young constable.

'I'm sorry, miss. You can't go through there, not with that there dog. There's been an incident. Police only.' He planted himself squarely in her path.

'Oh, don't be ridiculous. I'm with the inspector's party.' Kitty attempted to get around him.

'I don't thinks so, miss. I suggests as you and that dog waits over there.' He attempted to steer Kitty towards the onlookers who were watching the argument with avid interest.

Bertie, seeing Matt disappear from his view, threw back his head and started to howl in protest. A couple of the fishermen in the crowd started to chuckle sending a rush of colour into the constable's cheeks.

'And stop that there dog's noise,' he demanded.

'His master is with the inspector, which is where both I and Bertie should be. No wonder he is protesting.' Kitty drew herself up to her full five foot two inches and glared at the policeman.

'You tell him, missy,' one of the fishermen called out.

'And you can be quiet and all of you back up too.' The constable sensed he was losing credibility with the crowd and partially turned to square up to them.

Kitty took advantage of his momentary inattention to duck under his outstretched arm and ran along the quayside towards where she could see a small group gathered near the lobster pots.

'Oy, miss, you come back here,' she heard the constable shouting behind her as Bertie lolloped along beside her, his tongue hanging out and a happy expression on his furry face.

She slowed her pace as she neared the group gathered around what she presumed was the body of William Ford. Bertie trotted happily ahead and sat nicely beside Matt when Kitty joined him.

''Ere, miss.' The constable came puffing and panting along the quayside.

Matt looked at Kitty. 'Trouble getting through?'

She raised a brow. 'What do you think?'

Matt grinned and went to speak to the policeman. The constable scowled and turned away to return to his post, clearly still unhappy that Kitty had managed to get past him.

With the constable gone and Matt back by her side, Kitty began to take in the scene before her. Doctor Carter was kneeling, stooped over the body examining what appeared to be a large gash on the back of the man's head. As he turned the corpse back over, Kitty saw that it was definitely Billy Ford.

She could tell they had fished Billy from the water. His suit was sodden with rivulets of salt water trickling over the cobbles of the quayside. The two men who had found him stood nearby smoking. From their battered knitwear and work trousers tucked in their boots she guessed they were fishermen working the boats.

The inspector was methodically going through the contents

of Ford's pockets. Matt, like herself, was assessing the situation. A cold shiver ran along Kitty's spine. She had been starting to feel quite certain that it had been Ford who had killed Simon Travers. Now that Ford himself was dead, it seemed as if the case was not so clear-cut.

Matt seemed to sense her mood and placed his hand around her waist. 'The fishermen over there found him. It seems his body was partially concealed under another boat moored near theirs. When the tide changed, he floated free, and they raised the alarm.'

'My best guess is that he's been in the water since last night. Most likely time for something like this to happen and based on the tides and such that would be my supposition.' Doctor Carter stood and used his hands to brush the dust from the knees of his trousers.

'And the injury to his head?' Inspector Greville asked.

'I'd say before death rather than after. I'll take a better look at him when I get him back to the morgue. I can only see a few minor abrasions though, probably caused by the tide changes and the boats. I would have expected much more trauma to his head if it had occurred after he fell in the water.' The doctor smiled cheerfully at them.

Inspector Greville straightened up. 'Hit over the head and knocked into the water then.' He was clearly unhappy.

'Anything of significance in his pockets, sir?' Matt asked.

'The usual items, loose change, a few notes in his wallet, handkerchief, pocket comb, bus ticket. Oh, and your business card.' Inspector Greville looked at Ford's body.

Kitty was glad Ford's face was turned away from her again. 'He still has his wallet and if there is money still on his body, then I assume this wasn't a robbery gone wrong?'

Inspector Greville sighed. 'No, I'm very much afraid this looks like murder.'

He walked over to the fishermen who had pulled Ford's body from the sea and started to interview them.

'I wonder where everyone was last night?' Kitty mused, thinking of the other passengers who had shared the compartment.

'Unfortunately, because Mr Ford has been in the sea, I can't give you a definitive time. So, he could have been attacked before we met at the yacht club, during that time, or even shortly afterwards.' Doctor Carter seemed cheerfully unconcerned by his inability to narrow down the possible time of the attack.

'It may not have been one of the other passengers,' Matt said. 'There remains the possibility that Mr Ford was paid to murder Travers by someone who wasn't even in that compartment.'

'Lady Jacques was at the club, Miss Dubois was performing, Miss Briggs is very ill and I'm struggling to see Reverend Greenslade as the man.' Kitty wondered if Matt was right and there was some other person involved who had hired William Ford and then killed him.

Doctor Carter had closed his leather medical bag. 'I'll let you and Inspector Greville know if anything interesting turns up at the post-mortem.'

'Thank you.' Matt escorted Kitty as they walked along the quay back towards the constable still stood keeping guard. The doctor accompanied them.

'Any news yet on getting into Exeter Gaol to see Hammett?' Doctor Carter enquired.

Kitty shook her head. 'Nothing yet. I've tried all avenues so I'm hoping to hear something soon.'

'I'm afraid the Home Office can be quite slow in these matters. It is quite a daunting prospect visiting a prison, my dear. Are you certain you wish to confront Hammett in person?'

Doctor Carter peered at her, concern written across his countenance.

'Even if he refuses to tell me anything, or indeed if he has nothing to say, I owe it to my mother to at least try to find out the truth. Hammett is the only person left that is likely to know how she came to die and be buried under the streets in Exeter.' Kitty tried to make her voice sound confident, but truth be told, she was quite concerned about visiting Hammett in the prison.

However, Father Lamb, the priest she had met in Exeter when her mother's body had been found, had assured her that he would arrange for the prison chaplain to accompany her if permission were granted for a visit.

'Well, I can understand your need to confront the brute,' Doctor Carter said. They halted close to the constable who was doing his best to pretend they didn't exist.

'Now, can I give you both a ride anywhere? You came with the inspector I think, didn't you?' Doctor Carter looked around as if expecting to see Kitty's little red car.

Kitty and Matt were familiar with the doctor's love of speed and rather reckless driving style.

'Thank you, that's most kind, but I do need to call in at my office before we return to Dartmouth.' Matt smiled at the doctor and Kitty breathed a tiny sigh of relief.

'Jolly good. I'd best get off and finish my calls then before my chaps get our friend back to my mortuary.' The doctor beamed and gave them a cheery wave before jumping into his car and roaring off down the road.

Bertie gave a sigh as Kitty tugged gently on his lead and they set off to walk the short distance to Matt's office.

'Let's go and have a cup of tea and plan our next move,' Matt suggested.

After this latest turn of events, Kitty was more than happy to agree. It seemed they now had two murders to solve.

TWELVE

Matt's office was situated just over halfway along the main shopping street in Torquay. The entrance was through a discreet doorway beside a gentleman's tailoring establishment and up a flight of stairs. He shared a landing with a company that manufactured false teeth and the shared space often had a slightly chemical smell.

He unlocked the door and stooped to collect the mail from the mat before Bertie could assist him. Kitty followed him inside and immediately went to open the window a little since the air in the office was warm and fusty.

Kitty filled the small kettle and set it on the spirit burner to heat, while Matt crossed the landing to borrow some milk. Bertie made himself comfortable under Matt's desk and crunched on one of the shortbread biscuits that Matt kept in a tin on the shelf.

The kettle had boiled by the time Matt returned with a drop of milk in a small white crockery jug. He finished making tea for himself and Kitty as she contented herself with watching the passers-by in the busy street below and eating more of Matt's supply of biscuits.

'Do you still think William Ford murdered Simon Travers?' Kitty's question took Matt slightly by surprise. However, he could see that Kitty had been thinking about the case.

'It seems likely but it's not definite. The brigadier seemed to believe he was the culprit. I think that it still could have been any of the people in the compartment. Except Mrs C, of course,' he added as he took the now empty biscuit tin and placed it back on the shelf.

'Hmm. Inspector Greville will have quite a task on his hands if Mr Ford's killer was not one of the other passengers.' Kitty looked troubled.

That thought had crossed Matt's mind too. Privately he considered it might be almost impossible to discover who Ford's killer might be if not one of the other suspects for Travers's murder.

'I wonder who Miss Briggs wishes me to find?' He took a sip of his tea.

'She said it was personal and she clearly didn't wish Mrs Craven to know anything about it,' Kitty said.

'I understand she has been in India for quite some time, so whoever she is looking for may be difficult to trace.'

Kitty sighed. 'I don't think she has much time left either, Matt, and this must be important to her.'

They finished their tea and had just cleared away their cups when the telephone on Matt's desk rang.

'Torbay Private Investigative Services.' Matt picked up a pencil in his free hand and pulled a pad of paper towards him. 'Inspector Greville, yes, we were just about to leave.' He glanced at Kitty.

'Yes, sir, we'll walk down and meet you.' He replaced the handset and turned to Kitty.

'The inspector is at the police station. Miss Dubois is back in Dartmouth and has been detained. If we walk downstairs, he will give us a lift back.'

Kitty picked up Bertie's lead. 'I shall be interested to see how Miss Dubois responds when she hears of Mr Ford's demise.'

Matt followed her out of the office, relocking the door behind them. He too wanted to know how Miss Dubois would react. Like Kitty he did not trust that lady an inch.

Inspector Greville was waiting for them in the black police car. 'My constable picked her up as soon as the ferry docked. She wasn't very happy, he had a job to persuade her to accompany him to the station.'

Matt didn't suppose she would have been very pleased. 'Does she know anything yet of Ford's death?'

Inspector Greville shook his head. 'No. I told my men to keep it quiet. They've taken her to the police station for now. We can question her there.'

'Do you think she may have murdered Mr Ford, Inspector?' Kitty asked from her place on the back seat.

Inspector Greville sucked his teeth. 'It's quite possible. There's no honour amongst thieves and I suspect this may be to do with that missing jewellery. Billy the Fish may have murdered Travers for payment from Miss Dubois, or he may have seen her do it and wanted paying off.'

Miss Dubois was not in a good mood when they finally arrived at the tiny police station.

'I sincerely hope that you have a good reason for insisting on my presence here, Inspector?' She had leapt to her feet as soon as she saw Inspector Greville enter the room.

Her dark kohl-lined eyes flashed and under her make-up, her cheeks were flushed. She was dressed for a fine summer's day on the river in a pale lemon chiffon summer frock with a straw hat and carried a small Chinese-style parasol.

'My apologies, Miss Dubois. Normally I would never have dreamt of disturbing your day out, but something rather significant has occurred.' The inspector gestured towards the chair she had just vacated.

Matt saw her gaze dart swiftly towards himself and Kitty before she resumed her seat with an air of bad grace. 'What's all this about?'

The inspector took a seat opposite her, while Matt and Kitty tucked themselves discreetly out of Miss Dubois's eyeline in a corner of the compact, whitewashed room.

'It has come to my attention, Miss Dubois, that both you and Mr Ford were less than honest when you were both interviewed following the murder of Simon Travers.' The inspector's moustache had drooped but Matt noticed he was fully alert to Miss Dubois's body language.

The girl shrugged and took her cigarette case from her bag before inserting a cigarette into her holder. 'I know Billy by sight, that's all. I've run across him a few times. In my line of work you meet all sorts.'

The inspector took out his lighter and lit her cigarette. 'Then why did neither of you say something?' he asked.

Carlotta drew on her cigarette, then exhaled a thin plume of smoke. 'Billy's had run-ins with the police in the past and so have I. I didn't want to be fitted up for killing that bloke, and neither did Billy.'

There was a ring of truth about her words, Matt thought.

'When did you last see Mr Ford or speak to him?' the inspector asked.

Matt could see Miss Dubois was instantly on her guard. 'Why? What's happened? Has he done a runner?'

Her lips pursed in annoyance.

'Why would Mr Ford do that, Miss Dubois?' The inspector's tone was mild.

Carlotta realised she might have betrayed herself and affected a careless shrug. 'I don't know.'

The inspector gave a small smile. 'To return to my question, Miss Dubois. When did you last see or speak to Mr Ford?'

'Yesterday afternoon. Those two can vouch for me.' She looked at Kitty and smiled coyly at Matt. Kitty's fingers tightened momentarily on his arm.

'I think we told you of our conversation, sir,' Matt said.

Carlotta looked smug as she continued to smoke her cigarette, making use of the battered tin ashtray the inspector placed on the chipped wooden table in front of her.

'Did he say anything to you about knowing any of the other passengers in the compartment?' the inspector asked.

Carlotta shook her head. 'No. He recognised the man who was killed from his picture on the front of the paper. He knew me slightly, but that was it.'

'And he didn't mention any plans to meet anyone here during his stay, or his plans for the evening?' Matt interjected.

Carlotta favoured him with another smile, running the tip of her tongue over her crimson lipsticked lips. 'No, nothing. He kept hinting at free tickets to see the show, but I only offer those to special friends.'

Matt could feel the tension rising in Kitty at the singer's deliberately provocative behaviour.

'When we bumped into you yesterday, I couldn't help hearing a little of your conversation. Mr Ford said something about a hit and needing to find where the stuff was?' Kitty's tone was distinctly unfriendly as she asked her question.

Miss Dubois extinguished her cigarette in the ashtray. Her expression was carelessly blank. 'I have no idea what you're talking about.'

'Really, so you weren't discussing where the missing proceeds from the Tower Hill jewel robbery might have been stashed?' Inspector Greville asked mildly.

Telltale colour crept along Miss Dubois's cheeks. 'Billy was just speculating, that's all. He thought as that bloke who was murdered might have taken the stuff and hidden it. Possibly here in Torquay somewhere and maybe whoever killed him knew where the goods were.'

'Why would Billy think that? You have links to one of the gang members yourself, don't you, Miss Dubois? A Mr Frederick Haynes?' The inspector leaned forward a little in his seat, his gaze intent on Miss Dubois's face.

Carlotta shifted in her chair. 'I know Fred, yes. We had a bit of a thing going at one time, but I don't know anything about that robbery. I've already been questioned over that back in London. I read as some of the stuff was missing. Some silver and jewels, but I don't know anything except what I've read in the papers.' She paused and sucked in a breath to regain her composure. 'Billy thought as that Travers was crooked. He'd run across him before in some dodgy places. After he'd given his evidence at the trial Billy thought if anybody had took off with the loot then it would be Travers.'

Inspector Greville's eyes gleamed. 'Then it was not by chance that you and Mr Ford were both in the compartment with Simon Travers?'

Matt noticed Carlotta's hands were trembling as she tried to undo her bag to retrieve another cigarette.

'Billy had heard last minute as Travers was getting out of London. Don't ask me how he found out because I don't know. I was already booked on that train. My agent sorts out my travel. Billy followed him to the station and saw him hand over the dog, then he jumped in the carriage after him. I didn't know any of this till after Travers was dead. Billy told me to say nothing after we'd given our statements the day the murder happened. It was coincidence as I got in that compartment when the train company had messed up the seating by only having the one carriage.'

The inspector dutifully offered his lighter once more and

the singer took a pull from her cigarette to calm her nerves. 'Did Billy say what his plan had been when you disembarked at Dawlish after Travers's murder?'

'He swore black was white as he never killed him. I know it was done with a knife and all, but he swore as it weren't him. He wanted him alive so as he could get his hands on those jewels. He just planned to follow him and maybe persuade him that he should, you know, share the goods.'

'And you didn't think it was important to provide any of this information when you were questioned?' Kitty said.

Carlotta lifted her chin and stared insolently at Kitty. 'No. I ain't no grass and I thought if I were nice to Billy I might get me some of them jewels. You know what they do to grasses. I didn't want to end up with my face cut to ribbons in a dark alley somewhere.'

The singer's eyes narrowed. 'Anyway you can ask Billy all this when you gets hold of him.'

'I'm afraid that won't be possible, Miss Dubois,' the inspector said.

Carlotta laughed. 'Oh, don't worry, he'll turn up, even if he has done a runner for now. He always surfaces somewhere.'

There was a brief moment of awkward silence. Carlotta immediately tensed and looked from one person to the next. 'What's happened?'

'Mr Ford has indeed surfaced. He was found dead in the harbour in Torquay this afternoon. Murdered.' The inspector's eyes were sharp as gimlets.

Miss Dubois's hand stilled as she went to remove her cigarette holder from between her lips. Beneath her thick foundation her complexion had turned ashen.

'Murdered. Billy has been murdered?'

Matt saw a glimpse of fear show briefly in the singer's dark eyes before she composed herself.

'How?' If Carlotta was faking shock and surprise, Matt thought she was doing a good job.

'Mr Ford was killed sometime after leaving you at the theatre yesterday. Although based on the tides and the condition in which he was discovered, it most likely is that he was killed last night or during the early hours of the morning. He was struck over the head with a blunt instrument.' The inspector was watching Carlotta's reaction to the information closely.

'I don't believe it. Billy, dead? He wasn't the kind of man to go down without a fight. He was like me, brought up on the streets since we were children. We were both orphans, me and Billy. Well, his parents were dead, my mother abandoned me when I was a baby. He wouldn't turn his back and let someone cosh him like that.' Carlotta's voice was fierce. 'Mark my words, Inspector, if someone murdered Billy like that it would have to be someone he knew or who he didn't think was a threat. He always carried a knife with him.' She added the last piece of information almost in a whisper. 'It was his hallmark, see.'

Matt's brows raised at this last statement. The inspector had searched Billy's pockets and hadn't come across a knife.

Kitty clearly had the same thought. 'Where did he keep his knife?' she asked.

Carlotta blinked. 'Strapped to his ankle, above his boot. He could have that blade out in a trice, or so I've heard. Everyone knew so nobody messed with him. It doesn't make sense.' She finished her cigarette, a deep frown creasing her forehead.

Inspector Greville signalled to the constable, who had been stationed quietly beside the door, and murmured something to him. Matt guessed it was to get a message to Doctor Carter to check for Billy's knife.

Miss Dubois seemed to recover herself and returned her cigarette holder back to her bag. 'If there's nothing else, Inspector,' she said as she started to get to her feet, 'I need to get back to my lodgings. I have a performance tonight.'

'Of course, Miss Dubois, just a couple more things before you go.' The inspector turned his attention back towards her.

Carlotta subsided back onto her chair with a barely suppressed sigh.

'Where were you yesterday evening and during the early hours of this morning?'

The girl laughed. 'Singing at the Pavilion Theatre in front of several hundred people. I was then taken to supper at the Imperial Hotel by a gentleman admirer. I returned to my lodgings at about two in the morning. Then I rose at ten to meet my friends from the company for a day on the river.'

Inspector Greville had been taking notes throughout the interview. He scribbled this final piece of information into his notebook. 'Thank you, Miss Dubois. Do you have the name of your gentleman friend?'

The singer sighed and opened her handbag once more. She fumbled inside and produced a calling card, which she passed across. 'I'm sure he'll vouch for me and so will the staff at the hotel where we dined and danced.'

The inspector read the card and made a few more notes, before passing it back to Carlotta. 'Thank you, miss.'

The girl gathered her possessions and rose to her feet. 'I really must leave, Inspector. Though how I am to get back to Torquay I have no idea. My friends will have gone without me.' She tapped her foot and glared at Inspector Greville.

'My constable will be delighted to arrange a taxi for you, Miss Dubois. How much longer is your engagement for at the playhouse?'

'Four more days. Would you care to attend?' she asked.

'Most kind of you, Miss Dubois, but I am rather busy unfortunately.' The inspector nodded to his constable who had arrived back in the room. 'Please call Mr Potter for Miss Dubois.'

'Sir.' The constable escorted the singer from the room and closed the door behind them.

'Well,' said Kitty. 'What did we think of that?'

THIRTEEN

Kitty was woken the following morning by the arrival of Alice. Her friend was bearing a tray of tea and toast, with a side dish of gossip.

'Good morning, miss. Have you heard the latest news?' Alice popped the tray down on Kitty's bedside table before whisking back the curtains to let in a fresh, bright summer morning.

Kitty groaned and screwed up her eyes against the light. Normally she was an early riser, but the week or so long holiday had meant she was beginning to enjoy the luxury of an extra hour in her bed.

'I presume you are referring to Mr Ford's murder?' Kitty struggled to sit up and prop herself up on her pillows as Alice poured her a cup of tea.

'Our Dolly had it from the milkman this morning,' Alice explained, smiling with suppressed excitement.

Kitty scooted over in her bed and patted the counterpane, inviting Alice to sit on the edge and help herself to a cup of tea. She knew the extra cup hadn't found its way onto the tray by accident.

'I presume the milkman had it from the fishermen?' Kitty guessed. In a community connected by the river and the sea most of the news came via water rather than road.

Alice grinned and helped herself to tea. 'So, it's true then, miss? He was knocked over the head and dumped in the harbour?'

'I wouldn't have said he was dumped in the harbour. He could easily have fallen after being struck.' Kitty took a reviving sip of tea.

'It's like one of the films, miss. A lone figure at the harbour in the dark when a masked man rushes up and clobbers him.' The young maid's eyes were wide as she pictured the scene.

'It could just as easily have been a woman who attacked Mr Ford,' Kitty said as she helped herself to a slice of toast.

'Like that Miss Dubois?' Alice asked as she tutted at Kitty while spreading a white linen napkin across her lap to protect the sheets from crumbs.

'Could be, or Lady Jacques. Even Miss Briggs, I suppose, if she somehow managed to rise from her sickbed to venture out into the night.' Kitty tried imagining each of the three women in the scene Alice had conjured up.

Her friend sniffed and screwed up her small, freckled nose. 'I don't know, miss, happen as that vicar is the most likely culprit, him being a man and all.'

Kitty laughed. 'Alice! Why the Reverend Greenslade? We know that Miss Dubois knew Mr Ford, but what motive could the reverend have?'

Alice sipped her tea primly. 'Well, you said as how his church was near that jeweller's that was robbed. He could have found the missing jewels hidden in his church or something. Then, this man Travers might have known they were there and, when they went missing, he could have gone to the vicar.'

'I suppose that is possible, but then how does Mr Ford's

murder tie-in to this?' Kitty asked as she set her empty cup and saucer back down on the tray.

'If it were a film, the vicar would have killed Mr Travers and the other bloke would have seen him, so the vicar would have to kill him too.' Alice smiled triumphantly. She was clearly pleased with her hypothesis.

'Inspector Greville will no doubt be trying to determine where all the train passengers were during the evening when Mr Ford was killed.' Kitty smiled at her friend.

The maid finished her tea and added her crockery to the tray ready to carry it out of the room. She jumped up from the bed. 'My money is on the vicar.' She caught a glimpse of the time on Kitty's bedside clock. 'Oh, I'd best get moving or Mrs Homer will skin me alive.'

Kitty grinned. 'Thank you for the tea. I'll let you know if I hear anything else.'

Once the young maid had scurried off back to her regular duties at the hotel Kitty settled back on her pillows. Alice had a point about Reverend Greenslade, but there was no evidence to suggest the missing items had been hidden near the church. Or, indeed, that he had enough opportunity to murder Simon Travers. After all, he was the person seated farthest away from the dead man.

Miss Briggs had also resided near the church. She could have committed the murders too. But a lady of her ill health, just returned from India? Why would she have been interested in the jewels from the robbery? Her poor health meant she would have little strength to attack Billy Ford or to drive a knife into Simon Travers. Or would she? It was very perplexing.

Her thoughts turned to Meribel Jacques. The woman was known to be a gambler and to have money troubles. She could easily be bold enough and reckless enough to murder Simon Travers. Then she could have arranged to meet Billy at the harbour and dealt him a fatal blow if he had tried to blackmail her. But why? Could she have somehow managed to get her hands on the jewels? Had she been in league with Simon Travers? It didn't make sense.

It would be interesting to find out if the passengers all had alibis for the time of Mr Ford's murder. The problem was that, according to Doctor Carter, it was impossible to narrow the time down just from his examination of the body. The only way they could do that was to determine when he had last been seen alive.

Kitty dressed quickly in a pale green print dress and ran a comb through her blonde curls. If the inspector could discover how Billy had spent his evening that might help them to pin down the time of his death more accurately.

It occurred to her that there had been a bus ticket in his wallet. Perhaps he had taken a trip somewhere that evening. Surely that might be useful, if they could discover where he had been. He may even have been to meet someone.

Cheered by this idea she gathered her things and went downstairs to the lobby. She checked with Mary in case the post had already arrived, but there was still nothing for her from either the Home Office or the prison.

Kitty pushed all thoughts of Hammett from her mind and collected her car from its shed, before crossing the river to call for Matt.

Her fiancé was already waiting for her when she pulled to a halt outside his house. She was unsurprised to see that he was accompanied by Bertie.

'He ate my slipper this morning.' Matt secured the dog on the rear seat of Kitty's car before climbing into the passenger seat.

'Oh dear.' Kitty cast a nervous glance at her canine passenger in case he took a shine to nibbling her car seats.

'Not both slippers. Just the left one. I found them when I

went downstairs for breakfast.' Matt turned his head to glare at the dog. Bertie met his stare with brown, baleful eyes.

Kitty pressed her lips firmly together to keep from laughing. 'I take it we should call in at the shops after we have seen Miss Briggs to purchase new slippers then?' she suggested as she sped along the coast road.

Matt merely shot her a glance that showed he knew that she was finding his predicament amusing.

Kitty found a parking spot in the shade of a large tree near Miss Briggs's sister's house, and they decided that Bertie would be best to remain in the car. Matt checked that the leash was secure before they walked the short distance to knock on the door of the cottage.

She thought Mrs Pace looked slightly surprised to discover her on the step when she opened the front door.

'Miss Underhay, this is a nice surprise. I wasn't aware that Xanthe was expecting visitors today.' Her plump, pleasant face puckered into a frown.

'It's merely a short visit, Mrs Pace. I have no desire to tire Miss Briggs. She expressed a wish for me to call this morning with my fiancé, Captain Bryant.' She indicated Matt.

'Kitty thought your sister was troubled by what had happened on the train and wished to talk to me. I think it might allay her concerns,' Matt said.

Mrs Pace opened the door a little wider and stood aside to allow them to enter. 'Well, she has been very concerned about that poor soul who was killed. I know as she's been praying for him.'

She led the way along the corridor to the small parlour at the rear of the house. Miss Briggs was once more reclined on the sofa and the stifling heat of the room greeted them as they entered.

'You will excuse me, Miss Underhay, Captain Bryant, if I

get on?' Mrs Pace glanced at her sister and Kitty could see the worry on her face.

'Of course, you must be terribly busy. Please don't bother with any refreshments. We shall keep our visit short today as Matt has left his dog in my motor car.'

The worried frown disappeared from the woman's brow, and she took her leave of them. Kitty thought Miss Briggs looked considerably worse than when she had last seen her.

'Miss Underhay and Captain Bryant, I'm so pleased you were able to call.' Miss Briggs's voice sounded weak, and she could barely push herself up on her elbow in order to adjust the pillows under her head.

'Kitty said there was a personal matter that you wished to consult me upon. She had the impression that it was personal and deeply private.' Matt looked at the ailing woman.

Miss Briggs inclined her head in agreement before picking up the glass of water that stood beside her on a small pine what-not. 'That is correct.' She wet her lips with the water and placed the glass back down as if the weight of it were too much for her to manage.

'As you can see, Captain Bryant, and as no doubt Miss Underhay has told you, I am very ill and time is running out for me.' She paused and closed her eyes for a moment before opening them again and continuing. 'This is very difficult, but some twenty-five years ago I... made a mistake.'

Kitty shifted on the edge of her seat and wondered what Miss Briggs was about to confide.

'Rather foolishly I became involved with someone. A gentleman. I believed he was free to marry and that my affections were reciprocated. Sadly, when I told him that our relationship would result in the birth of a child his true nature emerged.'

Kitty's heart ached. She knew what Miss Briggs was about to say and she felt the woman's sorrow even now.

'It transpired that he was not free to honour his obligations. He was married already and had no inclination to aid me. Indeed, he cut me off and denied that he ever knew me. Fortunately, my late father had left me a small sum of money, or I would have been in very dire circumstances. I gave birth to the child, a girl, in London. I couldn't keep her; it would have been impossible.'

'What happened to her?' Kitty asked, her tone sympathetic as a single tear trickled down Miss Briggs's sallow cheek.

Miss Briggs dashed her hand across her face. 'Arrangements were made at the Christian home for the child to be adopted. When she was six weeks old, I left her there and returned to my life. Except, I couldn't bear to remain in England, there was no longer anything there for me. My shame and guilt were too much. I left for India and the missions.'

Kitty looked at Matt.

'And this child? Is this the person you wish me to find?' Matt asked.

'I want to know if she is well and happy. They promised me that she would be placed with a good Christian family. I can go to my grave in peace if I only know she is well.' Miss Briggs stretched out a thin hand and caught hold of Kitty's fingers. Her grip was surprisingly firm, and Kitty winced. 'Please will you look for her. I haven't much money, but I will gladly pay for the search.'

'It may be very difficult to trace her after all this time. Do you have any information for me to start the search with? Her date and place of birth? The name of the mother and baby home?' Matt asked.

Miss Briggs released her grasp on Kitty's hand. 'Over there on the sideboard is my handbag, Miss Underhay. In it there is a small black leather notebook. All the information you will need is contained in there.' She fell back against her cushions as Kitty obeyed her instructions.

She passed the battered book to Matt who opened it and took a cursory look at the contents.

'Thank you, Miss Briggs. I can see there is enough information here for me to commence enquiries.'

'If we find your daughter, Miss Briggs, do you wish to see her? Or have us make known to her that you have sought her out?' Kitty asked. Her hand still bore faint red marks from the pressure exerted on her by Miss Briggs's bony fingers. There was no doubt in her mind that the older woman desperately wished to find her child.

'I want to know her whereabouts and the name she is living under so that she might benefit by my will. I will leave the rest to your discretion.' She paused for a moment and her eyes closed once again. 'If she should wish to see me, then I hope God will grant me enough time on this earth to meet her.' Her voice was weak, and Kitty could see she was at the end of her strength.

'We shall do our best to find her, Miss Briggs. Now do please rest. Matt and I shall see ourselves out.' She nodded to Matt who got to his feet.

They left the room together and closed the door to the parlour quietly behind them. Matt tucked the notebook in the pocket of his jacket. An eerie wailing noise echoed along the hallway as they neared the front door.

'What is that noise?' Kitty clutched at Matt's sleeve.

'Oh no, I think I know all too well what that sound is.' Matt hurried to the front door and opened it.

Kitty peered around him to see Bertie sitting on the doorstep wagging his tail with excitement at seeing them again.

'Is that Bertie? How on earth did he get out of the car?' Kitty asked.

Matt picked up the chewed end of Bertie's leash. 'I'll give you five guesses.' He caught hold of Bertie's collar before the dog could bolt. 'We had better check your car for damage.'

They hurried across the street to Kitty's car but much to her relief it seemed the only harm done was to Bertie's lead.

'He must have chewed through his leash and then pressed against the door handle somehow.' Matt scowled at his dog.

'I suppose we should add a new leash to our shopping list too,' Kitty suggested as Matt heaved Bertie back onto the back seat of the car and endeavoured to secure him with what remained of the lead.

'Dog ownership is becoming expensive,' Matt grumbled as Kitty hopped into the driver's seat and started the engine.

Kitty smiled to herself as she drove the short distance into town so that Matt could obtain his purchases. The town was busy with shoppers and holidaymakers, and she was lucky to find a space to stop her motor car.

'I won't be long, Kitty. Would you like the key to the office, and we can look at Miss Briggs's notebook over a cup of tea when I've made my purchases?' Matt asked.

'By all means. I'll call in the bakery and get us some buns.' Her stomach had started to grumble, and she was in need of refreshment. She was also extremely thirsty after spending time in the stifling heat of Miss Briggs's parlour.

Matt handed her the key and went off towards a small iron-mongers at the top of the town that sold pet equipment. Kitty took Bertie on his makeshift lead and started to walk down towards the bakery near Matt's office.

FOURTEEN

Kitty had not gone far when she encountered a crowd of people on the pavement coming from the opposite direction. She was almost through when she bumped into a young woman hurrying along the street.

'I'm so sorry,' Kitty apologised and then realised she recognised the girl. 'Oh, it's Betty, isn't it? Alice's cousin?'

Betty was older than Alice and considered herself to be much more worldly-wise. There was a great deal of rivalry between the cousins and Alice's mother always described Betty as being 'fast'. Kitty guessed that this was because Betty was fond of cosmetics and the latest fashions. She worked in a variety of jobs, waitressing and as a maid. She never stayed in one position for long as she was always looking for a better situation, or a suitable young man to marry.

'Oh, Miss Underhay, I do beg your pardon. It was my fault; I wasn't looking where I was going.' Betty was dressed in the latest fashion, in a pretty summer dress with a chic little hat trimmed in blue. She eyed Bertie nervously. 'I didn't know as you had a dog, miss.'

'Bertie belongs to my fiancé. He's a very recent acquisition.' Bertie sniffed at Betty's stocking-clad legs with enthusiasm.

'Our Alice said as you and Captain Bryant was engaged to be married. Congratulations, miss. Have you set a date for the wedding as yet?' Betty asked as she skipped back a step out of Bertie's reach.

'No, not yet unfortunately. There's a lot of things to sort out first.' Kitty stepped to the side of the pavement to allow more people to pass by.

'I can imagine. Our Alice told me all about your cousin Lucy's wedding. It sounded proper lovely being in a castle and all.'

Knowing the rivalry between the cousins Kitty could imagine that Alice would have enjoyed queening it over Betty with tales of her role at Lucy's wedding.

'How about you, Betty? Where are you working now?' Kitty asked.

The girl immediately brightened up. 'I just got a marvellous new position as a personal maid. Proper step up it is, miss. In a grand house.'

'Oh, how lovely. Is it for anyone I might know?' Kitty asked.

'Lady Meribel Jacques. Her ladyship's mother has engaged me to look after Lady Meribel personally while she is here in the bay on her holidays,' Betty explained. 'Nice young lady with lots of life in her, she's got some lovely clothes. I might even get to go with her when she goes back to London after the summer.'

'How nice. Yes, I've met Lady Meribel a couple of times recently,' Kitty replied somewhat cautiously. It was good that it was Lady Meribel's mother that had employed Betty, presumably that would mean she was the one responsible for paying Betty's wage, given the parlous state of Lady Meribel's personal finances.

Betty's eyes widened as a thought obviously struck her. 'Of course, her ladyship said as there had been an incident on the train when she arrived. That bloke what was killed in her carriage. Are you and Captain Bryant looking into it?'

'Inspector Greville has asked Matt and I to assist, yes.' Kitty glanced around to make sure they were not overheard. It seemed Lady Meribel had either not yet been interviewed about Billy Ford's death or she had kept that to herself.

'Her ladyship was telling her friends all about it. It fair shook her up I think. Not what you expect when you'm in first class, is it?' Betty said.

'Not in any class of carriage, but I do see what you mean. It was most unpleasant so I'm not surprised Lady Meribel was distressed.' Kitty could see that Bertie was becoming restless, prowling around her feet emitting gentle whining sounds.

'Let's hope as you and Captain Bryant catch whoever did it soon. It's not a nice thought, a murderer running about the place. Oh well, I'd best get off. I have some errands to run for her ladyship.' Betty smiled importantly.

'Of course, it was lovely to see you and all the best in your new position. If, of course, you should hear anything that may be relevant to the case, however small, please get in touch. You know, if Lady Meribel remembers something or mentions something to her friends.' Kitty kept her tone light.

She did not expect Betty to place herself in any danger or risk her employment, but it seemed too good an opportunity not to enlist her aid.

Betty smirked and Kitty could see she liked the idea that she might be in a position to assist somehow. Or, even better, get one over on her cousin Alice.

'I'll keep my eyes and ears open, Miss Underhay. You can rely on me.'

Kitty thanked her once again and they parted company, leaving Kitty to continue on her errand in a thoughtful mood.

———

Matt arrived at his office a while later clutching a brown paper parcel containing a new pair of slippers, which he was careful to place out of Bertie's reach. Kitty was seated beside his desk eating a cream bun while the dog had a dish of water and a sausage roll.

'I've placed your post in the tray. Did you get Bertie a new lead?' Kitty asked as she licked a small dollop of cream from the side of her thumb.

'Yes, the man in the shop recommended this one. It's thicker and sturdier than his last one.' Matt took out the new leash and swapped it for the damaged one.

Kitty poured him a cup of tea and passed over a paper bakery bag. She told him of her encounter with Betty.

'Hmm, that connection could be useful. So, Lady Meribel has told her friends of Travers's death?'

Kitty nodded. 'Betty said she thought Lady Meribel was quite shaken about the murder, although I rather got the impression she had probably been making light of it in public. Betty didn't mention William Ford.'

Matt opened his bag and took out his bun. 'And now we also have this puzzle of Miss Briggs's illegitimate daughter to solve too.'

Kitty's expression sobered. 'Yes, and time is of the essence. Miss Briggs looked much more poorly today than when I last saw her. It sounded such a sad story.' She wiped her fingers on a paper napkin and crumpled up her bakery bag.

'Here, take a look at the notebook she gave us and we'll get things moving to try and find the girl.' He passed her the small leather-bound book to study while he ate his bun.

He had taken a cursory glance inside whilst they had been at Miss Briggs's home. The book had appeared to be a journal of sorts, written in black ink in old-fashioned copperplate handwriting. He had noted that the date and time of the child's birth had been recorded and the address of the mother and baby home.

It was a little surprising that Miss Briggs had not tried to find the child herself by visiting the address during her stay in London. He could only suppose that her poor health and perhaps embarrassment or shame had prevented her from applying in person.

He finished his bun and took a sip of his tea. Kitty continued to pore over the entries in the journal. Her small face screwed up in concentration as she read.

'Anything useful?' he asked.

'The main details are here at the start. Miss Briggs says that the baby's father died shortly before she left for India. There was a fire at his home. His wife and children survived but he was trapped in his study and could not get out.' Kitty gave a little shiver. 'Miss Briggs has noted that whilst sad, the wages of sin are death. Ugh, she has underlined that.'

Matt's brows raised. 'I suppose it's understandable that she would be bitter, but I see what you mean. It doesn't sound terribly Christian.'

'Oh dear, it seems that before she returned to England Miss Briggs did apply to the home, Cairn House, for information about her daughter but was refused.' Kitty looked at Matt, her blue-grey eyes held a perplexed expression.

'Does she give a name of the person she applied to?' he asked.

'A Sister Perpetua. Miss Briggs says here that the home replied that they did not give out such information once the children had been placed in a Christian home to avoid corruption from immoral influences.' Kitty's mouth formed a perfect 'o' of astonishment. 'How awful. If they will not give Miss Briggs any information, how are we to persuade them?' she asked.

Matt had encountered situations similar to this before

during the course of his work. 'I think if we are careful, they may help us. I presume Sister Perpetua believes that it is the mothers who are the corrupt influences since they are "fallen" women. We may have to take the train to London and make enquiries at Cairn House in person.'

Kitty nodded. 'I see what you mean. These things are always so beastly and complicated. I suppose though there are people who might try and snatch a child back or try to obtain money from the adoptive family or the child.' She sighed. 'Poor Miss Briggs, she seems to have spent her life trying to help others in order to atone for what she sees as her disgrace.'

Matt placed his empty bakery bag in the wastebasket. 'I think perhaps a telephone call first to see if Sister Perpetua will agree to meet us and then we shall pay a visit.'

Kitty gave a small smile. 'At least all of this is keeping me busy while I wait to hear if I can see Ezekiel Hammett before he is transferred for his trial.'

'Very true. I'm sure you will hear something from the prison or the Home Office soon.' He looked at the address in the notebook and dialled the operator to be connected to the mother and baby home, while Kitty cleared away their tea things.

'Yes, thank you, Sister. I do appreciate your kindness in agreeing to see us,' he concluded his conversation after having spent some ten minutes or so convincing Sister Perpetua of his credentials and respectability.

'She has agreed to meet us tomorrow. It seems a trip to London is definitely in order.' He looked at Bertie, who was now snoozing happily beneath his desk. 'What shall we do with the dog? I presume Simon must have put him in the guard's van because of the howling.'

'We can't take the poor thing all the way to London and back, especially if we are to try to persuade this Sister Perpetua to help us. It would be very awkward.' Kitty's brow creased as she thought about the problem. 'Wait, I think I know just the person to look after him for the day.' She smiled happily at Matt.

They were about to lock the office and leave when the telephone rang.

'Hello, yes, Inspector, Kitty and I were just leaving. We can call round to the police station.' He looked at Kitty who nodded her agreement. 'Yes, sir, we're on our way.' He replaced the receiver.

'What's happened?' Kitty asked as she followed him out of the office.

'You remember the bus ticket Billy Ford had in his pocket?' Matt asked.

Kitty waited for him to lock up before walking Bertie down the stairs. 'Yes, I'd wondered about that. I thought perhaps it might tell us where he had been before he was killed.'

He took the dog's new leather leash from her as they set off through the streets towards the police station. Bertie trotted ahead of them sniffing the air. They paused on the way to leave Matt's new slippers in Kitty's car.

'It seems as if the inspector may have some information on where Mr Ford went,' Matt said as they continued on their way.

They walked up the steps of the police station and entered the small reception area. Matt recognised the sergeant on duty behind the desk. He greeted them both, before raising the hatch to allow them through to see the inspector.

'Captain Bryant, Miss Underhay, if you'd care to follow me.'

Inspector Greville's office was a short walk along the whitewashed corridor. The sergeant halted and knocked on the door before opening it for them when he heard Inspector Greville's call for them to enter.

'Miss Underhay, Captain Bryant, please take a seat.' The inspector's office was in its usual state of chaos. Piles of manilla folders were perched in precarious heaps on the floor and all of the flat surfaces. A large pressed-glass ashtray was overflowing with spent cigarette stubs on the corner of the desk and the air was pale blue with smoke.

Matt managed to retrieve a chair for Kitty and one for himself. Bertie heaved a long-suffering sigh, sneezed and flopped down at his feet.

'I'm glad I managed to catch you both. I thought it might be useful to compare our findings.' Inspector Greville leaned back, making his seat creak ominously.

'On our side there is little to tell,' Kitty said and passed on her discovery that Betty was now Lady Jacques's personal maid and that Miss Briggs's health seemed to be sinking fast.

'You mentioned the bus ticket in Ford's pocket, sir?' Matt reminded the policeman.

The inspector's moustache twitched. 'Yes, we managed to decipher the print on the ticket. It was somewhat soggy from being immersed in the sea, but it seems that Mr Ford took a trip into Paignton shortly before his death.'

'Isn't that where Reverend Greenslade is staying?' Kitty asked.

'Indeed.'

Matt could see his fiancée's interest had been perked by this piece of information. 'Do we know where he went? Did he go to meet anyone?'

'My constable interviewed the driver of the omnibus who fortunately remembered Ford because he was trying to engage a young lady in conversation, and she was clearly discomforted by the encounter. The driver said Ford got off at the stop nearest to the pier on the seafront.'

'A pleasure trip?' Matt mused aloud.

'I don't think Billy was a pleasure trip kind of person, not when he thought there was a chance of getting his hands on that missing silverware and jewellery,' Kitty said.

'I am inclined to think your supposition is correct, Miss

Underhay. My constable is making enquires in the town and we are hopeful that we may uncover the purpose of Ford's visit soon.' The corners of the inspector's mouth lifted upwards in a brief smile.

'I don't suppose it is possible that he may have been murdered in Paignton, perhaps on the pier, and then his body washed up in Torquay?' Matt was really thinking aloud. He felt this was an unlikely scenario but nonetheless needed to be ruled out.

'I don't believe so. The tides would be unlikely to transport a body or debris in that direction. Not to finish up in the harbour at Torquay,' the inspector said.

Kitty nodded. 'I agree. If he did meet with the reverend though and he does turn out to be our man, would he have followed Ford back to Torquay to kill him there?'

Matt considered the possibility. 'He may have done so to avoid being linked to the murder, or it may have been that it was too busy and public a spot on the promenade by the pier.'

'That's if it was Greenslade who Ford was meeting,' the inspector reminded them. 'Don't let's get ahead of ourselves here.'

'Do you still think, sir, that Ford was the person who murdered Travers?' Kitty asked.

'I think it very likely. I can't rule out the possibility that there is an as yet unidentified person who could have hired Ford to kill Travers and then may have murdered Ford in order to acquire or retain the goods stolen from the jewellers.' Greville frowned. 'Obviously we will keep looking for those connections, but my resources are limited, and you have more freedom to explore the social connections of Miss Briggs, Lady Jacques and Reverend Greenslade.'

Matt told the inspector of their intended trip to London and the purpose of the journey.

'Very interesting. That information certainly sheds a new

light on Miss Briggs's character. Both Lady Jacques and Miss Carlotta Dubois were abandoned as babies. Lady Meribel was adopted by the Jacques family, while Miss Dubois remained in the orphanage until she ran away when she was a teenager. There is the possibility of a connection. Both young ladies are of the right age.' Inspector Greville stroked his moustache, his expression thoughtful.

'That had crossed my mind too, sir. It will be interesting to hear what Sister Perpetua has to tell us at Cairn House tomorrow.' Matt glanced at Kitty.

FIFTEEN

Kitty arranged for Mickey, her maintenance man at the hotel, to take care of Bertie whilst she and Matt were in London. Mickey was very fond of dogs, having had one himself for many years, and would put up with Bertie's nonsense.

She was relieved to discover that she and Matt had a compartment to themselves at the start of their journey to London. After Simon Travers's murder she couldn't help feeling slightly ill at ease when she took her seat in the first-class carriage.

Matt appeared to have picked up on her thoughts. 'I expect that Travers would have felt safer in a compartment without a corridor. I'm sure that would have been the thought of the minder from the brigadier's department when he escorted Travers onto the train.'

'Little thinking that one of those other occupants of the carriage would kill him,' Kitty said with a shudder.

The other seats were filled when the train halted at Exeter so there was no further opportunity to discuss the case, or their intended visit to the mother and baby home, until after they had disembarked in London. Although Kitty took note of where the train stopped on the journey and any tunnels they passed through.

Kitty had chosen her clothes carefully for the interview at Cairn House. A modest, lightweight navy-blue two-piece with a crisp white blouse and a neat navy hat and white gloves. She felt it would be important to convey the right image when meeting Sister Perpetua.

Matt was also dressed quite smartly in a light grey suit with a dark tie and hat. He assisted her down from the train onto the crowded platform. Kitty took hold of his arm, feeling slightly overwhelmed by the hustle and bustle.

'Do you know where we're going?' she asked.

'I have a pretty good idea. I looked up the location of Cairn House on a map last night after I got home. Come on, let's go and find a taxi.' He led the way out of the station to a nearby taxi rank.

Kitty was taken aback at first by the busy nature of the city. The air smelled of smoke, stale food and heat. Dartmouth seemed a very long way away and she realised it had been a good many years since she had last visited London. It made Exeter seem very small and provincial by comparison.

Matt gave the address of the mother and baby home to the taxi driver and Kitty contented herself with gazing out of the cab window as they made their way along the bustling streets, past the hawkers and barrow boys through to the slightly quieter suburbs.

''Ere you are, guv. That's the place, right over there.' The taxi had halted on an unprepossessing street lined with London plane trees. The buildings appeared to be constructed of grey stone, pitted and worn with age.

Matt thanked the driver and paid him as he and Kitty climbed out to take in their surroundings.

'Well, here we are,' he said as the taxi drove away.

'Let's see what Sister Perpetua is prepared to tell us.' Kitty brushed down the skirt of her suit and straightened her jacket, her fingers brushing against her mother's old women's suffrage brooch that was pinned carefully out of sight under the lapel.

Knowing it was there always gave her courage in difficult situations. She had a feeling that this meeting might prove to be just such a tricky occasion. The mother and baby home was separated from the street by a set of black painted iron railings, with the approach to the front door up three well-worn stone steps.

The front door was painted in discreet black gloss. A polished brass plate, stating *Cairn House* in gothic script, was affixed to the wall near the bell push. There was nothing to indicate the business of the building. Matt stepped forward and pushed the bell before falling back to stand at Kitty's side.

After a moment the door was opened by a stout middle-aged woman in a nun's black dress. The woman gave Kitty an all-encompassing assessing glance that swept her from head to toe. Despite the heat of the day Kitty shivered as she realised the nun was probably trying to judge if she was a girl in trouble or a prospective adoptive parent.

Matt reached inside the breast pocket of his jacket to hand the nun one of his business cards.

'Captain Bryant and Miss Underhay to see Sister Perpetua. She is expecting us.'

The nun glanced suspiciously at the card before opening the door a little wider to permit them to enter. They followed her into a wide cream painted corridor with a colourful patterned tile floor. Paintings depicting various religious scenes hung from the picture rail in the hall.

The nun opened a nearby walnut burred polished wood door and indicated that they should enter. 'Please take a seat and I'll go and see if Sister Perpetua is ready to receive you.'

They found themselves in a plainly decorated room with wooden chairs arranged around the edges of the parquet floor. A large dark wood cross hung from the wall of the chimney breast above the unlit fire. A green glass vase containing white daisies and crimson roses stood on top of an oak tallboy providing the only bright object within the room.

Kitty and Matt sat as instructed and waited for the nun to return. Kitty glanced at her fiancé and saw his mouth was set in a grim line as he surveyed his surroundings. The room smelled of carbolic disinfectant and soap. A fly buzzed angrily at a windowpane and Kitty thought that somewhere in the distance she could hear the plaintive wails of a baby crying.

'Sister will see you now.' The nun waited for them to rise before leading them along the hallway to another walnut burred door. She knocked and on hearing the summons from within she opened the door for them and discreetly withdrew as they entered Sister Perpetua's office.

Kitty's first impression of Sister Perpetua was her height as she stood from behind her desk. She was easily as tall as Matt and rail thin in her black robes. A wooden crucifix attached to a leather strap hung from her neck. Her handshake was firm and her grasp cool and dry. She indicated the carved wooden chairs placed before her desk and seated herself while waiting for them to take their places.

Another green vase containing daisies and scarlet roses stood on the corner of the desk and behind the nun Kitty saw there was a large blue and white statue of the Virgin Mary in a plasterwork niche next to the small lead-paned window.

'Captain Bryant, Miss Underhay, welcome to Cairn House. I must admit I was intrigued when I received your telephone call yesterday, which is why I agreed to see you.' Sister Perpetua had a low, musical voice.

'Why were you intrigued, Sister?' Kitty asked.

The nun surveyed her with shrewd grey eyes. 'I received a

letter from India some months ago from a Miss Briggs asking about a child born here and left in our care for adoption twenty-five years ago.' The nun paused for a moment and glanced at a slim file that lay in front of her on her desk. 'You must understand that we have to be very careful and discreet when answering any questions of this nature.'

'Of course, Sister,' Matt replied. Kitty could see his interest was piqued, as indeed was her own.

'Many of the women giving birth here are from straitened circumstances. A lot of them are of low moral character, have problems with alcohol, or are prostitutes. They may wish to get a child back for financial reasons or, if their own circumstances have improved, they may regret their decision. Miss Briggs, I gather from her file and the letter she sent to me, was a different case.'

Kitty understood what the nun meant about the mothers who might wish to contact the families or the children for financial support. She had said as much when they had been talking to Inspector Greville. She could also see how distressing it might be for a child now settled in a happy home with respectable people to be confronted by a potentially undesirable stranger claiming some connection with them. It would be an awful shock, especially if they were ignorant of the circumstances surrounding their birth.

However, given her own desperate search for her mother and quest for answers, she could understand and sympathise all too well with a mother's need to find out what had happened to a child.

Sister Perpetua confirmed this line of thought. 'There is also the feelings of the adoptive parents to consider. They may not wish to tell the child that they were adopted, although we always encourage them to do so. The child too may be distressed or upset if their lives are disrupted by the sudden arrival of the woman who gave them up.'

'We assumed this was why you were unable to assist Miss Briggs,' Matt said.

Sister Perpetua nodded. 'Indeed, I was uncertain about her reasoning for seeking the child out now. The baby she was enquiring about was born here twenty-five years ago. My predecessor, Sister Michael, was in charge of Cairn House then. Miss Briggs left her daughter, Dorothea, in our care and, according to the file, expressed a wish to become a missionary. From reading the notes it seemed she wished to remove herself from the scene of her disgrace by quitting the country. It seems too, that she was dealt a further blow when the alleged father of the child was killed in a quite terrible house fire shortly before her ship sailed for India.'

Kitty looked at Matt. 'That is what Miss Briggs has told us had happened.' She was still puzzled about why the nun had felt the need to see them when she had already explained to Miss Briggs that she couldn't, or wouldn't, assist her.

'I had thought the matter to be at an end, but then just a few weeks ago I received another application for information for the same case.' The nun steepled her long, slender hands together as she looked at Matt and Kitty.

'Who was the request from?' Kitty sat up straighter in her chair. This was a most unexpected development.

Sister Perpetua's lips lifted in a slight smile. 'This was from the child herself.'

'Miss Briggs's daughter? Dorothea?' Matt asked, a frown puckering his forehead.

'Yes, Dorothea herself. She asked for a meeting with me as she had some questions about her birth and her birth parents that were troubling her.'

'I don't understand. What kind of questions were they? Did she come to see you?' Kitty asked, her eagerness for information causing her to rush for answers.

'In brief, she especially wished to know who her mother was

and if there was any predilection, as she phrased it, for badness in either of her parents.' Sister Perpetua raised her thin, black clad shoulders in a slight shrug. Her grey eyes betraying her amusement at Kitty's eagerness to discover the reason for the visit.

'Did you agree to meet with her?' Matt asked.

The nun nodded. 'Yes, I agreed to meet her. If a request comes from a child, I will often try to give them some peace of mind where possible.' She frowned. 'The nature of the questions concerned me. It spoke of some trouble in the girl's mind and I wished to reassure her.'

'Did you tell her that her mother, Miss Briggs, had written to you?' Kitty asked.

Sister Perpetua relaxed her posture and fingered the edge of the file. 'I confess that I did not. I did not feel it would be appropriate to do so.'

Kitty thought the woman looked uncomfortable.

'What had Dorothea to say for herself when you met?' Matt took over the questions.

'Dorothea has been very fortunate in her adoption. Her adoptive parents are wealthy, titled, respectable people who have provided her with every advantage in life. She is, of course, known now by a different name. I assured her that her mother, before her fall into sin, had been a respectable woman who had been deceived and that she had atoned for this by undertaking Christian work overseas.'

Kitty sensed the nun had more to say so held her patience when she paused as if gathering her thoughts before continuing with her story.

'I must admit that I was not impressed by the young woman who came to see me. You will, I am sure, understand that I have long experience of meeting women in all kinds of difficulties. I was somewhat disappointed that despite all the advantages she had received she had somehow lost her way. She confessed to me when I questioned her that her adoptive father was thinking of disinheriting her. She had fallen into drinking, gambling and, although she did not say so, I suspected the use of opiates. She wished to know if these traits could have been inherited.'

Kitty blinked. 'Goodness, why did she wish to know that?'

'She thought that if it were built into her that she could not help these traits then nature would take its course. A somewhat fatalistic view, which I think she thought absolved her in some way of taking any personal responsibility for her actions. However, she appeared relieved when I assured her that these were not issues known to affect either of her parents. She muttered that she could change her habits and intended to go away to assure her father of her good intentions.' Sister Perpetua opened her hands.

'Sister, could we ask that you share with us Dorothea's adopted name. I can assure you of our discretion and confidentiality. It is very important and may affect a murder investigation that is currently underway if Dorothea is now the person I think she is.' Matt met the nun's gaze and held it.

Kitty held her breath.

'Dorothea Briggs is now Lady Meribel Jacques.'

Kitty swallowed. 'Sister, may we also ask if you told Lady Jacques the name of her birth mother?'

Sister Perpetua nodded. 'I saw no reason not to do so, given Miss Briggs's earlier letter to me and I believed her to still be in India so thought there could be no harm caused. There seemed little chance that their paths would cross. However, Captain Bryant mentioned yesterday on the telephone that Miss Briggs has now returned to this country.'

Matt shifted in his seat. 'She has indeed, Sister, and unfortunately is most seriously ill. We believe she may not live much longer. Hence her desire to be assured of her daughter's well-being.'

The nun bowed her head. 'I see. I am most sorry to hear that. We shall pray for her.'

'Thank you, Sister,' Kitty said.

The same nun who had taken them to see Sister Perpetua saw them to the door and closed it firmly behind them as they left.

SIXTEEN

By mutual unspoken consent Matt and Kitty left Cairn House without telephoning for a taxi. Instead, they walked along the grey, gloomy street towards a small green park that they had passed on their journey to the home.

Kitty was relieved to be outside and away from the claustrophobic sterility of the home with its oppressive atmosphere. Matt was unusually silent as they walked, seemingly lost in his own thoughts. Visiting Cairn House had clearly affected him and she sensed he needed time before he could share his thoughts with her.

After a few minutes they reached the wrought-iron gates of the park entrance and stepped inside the green oasis away from the grimy London streets. Up ahead Kitty spied a rose garden and a small blue painted wrought-iron bandstand. The sounds of the city seemed muffled by the rustling of the leaves on the trees and birdsong.

Eventually they reached the bandstand and sat to rest on one of the wooden benches that were arranged on the gravel path that surrounded it. Kitty took a seat next to Matt and breathed in the welcome scent of the delicate pink roses that surrounded them.

Kitty could see that something was still clearly bothering Matt. 'What's wrong? You've been very quiet ever since we left Cairn House.'

He gave a small shake of his head, the corners of his mouth lifting in a grim smile. 'I'm sorry, Kitty. It was just that place. It affected me in a way that I was not expecting. I was thinking about Edith and what might have become of her and Betty. If I had not met her when I did…'

Kitty reached across to take his hand in hers. Edith had been Matt's first wife, who he had met when he had been injured during the war. She had been his nurse at the convalescent hospital. He had only recently confided in her that he had married Edith to save her from disgrace when she had discovered she was pregnant by a married fellow officer. Everyone had believed Betty to be Matt's baby and he had never enlightened them.

Matt had adored his wife and baby Betty. Their uncertain courtship having bloomed into a deep affection, until their happiness at having found one another had been brutally snatched away in a bombing raid during the war. It had taken him a long time to recover from the loss.

Kitty could see that he was picturing Edith being forced to abandon Betty in just such a home if they had not met, fallen in love and married. The idea was sobering and she squeezed his fingers tenderly.

'Edith and Betty were fortunate to have had you.'

He responded to her touch, returning the pressure on her hand. 'I'm sorry, Kitty. It's just sometimes it all comes back to me.' He turned and smiled at her. 'I wonder that you put up with me, old thing.'

Kitty smiled back at the familiar term of endearment. 'Come on, while we are in the city, I should very much like to see Reverend Greenslade's church and the scene of the robbery. Is it far from here, do you know?'

To her relief he followed her cue and jumped to his feet. 'When I was studying the map yesterday to find Cairn House, I noticed St Mark's didn't appear to be too far away. I think if we leave this park by the other gate and walk for about fifteen minutes we should be almost there.'

Kitty stood and brushed a small dead leaf from her skirt. 'Then let's go over there and take a look for ourselves. I must admit I'm quite curious to see St Mark's for myself, and the site of the actual robbery. After that, I think you owe me a rather nice late lunch.' She grinned impishly at him, and he laughed.

———

Matt's mood lightened as they put more distance between themselves and the mother and baby home. When he had first discovered Edith's predicament, he knew that a place like Cairn House had been the one thing she had dreaded more than anything. That she would be forced to stay in such a home and give up her child.

He hadn't thought of that aspect of his first marriage for years but the interview with Sister Perpetua and the feel of the home had brought it all back. Kitty's hand rested lightly on the crook of his arm, and he reflected again on how fortunate he had been to meet her. For a long time he had been convinced that he would never marry again, until Kitty had entered his life.

The incident a few months ago when she too had almost died on the orders of the Hammetts had frightened him. He knew Kitty was setting great store by obtaining permission to confront Ezekiel Hammett in prison before his trial. While he understood her desire to obtain some form of closure from her mother's killer, he couldn't help secretly hoping that permission might be refused.

They stopped to ask a passing police constable for directions to the church. He was relieved to find that his memory of reading the map was correct and they were only a couple of streets away. The buildings around them had been changing during their walk. From the grey bleak stone of the streets surrounding the mother and baby home, which had been on the edge of the slum area, to more elegant and gracious Georgian-style buildings interspersed with shops and eating houses.

'It is quite warm now,' Kitty said as they paused on a street corner to get their bearings. She released his arm to fan her face with her hand. Her cheeks were pink and her face flushed beneath the brim of her hat from the exercise and the heat of the day.

'Would you like to stop for lunch?' Matt asked. He knew his fiancée had a healthy appetite and Kitty always had her best inspirations on a full stomach.

'Perhaps there will be a tea room or café near the church,' she suggested.

They walked on and rounding the corner they discovered themselves in a busy street lined with fashionable shops and cafés.

Kitty clutched at his arm. 'Look, over there is the Tower Hill Jeweller's shop.'

The jeweller's shop had an impressive black marble double frontage with elaborate gold lettering and the royal crest above the door. Behind the heavy glass windowpanes silver and gold pieces set with precious stones gleamed on black velvet cushions.

They paused to peer in through the window at the display.

'There are some very lovely things,' Kitty said, apparently admiring a gold bracelet set with emeralds in the shape of a panther's head.

Matt wondered if she might have preferred a new engagement ring instead of the family ring he had given her a few days ago.

'And very expensive, I imagine. I can see why the robbers would have targeted the business. The shop assistant was brutally attacked during the raid. He was fortunate not to be killed.'

'I read that in the newspapers. They said he is making a good recovery although he was still too unwell to be present at the trial,' Kitty replied as they continued their stroll along the street taking in the sights.

'There is Reverend Greenslade's church, just up ahead.' Matt saw that at the end of the row of shops there was a small square. The road ran all around it leaving a grassed area with a couple of benches and a statue of some long-forgotten worthy gentleman surveying them haughtily from his stone podium in the centre.

On the far side of the green was St Mark's Church. A red-brick building with a spire surrounded by a somewhat unkempt looking graveyard. Kitty hastened her steps to keep up with his longer strides as they hurried towards it.

Matt halted in front of the wooden church noticeboard. The faded gilt lettering announced the times of the services and at the bottom gave the reader the information that the Reverend Greenslade was the main point of contact for the church.

'We are at the right place, then,' Kitty said, after studying the sign.

'Shall we enter the grounds and explore?' Matt suggested.

Kitty happily agreed and they entered the churchyard through the small green painted wooden gate. They followed the narrow-paved path and Matt realised that the graveyard continued on back behind the church, much further than they had realised when they first approached from the front entrance.

At the entrance of the church, they had passed larger

ornate stone memorials presumably housing the remains of some of the grander local families. Now, as they rounded the rear of the building, the grass was longer and small rabbit trails led away between the older gravestones that leaned drunkenly in the summer sunshine. Large white butterflies skittered around the stones and brambles spilled out from the boundary bearing blackberries, which were gradually ripening in the heat.

A ginger cat sat in a puddle of sunshine placidly cleaning his paws as it watched them through unblinking green eyes.

'It's like another world back here, isn't it?' Kitty said as she gazed around her.

'Yes. I believe this must be where Travers claimed he over-heard the robbers planning their escape and dividing up the proceeds of the raid.' Matt frowned as he took in the layout of the grounds.

'Where was he? And what was he doing here?' Kitty sounded puzzled.

'I rather think that he said he had been walking Bertie and heard voices. He hid in some bushes in here as he felt afraid.'

'Hmm, that's possible, I suppose.' Kitty chewed her bottom lip, clearly trying to picture the scene as she looked around the grounds.

'There is another entrance over there. I presume that leads into the next street.' Matt pointed it out to Kitty.

'He could have been walking Bertie from that direction. I expect the local people use this as a shortcut,' Kitty said.

They turned around and made their way back along the path to the front of the church where they encountered an elderly woman engaged in locking the front door. A battered olive-coloured leatherette shopping bag was hung over her arm and she wore a navy pinafore under her summer coat. Matt guessed from her appearance that she must have been cleaning inside the church.

The woman pressed her hand to her heart, clearly startled by their sudden entrance from the back of the churchyard.

'Oh my days, you fair gave me a fright. Never 'eard you coming, I didn't.'

'We're terribly sorry. My fiancée and I were just looking around the church. An acquaintance of ours suggested that Reverend Greenslade might be willing to marry us here, so we thought we should take a look,' Matt said suavely.

'Lor' bless you, the vicar is away from 'ome at the minute. Got bad nerves 'e 'as from the war. Then all that bother with the robbery at the jeweller's over there made 'im bad. 'E's gone to the seaside for a few weeks to recover 'imself.' The woman sniffed and dropped the large iron key to the church door inside her bag.

'Oh, that's a shame,' Matt said.

'I don't blame 'im me'self. We've 'ad all sorts of strange folks poking around 'ere lately, asking questions. Reporters and the like, what with the trial being reported in the papers.' The woman hitched the handle of her bag more firmly on her arm.

'That must have been very difficult for him. Indeed it must have been very trying for all of you. Miss Briggs will be disappointed we have missed him.' Kitty played along with Matt's subterfuge.

The woman pursed her lips, a slightly sour expression appearing on her pleasant, wrinkled face. 'Miss Briggs? That would be the missionary woman back from India? Friend of yours, is she?'

'Just an acquaintance.' Kitty judged from the woman's reaction that it would be wise to play down their meetings with Miss Briggs.

'Best kept as an acquaintance, that one, if you ask me. Something not quite right with that woman. I know she's very poorly and all but still...' The woman broke off and gave Kitty a significant look.

'Oh dear, why?' Kitty asked, her eyes wide.

'Got a nasty streak, she 'as.'

The ginger cat they had seen earlier came strolling around the corner to wrap himself affectionately around the woman's legs. 'I saw 'er try to kick old Tibs 'ere when she thought as no one was looking. Sly, that's the word for 'er.'

'That's dreadful,' Kitty sympathised.

'She 'ad the reverend fooled though. Took 'im in good and proper, 'ad 'im running 'er 'ere, there and everywhere she did. Got a kind 'eart 'e 'as, Reverend Greenslade. Kept taking 'er things when she was staying in that women's 'ostel over there. Little treats of cakes and chocolates.' The woman tutted and waved her free hand in the direction of a building on the other side of the street. 'It would be nice to 'ave a wedding 'ere. There was another bloke 'ere asking about weddings just before the reverend went on his 'oliday. Got a foreign-looking girlfriend with a funny name. Singer she said she was.'

Kitty exchanged a glance with Matt.

'Miss Dubois?'

'That's it! She famous then? 'Ave you 'eard of 'er?' The woman peered at Kitty.

'I think I may have seen her name on a poster,' Kitty said.

'They was 'ere asking after the reverend and poking about in the church. Flash they was, the pair of them.' The woman sighed.

'We must come back when the reverend is returned from his holiday,' Matt said.

The woman's face brightened. 'Oh yes, I like a good wedding and your young lady will make a lovely bride.' She beamed at Kitty, who blushed guiltily at the woman's approbation.

They said their farewells and the woman scuttled away with the cat following along behind her.

'I think we can probably assume that Mr Ford was Miss

Dubois's escort when she came here. Do you think they were looking for the missing jewellery?' Kitty asked.

Matt grinned. 'I very much doubt they were arranging a wedding.'

They walked out of the churchyard and Matt spotted a tea room further along the street. 'Let us go and have some lunch before we get the train back to Devon. It seems we have uncovered a great deal of interesting information today.'

———

Once they were seated in the small upmarket tea room and the waitress had taken their order, Kitty drew off her gloves and placed them on top of her bag. 'Miss Briggs's request for information about her daughter has certainly been enlightening.'

Matt settled back in his seat. 'It seems that Miss Briggs is unaware of her daughter's identity, but Meribel Jacques knows the truth. Surely she must have recognised Miss Briggs's name after Travers was killed, when the constable was taking everyone's details?'

The waitress returned with their order, and he waited until their plates of ham, egg and chips were in front of them before continuing the conversation.

'This looks delicious.' Kitty sighed happily as she picked up her knife and fork. 'Meribel has not mentioned her connection to Miss Briggs, not to Inspector Greville or to Miss Briggs herself.'

'Perhaps she wishes to distance herself from the connection.' Matt speared a piece of ham with his fork.

'Even so, she should have declared it to the inspector. He would have respected her wishes if she did not wish to make her identity known to her mother.'

Matt could see that Kitty was troubled by Meribel's omission. 'She may have her reasons. Certainly, it is something we need to discuss with her before we see Miss Briggs again.'

'The lady we met at the church did not seem to care for Miss Briggs. It was a strange reaction since she surely cannot have met her many times.' Kitty applied herself to her fried egg.

'And kicking the cat when she thought no one was looking? Very odd. Even if she were allergic and disliked cats that seems unnecessarily cruel,' Matt said.

Kitty swallowed her food and picked up her teacup to take a drink before replying. 'In my opinion you should never trust anyone who is unkind to an animal.'

Matt smiled at the firm tone in her voice. 'You are feeling less sympathetic towards Miss Briggs now?'

Kitty frowned. 'It is impossible not to feel sympathy for a woman in such poor health and who has clearly suffered in her life, but I must admit my perception of her is slightly altered.'

Matt took a sip of tea from his own cup. 'I agree.'

'I think the inspector may wish to know about Miss Dubois's connection with the church and Reverend Greenslade too. Miss Dubois and Billy Ford had clearly seen the reverend's name on the church sign. They would have recognised it in the waiting room after Travers's death in the same way Lady Jacques would have recognised her mother's name,' Kitty said.

Matt agreed with his fiancée. He was certain that Inspector Greville would be very interested in all the information they had uncovered. It had been a very worthwhile train trip.

SEVENTEEN

Once back in Torquay, Kitty dropped Matt back off at his home at Churston and motored back the short distance down the lane to Kingswear to cross the river back to Dartmouth. She had arranged for Mickey to take Bertie back to Matt later that day when he had finished his chores at the hotel. Kitty hoped the dog had not proved too distracting or destructive.

She felt completely worn out by the time she had parked her car in its shed and walked the short distance along the street to the Dolphin. The air was growing cooler now that evening was approaching, and she longed for a nice bath and a good supper with perhaps a cocktail or two.

'Have you had a nice time in London, Miss Kitty?' Mary, the receptionist, greeted her with a smile as she entered the lobby.

'It was very interesting, but I must confess I feel quite exhausted now.' She paused at the desk while Mary gathered up a small collection of post that had come for her.

She flicked through the pile, pausing when she saw one letter in a brown envelope that looked official.

'Mary, may I use your letter opener?' Kitty placed the other letters down on the counter and took Mary's small brass paperknife to open the envelope.

Her fingers trembled as she extracted the letter from inside. She scanned the contents quickly. 'This is it, Mary. It's finally come. I have permission to visit Hammett in the prison at Exeter.'

'Gracious me, Miss Kitty.' Mary was clearly taken aback by Kitty's excitement at this news.

'I must go and tell Grams. Is she in her salon?' Kitty gathered up the rest of the post. Her exhaustion replaced by a surge of energy.

'Yes, miss, she went up an hour or so ago.'

Kitty beamed at the bewildered receptionist and ran lightly up the stairs, her pulse racing with excitement.

She knocked on the door to her grandmother's apartment and hurried inside. Her grandmother was seated on the sofa, her pre-dinner glass of sherry already in her hand.

She turned her head at Kitty's slightly breathless entrance.

'Kitty darling, you're back, just in time for dinner. How was London?'

'Hot and busy, but interesting. Grams darling, look, it came, the letter. It finally came. I have permission to go to the prison in Exeter to see Hammett before he is transferred to London.' Kitty passed the letter to her grandmother to read while she divested herself of her hat and jacket.

'The appointment is for the day after tomorrow for thirty minutes. The permission is granted for you alone, although a member of the prison staff may accompany you during the interview.' Her grandmother read parts of the letter aloud, a troubled expression on her face.

'Kitty darling, you are quite certain about this, aren't you? I mean, actually visiting a prison. It is hardly a fitting place for you to go. Exeter Gaol always looks the most forbidding place, and this terrible man and his sister have tried to kill you.'

Kitty stood behind her grandmother and wrapped her arms around her grandmother's slender shoulders. 'Father Lamb said that if I were given permission to visit then he would ask his colleague to accompany me. He is the prison chaplain there so would be allowed to support me whilst I see Hammett. A guard will be there too, so it isn't as if I shall be alone with him.'

Her grandmother set the letter down on the marquetry topped occasional table and sighed. 'I would feel much better about this if Matthew were accompanying you.'

'It's only for thirty minutes, Grams, and I will have people with me who are used to such criminals. I need to do this. I owe it to Mother to try and get answers from Hammett about what happened that day.' Her hand automatically strayed to the brooch pinned under her lapel.

The older woman placed her hand on top of Kitty's and patted her tenderly. 'If you promise me that this will be the end. Your mother is at rest now and you must move on. You have your wedding to plan and your life to look forward to. Promise me this will finally close the door.'

A tear escaped from Kitty's eye as she lowered her head to kiss her grandmother's wrinkled cheek. 'I promise.'

Her grandmother seemed satisfied at having extracted Kitty's word of honour on the subject and rose from her seat to pour her a pre-dinner sherry.

'Millicent Craven came for tea this afternoon. She informed me that there had been another death, the brush salesman, she said.' Her grandmother handed Kitty her drink in a delicate crystal glass.

Kitty mentally cursed Mrs Craven. 'Yes, that's right. The inspector thinks that Mr Ford may have been responsible for killing Mr Travers on the train.'

'Hmm, if that is so, then who does the inspector think killed Mr Ford?' Her grandmother asked before taking a sip of her sherry.

That, Kitty thought, was the question. 'He isn't sure yet. I believe he and his men are tracing Mr Ford's last known actions to try to determine exactly when he was murdered.'

Her grandmother raised a delicately arched eyebrow. 'I presume your excursion to London today was to assist Matthew with this case?'

Kitty sighed and took a seat beside her grandmother. 'Not exactly. We were tasked with a personal request from a dying woman about another matter. However, it does seem that what we have learned today may be useful to the inspector as well.'

'I do hope that when you are married, Kitty, that you will pay more attention to managing your home and spend less time chasing about after these dangerous criminals.' Her grandmother's lips pursed, and Kitty jumped up quickly, eager to forestall the impending lecture.

'Darling, I must go and take a bath. I feel absolutely grimy from the train, and I want to telephone Matt and tell him about my letter.' She gave her grandmother another hasty kiss on her cheek and escaped the room clutching her glass of sherry before her beloved Grams could stop her.

She had scarcely made it up the stairs to her own quarters when there was a knock at her door.

Alice came in at her invitation to enter, her auburn curls escaping from under her cap. 'Mary said as you'd had your letter come, Miss Kitty, about going to the prison to see that man.'

'Yes, it came just now. Here, take a look.' Kitty passed the letter across to her friend to read.

She perched herself on the edge of one of her fireside chairs and took another sip of sherry while Alice studied the contents of the letter.

'There's a lot of rules, what you can't take inside and such. I think you'm being brave to do it. To face that man all on your own without Captain Bryant beside you and inside a prison and all.' Alice passed the letter back to Kitty, a troubled look on her face.

'It's for thirty minutes only and the timing is very strict. I presume that must be due to the high-risk category. I am to be there fifteen minutes beforehand at the governor's office and I shall be escorted by a guard throughout the visit. Father Lamb's colleague will also be present to give me support.' Kitty swallowed the last of her drink and set the empty glass down on a small rosewood side table.

'Do you think as that Hammett will tell you anything about what happened to your mother, miss?' Alice asked.

Kitty shrugged. 'I don't know quite what to expect from him. The last news I had was that he was refusing to speak to anyone. Inspector Greville said he would not even acknowledge his own defence barrister. However, presumably he has consented to see me.'

Alice picked at the hem of her starched white apron. 'Then what do you think he might say? He surely won't admit to anything that would help fasten the noose around his neck.'

Kitty had considered this point. She had played out what might happen a million times in her head when she finally came face to face with the man she was convinced had murdered her mother.

'Even if he says nothing at all then I shall have the satisfaction of knowing that he is finally behind bars. I will force him to look me in the eyes and I hope that seeing me will bring my mother back to his mind and haunt his every moment until he pays with his own life.'

She knew she was the image of her mother and was now of a similar age to when her mother had been killed. Normally she was a kind, forgiving person, but she hated Hammett for everything he had done to her mother and what he and his sister had tried to inflict upon her.

Alice gave a visible shiver, whether at her words or the fierce tone of Kitty's voice, she wasn't sure.

'It's been a long time a-coming, miss.'

'It has, Alice, it certainly has.' Her mother's whereabouts had been unknown for years until Kitty had finally uncovered the clues leading to the discovery of her body. At least her mother now was at rest in the churchyard of St Saviour's in the town. She and her grandmother had a place to lay flowers and grieve properly.

Instead for the longest time, everywhere they had gone subconsciously they had looked for her. Strangers with the same shade of hair, or a mannerism had caused them to turn and check, always wondering where she had gone.

Now the man responsible was imprisoned, Kitty felt she owed it to her mother and her grandmother to at least see for herself that this was at an end and that Hammett would pay for his crimes.

Alice insisted on preparing Kitty's bath for her. Kitty in return told Alice about everything they had learned from Miss Briggs and the excursion to London.

'Our Betty is working for that Lady Meribel Jacques. She said as Lady Meribel's mother was the one as employed her. Here in disgrace, she is apparently; her father has threatened to cut her off if she gets herself in any more financial scrapes. Our Betty says as she owes money all over London what with her gaming and her extravagance. Lady Jacques's mother has asked our Betty to keep her eye on her.' Alice added a generous scoop of bath salts to the bath water and swished vigorously with her hand. Clouds of rose-scented steam filled the air.

'Does Betty report directly to Meribel's mother then?' Kitty asked. She had forgotten to ask that question of Betty when she had bumped into her on the street.

Alice straightened and dried her hands on a towel. 'I think as she is to let her know if Lady Meribel is running into trouble.

Our Betty says she has a bit of a wild group of friends staying with her. All cocktails and japes they is.' Alice gave a sniff of disapproval.

'It will be interesting to talk to her again and find out exactly what she thinks about discovering that Miss Briggs is her birth mother.' Kitty fetched a pile of towels out of her cupboard.

'That it will, miss. She must have been proper shocked when you was all in the waiting room and giving your names to the constable to realise that her mother had been right next to her in the compartment,' Alice mused.

Kitty searched her memory. Everyone had seemed quite shaken in the aftermath of discovering Simon Travers's murder. She couldn't recall anything special in Lady Jacques's responses. Or for that matter any reaction from Miss Dubois and Billy Ford on hearing Reverend Greenslade's name. Then again, Mrs Craven and Miss Dubois had been a distraction as they butted heads.

Kitty thanked her friend for her help and Alice left her to soak in the rose-perfumed water. She intended to telephone Matt and Father Lamb once she had dressed for dinner. There was a lot to do ahead of the visit to Exeter Gaol to see Hammett and still a murder mystery to solve.

———

Matt also had telephone calls to make on his return to his cottage. Mickey had dropped Bertie off shortly after his return, declaring him a lovely dog but needy. Now, with his new dog lying peacefully at his feet, Matt took a sip of whisky and made the first of his calls.

Inspector Greville thanked him for the update and the new information.

'I think, if you are agreeable, Inspector, Kitty and I will see Lady Meribel and hear what she has to say on the subject of her parentage. We still have to let Miss Briggs know what we have discovered, but we need to speak to Lady Meribel first.'

'Quite, quite, no, I think you are probably best placed to have that conversation with her ladyship. My hands are quite full here at the moment tracking down sightings of Mr Ford so I can get a better fix for his likely time of death.' Matt heard the gust of the inspector's sigh echo down the line.

'Did you manage to discover if Ford called to see Reverend Greenslade, sir?' Matt asked.

'A man answering Ford's description did call at the reverend's lodgings. Reverend Greenslade was not at home at the time, so we believe a note was left. We are still trying to find someone who may have seen them together in Paignton.'

Matt frowned. 'Could you not simply ask the reverend if he had seen Ford that evening, sir?'

'I could, but if he denied it then that would pre-warn him if he is our man and give him time to escape or prepare a defence. No, I would rather have a sighting first. Something concrete that he can't deny, then if he is the one, I can pin him down properly.' The inspector's tone was thoughtful.

'You feel he may have killed Ford?' Matt must have sounded dubious.

'I can't rule it out. He may have murdered Travers too and Ford may have realised and tried a little extortion,' the inspector said.

'If the reverend stumbled across the proceeds of the robbery and kept them for himself?' Matt suggested as he mulled over this possibility.

'It could have happened. You just said you visited the church yourself today. What did you think?' Greville asked.

Matt recalled the path cutting across the graveyard and the wild rear of the site. Both he and Kitty had seen empty beer bottles and cigarette ends in the long grass. It could quite easily have provided a place for the robbers to rendezvous or hide some of the proceeds.

'I agree, sir. Considering the position of St Mark's to the jewellers, then I would say it is possible.'

He finished the call after promising to report any new information to the inspector. After replacing the receiver back in its cradle, he sat for a moment thinking about everything they had learned in the last two days.

Bertie rolled over at his feet and sighed loudly before placing his nose on the toes of Matt's new house slippers. Matt took another sip of his whisky and picked up the telephone receiver again to place his calls to London.

The discussion with Sister Perpetua was playing on his mind and he realised that he needed more information. Once he had spoken again to the sister he hung up, and this time he called Brigadier Remmington-Blythe.

The brigadier was still in his office and listened intently as Matt gave his report.

'Hmm, interesting stuff, what. The verdict in the trial is expected tomorrow. I take it you want me to do a bit of digging for you, eh?'

Matt outlined the information he needed, and the brigadier agreed to use his connections.

'All a bit more complicated than we thought. It would be very beneficial if we could recover the loot, as they say.'

'Let us hope so, sir. I feel as if the solution cannot be too far away now,' Matt said and ended his call. He hoped he was correct with his assurance as there were still a lot of unanswered questions.

EIGHTEEN

Matt was still at breakfast when Kitty called at his house the following morning. Bertie greeted her happily, his tail wagging, as she entered the dining room at the front of the house.

'Good morning, darling.' Matt rose from his seat to place a kiss on her cheek as she drew off her gloves and took a seat beside him at the table. 'I've taken the liberty of telephoning Lady Meribel. She is expecting us at the manor after ten.'

Kitty helped herself to a triangle of toast from the silver toast rack on the table. 'What was her reaction when you called?' she asked as she spread a pat of rich yellow butter lovingly onto her toast.

'I didn't provide her with a reason for our visit. She tried to get out of seeing us, however I told her that it was either us or the police that called to see her.' Matt passed the glass dish of marmalade to Kitty.

She smiled her thanks at him and applied herself to the marmalade. 'And what was her response to that?'

Matt grinned, the dimple flashing in his cheek. 'She became amenable to our visit. However, she requested that we not call very early. It was quite noisy in the background.'

Kitty's eyebrows lifted at this. It sounded as if Lady Meribel had been enjoying a social evening and no doubt required time to recover herself. She smiled as Bertie seated himself beside Matt, placing his nose on Matt's knee.

'Is Bertie in the good books this morning? No more eating your slippers?' She took a bite of toast savouring the tang of the home-made marmalade. 'Mickey said he had no problems with him yesterday.'

'He is being suspiciously good this morning.' Matt glanced down at the dog.

'I take it he will be accompanying us to see Lady Jacques?' Kitty finished her toast and wiped her sticky fingers on the white linen napkin that was beside Matt's plate.

'I'm afraid so, I don't think I can safely leave him here. Let's hope that he behaves himself whilst we are at Cockington Manor.'

With breakfast completed Matt secured Bertie once more in the back of Kitty's car and they set off towards the picturesque village of Cockington. Lady Jacques's family had secured the purchase of a small manor house not far from the centre of the village. Mrs Craven had suggested that the house had been purchased as a holiday home since it was known to have good tennis courts and was in a pretty spot.

As Kitty pointed her car through the narrow lanes that were lush with greenery and sprinkled with daisies, she wondered if Lady Jacques senior hoped the location might keep Meribel out of mischief.

Finally, they rounded a corner and the manor house stood before them at the end of a gravelled drive. The house was of red brick capped with a grey slate-tiled roof. A creamy stone portico graced the front and on either side of the driveway the lawns were a manicured emerald green.

'Nice place,' Matt commented as Kitty pulled her car to a stop near the front door.

'Mrs C said she thought the house was quite old. It was quite run down when Meribel's family acquired it.'

'It certainly appears very well maintained now,' Matt remarked as he opened his door and started to untie Bertie's leash. He got the dog out and crossed around the front of the car to open Kitty's door for her.

'Well, let us see what Lady Jacques has to tell us about her visit to Sister Perpetua,' Kitty murmured as she tugged on the black cast-iron bell pull at the side of the front door.

To her surprise instead of a maid or manservant answering the door, a young man in casual attire appeared.

'We have an appointment with Lady Meribel,' Kitty said. She thought she recognised him from the evening at the yacht club when he had been paying Lady Meribel a great deal of attention.

'Oh yes, Meri is expecting you, she's out on the terrace.' The man made no attempt to introduce himself. Kitty gave a slight shrug of her shoulders and she and Matt followed the man through the house.

The house had clearly been fully renovated and was furnished in a modern style with light walls and sleek minimalist furnishings. They were led through the hall and along a short corridor via a spacious, if untidy, drawing room, out through the open French doors and onto a wide stone-flagged terrace.

Lady Meribel was reclining on a rattan garden lounger beneath a pale green sunshade. Black sunglasses with circular lenses covered her eyes and the pallor of her face was heightened by the bright red slash of her lipstick.

'Meri old girl, got your private eye people for you,' the man who had answered the door called as they approached.

'Do be quiet, Johnny, you are such an ass.' Lady Meribel moved her sunglasses to peer at them over the top of the lenses.

'I'll leave you to it. Got a tennis game on in a minute and

need to change into my whites.' The man winked at Kitty and strolled off back inside the house, leaving Kitty, Matt and Bertie standing around on the terrace next to Meribel.

Lady Meribel pushed herself up on her lounger and adjusted the bright cotton lounging pyjamas she was wearing. 'I'm sorry but will this take long? I have guests here at the moment and I thought I had answered all the questions that the police wished to ask.'

Matt looked around and spied some cane chairs nearby. He pulled one over for Kitty and another for himself.

'There are a few things that have come to light since your first interviews, Lady Jacques, which we hope you might be able to help us with,' Kitty said.

'We were entrusted the other day with a private commission. Something which we originally thought had no bearing on the investigation into the murders of Simon Travers and William Ford,' Matt continued where Kitty had left off.

Lady Meribel had been taking a cigarette from the silver case that lay on the table beside her. Her hands stilled for a moment when Matt spoke.

'That policeman has already asked me where I was when Ford may have been killed. So this commission of yours involves me how exactly?' she asked as she secured her cigarette into a carved jade holder.

'The commission we were given was from a mother looking for her child. A baby she was forced to relinquish at birth for adoption.' Kitty jumped as Meribel's hand trembled as she attempted to light her cigarette causing her to singe her fingers with the flame from the lighter.

'Ouch, so clumsy of me.' Meribel winced and refocused her attention on Kitty.

'We went to see Sister Perpetua at Cairn House mother and baby home. She said that you had visited there yourself not too long ago,' Matt said.

Kitty watched Meribel closely, wishing the other girl wasn't wearing her dark glasses so that she could read her reactions more accurately.

'It's no secret that I was adopted as a baby.' Meribel blew out a thin stream of smoke.

'You were asking Sister Perpetua about your birth mother,' Kitty said.

Meribel shrugged. 'I was curious, that's all. It's also no secret that my adoptive father and I do not get along terribly well. He had accused me of all kinds of things, saying that my mother had been an immoral woman, so I had no doubt inherited these undesirable traits.' Meribel paused, her shoulders drooping. 'His comments had played on my mind, so I decided to go and see Sister Perpetua to try and discover who my parents had been. I wanted to know if she was some street girl or simply a woman who had made a mistake.' She lifted her chin defiantly.

'In the course of that conversation with the sister you discovered your mother was, in fact, Miss Briggs,' Matt said.

There was a moment's silence as Meribel seemed to be deciding what she should say.

'Yes, Sister Perpetua told me that my father had been a married man with two children. He died in a house fire just after I was born. Miss Briggs had been deceived by him, believing him free to marry her. She had me at Cairn House and decided to leave for India to enter the missions. I believed that was where she had remained. I had no desire to disrupt her life by contacting her.' Meribel stubbed out her cigarette in the large Lalique glass ashtray. 'We clearly could have nothing in common and my curiosity was satisfied. My adoptive father, as usual, was wrong about everything.'

'It must have come as a shock then, after Simon Travers was killed, when you were all giving your names to discover that the

Miss Briggs who had shared your compartment was your birth mother?' Kitty said.

Meribel sat up straighter in her seat. 'I was late arriving for the train. I only made it due to the good offices of the guard who virtually threw me into the first-class compartment.'

Kitty saw the girl suck in a breath as if trying to keep her composure.

'I thought I heard the reverend mention her name when she fainted, and we were attempting to revive her, but Briggs is a common surname, so I convinced myself it was merely a coincidence.'

Matt cut in. 'Then you heard her give her first name to the constable. Xanthe is a more unusual name, and she said she had recently returned from India. You had to have realised at that moment who she was.'

Lady Meribel was silent once more. In the distance Kitty could hear shouting and laughter combined with the thwack of tennis balls hitting racquets. Bertie gave a loud snore from where he had fallen asleep at Matt's feet.

'Yes, it was a shock.' She broke her silence. 'It was bad enough that a man had been stabbed only a few feet away from me without any of us noticing.' She shook her head as if trying to make sense of it all. 'Then to discover that my mother, who I believed to be half a world away, was right beside me and I didn't know.' Her voice trembled and broke. 'Does she know who I am? You said she had commissioned you to find me.'

Kitty couldn't tell from the tone of Meribel's voice if she wanted Miss Briggs to be made aware of her identity or not.

'We have not informed Miss Briggs as yet that we have discovered the identity of her daughter.'

Lady Meribel's body sagged back in her seat.

'Would you prefer us to keep your identity concealed from her?' Kitty asked. She could see that the girl was confused.

'I don't know. It's something that I need a little more time to process.' Meribel rubbed her temple with her hand.

'Miss Briggs is ailing quite quickly. If you did wish to make your identity known to her, then I would advise you to do so sooner rather than later.' Matt's response was gentle.

'Thank you.' Meribel straightened her back.

'Why did you not reveal the relationship to Inspector Greville?' Kitty asked.

Lady Meribel sighed. 'I was in shock. Then, afterwards, I couldn't see what difference it would make to the investigation.'

Kitty could understand Lady Jacques's point. Yet nothing seemed to make any sense about who might have murdered Simon Travers, or what any of these random discoveries might have to do with his death.

Matt moved and Bertie lumbered to his feet with a long-suffering sigh.

'Thank you for your time, Lady Jacques. I hope that you do make your decision swiftly. In the meantime, we shall tell Miss Briggs that we have traced you and seen you and that you are well.'

'Yes, please do. Thank you for that. I have many questions that I should like to ask her, but I am not sure that I'm ready for the answers she might give me. Cowardly of me, I know.' She opened her cigarette case once more.

Kitty and Matt made their farewells and left Meribel to her cigarette. They walked back through the house seeing no one.

'I wonder where all the servants are?' Kitty said as they reached the hall.

'It is very odd,' Matt agreed as they peeped into what was obviously the dining room.

'What shall we do next?' Kitty unlocked the door of her car and waited for Matt to secure Bertie on the back seat once more.

He finished fixing Bertie's leash before moving his cuff to check the time on his watch.

'We have been here for a while. What do you say to a drive into Torquay for an early lunch on the seafront? We could go to Bobby's café or perhaps instead try the Pavilion tea rooms and sit out on the green.'

Kitty beamed as she slid behind the steering wheel. 'Well, my holiday is almost over so I suppose I should try and do something pleasurable before I return to the books and balance sheets at the hotel.'

Matt returned her smile as he took his place beside her. 'Absolutely.'

They set off back along the narrow lanes, this time heading towards the sea at Torquay. Kitty was quietly pleased that she was wearing her pale blue crepe de chine summer frock and her hat with the matching ribbon. At this time of day in the season everyone wore their most fashionable attire to see and be seen in on the promenade.

Before long they had reached the outskirts of the town.

'Kitty darling, just pull over a moment,' Matt requested, his tone urgent, as they passed a small row of shops.

'What is it?' At first, she was alarmed thinking perhaps Bertie had freed himself.

'The newsboards are out for the midday edition of the *Herald.*' Matt indicated one of the wire-framed boards that shouted the latest headlines. 'The verdict is in on the Tower Hill jewel robbery trial.' He jumped out of the car and hurried inside the newsagents, returning shortly afterwards with a newspaper folded up under his arm.

Once he had closed the door, Kitty pulled out once more and they continued towards the seafront. Ahead of them through the buildings the sea sparkled bright blue in the sunshine and the palm trees swayed gently.

Kitty turned near the memorial clock tower and drove along

the front looking for a suitable place to stop. The promenade was busy with people out enjoying the summer sunshine. The fountain played amongst the flower beds and small children laughed and ran around on the grass under the watchful gaze of their nurses and mothers.

There was a space not far from the Pavilion Playhouse, so Kitty pulled in and turned off her engine.

'It is quite busy along here today as it's such a lovely day.' She looked around her as she spoke.

'Let's walk down and see if there are any tables free at the Pavilion tea room. It would be pleasant to be outside for a while.' Matt rescued Bertie from his perch on the back seat and they set off along the promenade.

'Look, at that table over there.' Kitty nudged Matt.

The tea room was busy as she had predicted, but on a table by herself Kitty had spied Carlotta Dubois. The girl was dressed in her usual slightly flamboyant style in a navy drop-waist dress with canary yellow trim and a matching yellow hat.

'Most fortuitous,' Matt murmured, and they made their way through the seating area to Miss Dubois's table.

NINETEEN

'Good afternoon, Miss Dubois, gosh it's frightfully busy here today, isn't it? May we join you?' Kitty had already pulled out a chair as she was speaking so the other girl had little option but to agree.

Kitty noticed the singer's eyes looked slightly puffy and she had been gazing moodily into the distance when they had arrived. As if aware of Kitty's scrutiny Carlotta quickly donned a pair of dark-lensed glasses.

A waitress came to clear Miss Dubois's cup and to take their order.

'We were intending to have lunch, Miss Dubois, will you join us? The sandwiches here look very good,' Kitty said as the waitress stood by holding her notepad and pencil.

'Made fresh every day, miss. Done while you wait, they are. I recommend the crab or the cheese with pickle,' the girl said.

'That sounds excellent. We'll take a selection and a pot of tea for three,' Matt jumped in with the order, so Carlotta was compelled to remain in her seat.

The waitress beamed her approval and cleared away the used crockery before returning with a fresh tea tray.

'Your lunch will be out shortly, sir, miss.'

Matt murmured his thanks and set his newspaper down on the table beside his place setting.

'Forgive me, Miss Dubois, but are you quite all right?' Kitty asked in a kindly tone.

The girl sighed and fidgeted with the fresh empty china teacup that Kitty had placed in front of her. 'No, I'm not. I was wishing that I'd never agreed to come here.' Her gaze appeared to fall on Matt's newspaper, and she gasped and pressed the back of her hand to her mouth. She removed her glasses to read the headline.

Guilty verdicts returned in notorious jewel raid.

'I believe you know some of the men involved in the trial,' Matt said as she lifted anguished dark eyes towards him.

'One of them is my older brother. Well, half-brother really, Norman. He's all I've got. We've always stuck together me and 'im. I don't have no one else. Then, there's my bloke, Fred...' A tear rolled down her cheek. She fumbled in her handbag for her handkerchief.

'I'm sorry.' Kitty couldn't help feeling for the girl as she was clearly distraught.

'Here, please read it for yourself.' Matt passed Carlotta the newspaper so she could read all of the article.

'Twenty-five years.' The words escaped her in a frightened gasp. 'What am I going to do?'

The waitress returned at that moment with a tiered plate stand containing a selection of sandwiches. She placed them in the centre of the table and hurried away.

'Here, let me pour you some tea. You've had a nasty shock.' Kitty picked up the floral china patterned teapot and served them all with tea.

Carlotta had grown pale beneath her thick layer of make-up. She seemed to have shrunk down in her chair. The faint air of belligerence that had been present when they had first approached her had now vanished completely.

'We've always been together since we was kiddies and we was left at the orphanage. There was me and Norman and Billy and Fred.' Carlotta gave a gulping sob.

'Who exactly is Fred?' Kitty asked as she spooned sugar into Carlotta's cup.

'He was my gentleman friend. We had thought of getting married. He's being sent down as well though. He might never come out.' She pushed the newspaper away from her as if unable to continue reading any further.

'Drink some tea,' Kitty urged and was relieved when the girl finally accepted the cup and took a sip of the hot, sweet liquid. She guessed that Fred must be the man that Inspector Greville had referred to when he had said Miss Dubois was connected to the trial.

She could understand the girl's distress at the length of the sentences but if the assistant they had assaulted had died, they would have faced the noose.

'Forgive me for asking this, Miss Dubois, but did you see Billy Ford again after you left us outside the playhouse?' Matt asked. 'It's really important if we are to find who may have murdered him.'

A faint flush of colour crept into the girl's powder-caked cheeks. 'I saw him after the end of my show. He was waiting for me at the stage door. It was just for a few minutes.'

'What did he want?' Kitty asked, acutely aware that Carlotta had once again not seen fit to share this information with Inspector Greville.

'I had a gentleman waiting for me, so I didn't talk to him for above a few seconds.' Carlotta looked pleadingly at Kitty.

'What time was this?' Kitty knew Carlotta may have been

one of the last people to see Billy Ford alive if she was telling them the truth.

'I don't know for sure. The show finished at ten so it must have been close to half past by the time I'd changed out of my dress and got out of the theatre. Pretty much everyone had gone except the stage-door Johnnies who like to bring you flowers and stuff. Billy was waiting in the shadows, and he nabbed me as I was about to go off in the taxi with my admirer.' Carlotta sounded a little sulky as she explained her movements.

Matt had helped himself to sandwiches and was busy eating while Carlotta told her story. Kitty gave him a pointed look and he promptly placed some on a plate for her while she carried on interviewing the distraught singer.

'What did Billy have to say to you? It must have been something he thought was important if he was prepared to wait outside the theatre for you to finish your show?' Kitty asked.

Carlotta pouted. 'It was about the stuff. You know, the missing things from the jewellery raid. I might as well tell you now. I can't make anything any worse for Norman or Fred and poor Billy is dead.' She gave another sob and had to pause to collect herself. 'Billy was supposed to receive some of the goods, and I was to keep them for a bit until everything died down. Then we was going to sell them, or melt some stuff down.'

Matt nodded as he finished off a crab sandwich while Kitty glared at him.

'I take it something went wrong with the plan?' Kitty said.

Carlotta gave a miserable nod. 'The gang hid some of the stuff temporary like in a spot in the grounds of the church near the jewellers. We couldn't afford for none of us to get caught with anything. That would have given the game away good and proper.'

Kitty began to see how Reverend Greenslade could fit into this puzzle.

'Well, this Travers bloke, he must have seen where they

stashed the stuff and took it for himself and hid it someplace. Then he turns evidence to make sure as Norman and Fred and the others is out the way so he can hop it with the goods. We was hoping as we could find out what he'd done with the stuff.' Carlotta was flushed with indignation.

'Then, surely, if Billy thought that Travers knew where the goods were, he would have had no reason to kill him. With Travers dead you would never find out where he might have hidden the goods.' Kitty frowned. There was something amiss in this story. If Travers was dead, then Billy and Carlotta would have had no chance of getting the jewels back into their possession.

'Billy didn't kill Travers. He swore to me as he hadn't done it. Why would he? He knew as Travers was our best chance of finding the stuff.' Carlotta finished her tea and set the cup back down on the saucer.

'Then who did kill him?' Matt asked. 'The pool of suspects is becoming even smaller.'

Carlotta shrugged and helped herself to a cheese sandwich and nibbled at the crust while she considered Matt's question.

'Reverend Greenslade, perhaps?' Kitty suggested. 'He may have seen Travers remove the stolen goods from the churchyard. What did Billy say to you when he came to the playhouse?'

Carlotta chewed and swallowed. 'He said as he had been to see somebody to have a word and he thought as how he knew who had taken the stuff. He told me not to worry as he would soon have it sorted.'

'Did you believe him?' Kitty asked.

Carlotta brushed the crumbs from the front of her dress. 'Got no reason not to. He weren't going to double-cross me. I'd got too much on him and he knew it. Always was sweet on me, Billy was, God rest his soul.' Another tear leaked down her cheek.

'It's a pity he didn't tell you who this person was. I presume he was expecting to meet them later on that night?' Matt looked at Carlotta.

The girl nodded. 'That's what I thought. He said as they were going to hand over the stuff and we would be off and in the clear. He said we would have a good time coming soon.'

'Instead, Billy ended up floating in the harbour dead.' Matt's words caused Carlotta to begin sobbing again.

Kitty glared at him.

'I'd best be going. Thank you for the lunch, Miss Underhay. I want Billy's murderer caught. I know he weren't exactly the most honest, but he were good to me. If you find out who killed him, I want to know.' Miss Dubois rose from her seat and dabbed at her eyes with her handkerchief.

'Of course, I do understand, and I am sorry,' Kitty said as the girl gave her a watery smile and hurried off along the promenade.

Matt shook his head. 'I think your sympathy is misplaced there, old girl.'

Kitty sighed and selected one of the sandwiches Matt had put on her plate. 'Perhaps, but I can't help feeling a little sorry for her. She's had a hard life.'

'That's as maybe but she has also lied to us, and the inspector, several times now. She has admitted to being involved with the gang who committed the robbery at the jewellers, and I'm sure has no scruples about murder.' Matt looked at Kitty.

Kitty frowned. 'I am aware of all of those things, but I still do feel for her. Do you think she could have killed Billy Ford? He could have met her as she said and told her where the stolen goods were hidden. I just don't know, she seemed so genuine just then when she was talking to us.'

Matt poured the last dregs of tea from the pot into his cup and added a splash of milk. 'It's possible, I suppose. By Miss Dubois's own admission there is a window of time when she could have met with Billy and killed him. We only have her word that she saw him at ten thirty at the stage door before she left for the Imperial with her admirer.'

'I see what you mean. She could have met him after she came off stage before she changed and went to the stage door. The harbour is very close to the theatre.' She watched as Matt took a last gulp of tea. 'Shall we order a second pot? I'm sure that must have been horribly stewed and bitter.'

He shook his head. 'It was not the best, but I'm fine now. Have you had enough to eat and drink?' He looked at her now empty plate.

'Quite enough, thank you, although I did wonder if our friend Inspector Greville's influence had rubbed off on you when I saw all those sandwiches disappearing.' Kitty gave him an impish grin and he laughed aloud.

'Our waitress was right, they were very good sandwiches. Bertie certainly enjoyed his portion.' He patted the top of the dog's head and Kitty shook her head in mock despair.

'You are quite incorrigible.'

Matt called the waitress over to pay for their lunch. Kitty slipped her hand onto the crook of his elbow as they walked away from the table and headed onto the promenade. Bertie trotted happily ahead of them sniffing at anything interesting that he encountered.

Overhead the seagulls wheeled and screamed and the beach below them was busy with children playing on the sands and paddling in the blue water. Kitty's mind was busy thinking over everything they had learned.

'Are we any closer to discovering who murdered Simon Travers?' she asked as they paused to take in the view across the bay.

'I don't know. It could still have been Billy Ford who murdered Travers. Although I must confess after listening to Miss Dubois I do have some reservations about that theory. But that would mean either Lady Meribel or Reverend Greenslade is our killer, or the unreliable Miss Dubois.'

Kitty could see that Matt's thoughts were running on the same lines as her own. 'We cannot rule out Miss Briggs either, I suppose.'

The older woman was very ill, but she had managed the journey from London and the woman they had met at the church had said she thought her devious. She could even have risen from her sick bed to murder Billy Ford, although Kitty couldn't make the pieces fit together for that.

Matt glanced at her. 'No, I'm afraid we can't exclude Miss Briggs either. Let's forget about the case for the rest of today. Perhaps our thoughts may be clearer after a little break. You have an arduous ordeal ahead of you at the prison tomorrow, my dear. For now, what do you say to devoting the rest of the day to continuing our stroll, perhaps taking in an ice cream and then supper out tonight?'

Kitty's gaze met his. 'Why not.'

It was true she could use a nice afternoon's outing before venturing to see Ezekiel Hammett tomorrow. While she had been longing for permission to be given for her visit, she also had quite a few qualms creeping in as the appointment grew nearer.

———

Kitty dropped Matt and Bertie back at his house at the end of the afternoon. He arranged to meet her at the Dolphin for a supper and dance at one of the other hotels in Dartmouth in a few hours' time.

There was the question of what to do with Bertie while he was out with Kitty. However, since the dog appeared tired from the long walk he had been on during the afternoon, Matt decided to chance shutting him in the back scullery with a blanket and his water bowl. With luck there was nothing he could destroy in there, and he would sleep for a few hours while Matt took Kitty dining and dancing.

When he let himself into his house Matt found several notes waiting for him on the small oak hall table at the foot of the stairs. His housekeeper had clearly taken down his messages for him during his absence and placed them where he would be most likely to find them.

The first of the notes was a response from Sister Perpetua at Cairn House.

Sister Michael had kept a cutting containing the news report. Have put it in the post for you.

Matt gave a small grunt of satisfaction at that. It would no doubt prove a red herring but nonetheless he wished to follow it up.

The second was from Brigadier Remmington-Blythe.

Hospital confirms diagnosis is terminal, matter of weeks. Have followed up on the India question, will telephone again when have more information.

At least that answer told him that Miss Briggs was indeed as ill as they believed. He and Kitty had decided they would call on Miss Briggs the day after Kitty's visit to see Hammett.

They needed to tell Miss Briggs that they had succeeded in tracing her daughter. He wondered if Lady Meribel would wish to call on her mother and reveal their connection. It was a delicate situation made worse by Travers's murder. He could understand her wariness to make a connection after so long a time.

He gave Bertie his supper and made a telephone call himself to let Inspector Greville know how their day had gone and to discover if the inspector had made any headway in his own enquiries.

The inspector listened intently as Matt first provided him with a concise report of everything he and Kitty had uncovered from their meeting with Lady Meribel.

'You'll have seen that they've reached a verdict in London on the jewel robbery trial?' the inspector asked.

'Yes, sir, we had the good fortune to encounter Miss Dubois shortly after the midday edition of the newspapers had been delivered.' He told the inspector what the singer had said during lunch.

'It's taken her long enough to admit to seeing Ford before he was killed. If she's telling the truth, then it narrows the time down a little further.' The inspector's tone was thoughtful.

'Unfortunately, I'm not sure Miss Dubois is the most reliable of witnesses.' Matt wished he could trust Carlotta's testimony.

'I take your meaning. Still, it does mean that we can place him back in Torquay that evening between ten and ten thirty and not far from the harbour.'

Matt envisaged the inspector tugging at his moustache as he sat in his smoky office surrounded by files while he considered the problem.

'What about Reverend Greenslade, sir? Any sightings yet of him meeting with Ford?' Matt knew that the inspector had been busy around the town asking questions.

'Nothing confirmed as yet. The reverend was reported to have attended a lecture that evening at the church hall in Paignton. Birds of the British Isles, apparently. It ended though at nine thirty so time enough for him to nip to Torquay and murder Ford.' The inspector sighed heavily.

'The reverend does seem to be coming more into the frame,' Matt said.

'I take your point. You would have thought a case like this

would have been simple. A man stabbed in the compartment of a train, six other people present so one must have done it and surely someone should have seen or heard something.'

Matt sympathised with the inspector's complaint. They were not even certain when Travers's murder had been committed. It was only a supposition that it may have occurred when Miss Briggs had collapsed.

'We'll let you know, sir, if we discover anything else. Kitty has her appointment to see Hammett tomorrow, however, at the prison,' Matt explained. He was not entirely happy about his fiancée's determination to press ahead with the visit, but he knew that Kitty was determined.

'Well, rather her than me, that's all I'll say on the matter. That Hammett is as nasty and slippery a character as I've met. Miss Underhay has a great deal of courage about her. There is many a man who would not be brave enough to do what she intends to do,' Inspector Greville said.

Matt bid the inspector a good evening and replaced the telephone receiver with a thoughtful air. He hoped that Kitty would be all right during her visit tomorrow. She might be insistent on seeing Hammett and he might not be permitted to accompany her, but there could yet be a way he could make sure she was safe.

TWENTY

Kitty woke early the next morning. She had enjoyed her evening out with Matt. He had taken her to another of the hotels in Dartmouth where they had enjoyed a delicious four-course supper, before dancing on the pocket-sized dance floor until almost midnight.

After he had updated her on his conversation with Inspector Greville and the responses to his telephone calls of the previous evening, they had not mentioned her visit to Hammett or the ongoing investigation again.

Instead, they had concentrated on enjoying themselves and had discussed some ideas for when their wedding should take place. She had begun to adjust now to her engagement and had started to feel excited at the thought of planning her wedding. It had been a most delightful distraction from everything that had been happening.

She propped herself up in her bed and reread the letter giving her permission to visit the prison. There were several rules and instructions and she wished to be certain that she understood them all before setting off for Exeter. Butterflies flapped in her stomach, and she wished she did not feel quite so nervous. After all, she had been waiting for this day for so long.

The time of the visit was fixed, and she was to report to the governor's office fifteen minutes beforehand. Any valuables on her person, or her handbag, could be locked in the office until her return as she was not permitted to take anything inside the prison. The chaplain and a warder would escort her to a visiting room and remain with her for the duration of her thirty-minute permitted interview.

Kitty set the letter down on top of her rosewood bedside table and rubbed her eyes. She wished that Matt could accompany her, but at least Father Lamb had arranged for an extra person to be beside her in the form of the prison chaplain. It was a small comfort to know that she would not be entirely alone when she faced Hammett.

There was a soft knock on her door and Alice's narrow cheery face appeared. 'I brought you some toast and tea, miss. I knew as you'd need to be setting off soon if you'm to get to Exeter in time.' The girl carried in a fully loaded breakfast tray and Kitty moved the letter out of the way so she could set it down.

'Thank you, Alice, this is very kind of you.' She managed a smile for her friend.

'I do wish as Captain Bryant was able to go with you, miss. Are you sure as you still want to go on with it?' Alice asked, her pale face anxious.

'Yes, I'm quite sure. I shall be fine, I promise.' Kitty forced herself to look unconcerned as she helped herself to tea and toast.

'Well, I shall be thinking of you. You will let me know how it went when you gets back to the hotel?' her friend asked.

'Of course.' Kitty was touched by Alice's kindness and concern.

'I'd best get a hustle on, Mrs Homer is on the warpath this

morning as Annie hasn't turned in and we'm one maid short.'
Alice smiled at Kitty and moved towards the door to return to
her duties.

'Thank you for this.' Kitty smiled at the young maid and
Alice let herself out of the room to get back to her work.

She finished her breakfast and dressed carefully ready for
her meeting. The clothes she picked out were chosen deliberately to try and provoke some reaction from Hammett. Even if
he decided he would not speak a word to her she wanted to
make a point.

When her mother had gone missing, she had been wearing
a distinctive dove-grey travelling suit with pale pink accessories.
Her women's suffrage pin had been displayed on the lapel of
her jacket. The same pin that Kitty now carried with her at all
times.

Kitty had selected a suit in the same pale-grey colour with a
pastel-pink silk blouse. Her hand shook as she transferred her
mother's prized brooch to open display near her coat collar. She
surveyed her reflection with grim satisfaction when she was
done. Hammett would think he had seen a ghost when he laid
eyes on her. At least, she hoped that was the impression she
would give.

She left the hotel without going to see her grandmother,
afraid her appearance would provoke frightening memories.
Mary called out a good luck message to her as she passed the
reception desk. Kitty waved her hand briefly in acknowledge-
ment and hurried off to the shed where she garaged her car.

Despite the time of year, the early morning air felt cool and
fresh as she made her way out of the town, up the hill past the
Royal Naval College and on towards Exeter. She had allowed
plenty of time for the journey in case there should be any
problem with either the traffic or her car.

Kitty's heart hammered in her chest as she approached the
street leading to the front of the prison. She parked her car at

the kerb and took a deep breath as she surveyed the building. In front of her was a massive locked wooden gate housed in a creamy-white stone portico. This was flanked on either side by two houses that reminded her of a doll's house she had once owned as a child.

She surmised that one of these must be the governor's residence where she was meant to report. On either side of each house, running around as far as she could see, was a twenty-foot-high wall built of red brick. The stark red-brick block of the prison lay secure behind this wall, its entrance fronted by another portico of Moorland stone.

After checking the time on her watch and seeing that she was a little early she opened her handbag to transfer her handkerchief and her lipstick into the pocket of her jacket. She decided to lock her bag in the boot of the car so she would have no need to take it inside the governor's office.

She made her arrangements carefully, using the time to steady her nerves before it was time to approach the prison. The letter from the Home Office crackled in the breast pocket of her grey jacket, ready should she need to provide proof of her identity.

The road had few cars passing by and only one horse-drawn wagon delivering milk further along the road went past. The noise of the city was mainly from the goods yards and industrial workplaces on the far side of the street. No one walked by on foot and Kitty found the experience quite isolating.

She straightened her shoulders and drew in a breath ready to cross the street and knock on the door to the offices for admission. She was stepping off the pavement when she heard the faint sounds of a commotion somewhere close by. Kitty paused beside her car. She couldn't be certain but the sounds seemed to be coming from the direction of the prison.

As she hesitated, wondering if this could be normal for such an institution, she heard more shouting and the sound of whistles. Alarmed by the ruckus she decided to sit back in the driver's seat of her car for a moment to see if it settled down. There had been trouble at several prisons lately, or so her grandmother had informed her from her daily perusals of the newspapers.

Kitty had barely taken her seat behind the wheel when several men came running from the side of the prison. She watched in alarm as they scattered in various directions and vanished into the goods yard and the city. All except one man, with an altered gait, who was making straight for her at speed.

She fumbled for her car key to insert it in the ignition to make good her escape, frightened of what the man might intend. Surely this could not be a breakout like the one from the prison on Dartmoor? The sounds of shouting and noise from inside the prison grew louder and she saw the large wooden gate was beginning to crack open.

The car engine turned over and she hastily put the motor in gear ready to drive away, all thoughts of her visit to Hammett abandoned. She had almost made it when the man caught up to her and inserted himself into her passenger seat.

Kitty let out a scream and went to push the intruder back out of her car.

'Well timed, Miss Underhay. Best get your toe down and away from here as quick as you like.' The man's voice was rough with a local burr, and she realised to her horror that he had some kind of a switchblade in his hand.

Left with no choice in the matter, Kitty obeyed her kidnapper and drove off as the huge wooden gate between the houses opened wide and a group of uniformed warders ran out into the road after them. She thought she might be sick as realisation dawned that her unwanted passenger was none other than the man she was supposed to see inside the prison.

It was clear that he must have orchestrated the whole meeting with her as cover for his escape from custody, presumably aided and abetted by the other convicts who had escaped with him.

'Can't this tin box go no quicker? For mercy's sake, wench, drive faster,' Hammett growled as he waved the blade closer to her face.

'I'm going as fast as I dare, my car doesn't have a very big engine. I don't want us to crash.' Kitty tried to keep the tremor out of her voice. 'Where are we headed anyway? I don't know my way out this side of the city?' She strained her ears hoping to hear some sound of a police siren behind them.

Surely the police would be after them quite quickly. The police station was not too far from the prison, and she had read of escapes such as this from there before. With the car's open top and the noise from the narrow-tyred wheels she could hear little except her own motor and perhaps another motor somewhere in the distance behind them.

'That's for me to know and you to find out, Miss Nosey. Just you do as I say and take the turn to the left just along of here,' Hammett directed.

He was leaned in close to her seat, the blade pointing towards her neck. She could smell the rank scent of stale sweat emanating from his body. His early morning breath made her crinkle her nose as she took the turn.

The lane they had turned into was barely wide enough to admit her car and was clearly designed for horses rather than motor cars. The bushes at the side of the road touched the sides of her car and she jumped as a bird flew out suddenly in front of them, disturbed by their passage.

'Keep on going,' Hammett ordered as Kitty automatically slowed her speed to ensure she could get through the overgrown track.

She kept listening, sure she could hear a faint slightly familiar engine rumble from somewhere behind them in the distance. The car jolted and bumped over the rutted track and Kitty was forced to cling on tightly to her steering wheel.

'If this gets any narrower I won't be able to get through,' Kitty said. She hoped the brambles were not doing too much harm to the crimson paintwork of her beloved car.

'You'll keep going for as long as I tells you. There's another turn in a minute, take the left.' Hammett leaned in as close as he could and leered at Kitty. 'Not got such a sharp tongue when there's a knife at your pretty neck, have you?'

Kitty gritted her teeth and forced herself not to respond to his taunting. She would not give him the satisfaction of knowing that she was scared witless. There had to be a way out of this situation, and she was determined to find it.

'Is that what you did to my mother? Held a knife to her throat? What had she done to you?' Kitty asked as she took the turn Hammett had described.

To her relief this lane was a little wider with fields on the one side running down to what she assumed was the river glinting in the distance.

'She was nosey too. Sticking her oar in where 'twasn't wanted. My old man saw her and stopped her from running off and opening her big mouth. I knew I had to put a stop on her, or the jig would be up and we would be for the scaffold.' Hammett grinned evilly at Kitty, revealing a mouth full of black and broken teeth.

'What did she see that you didn't want her to tell anyone about?' Kitty asked. The car hit a deeper pothole and she and Hammett were swayed about on the slippery leatherette seats.

The convict cursed and tightened his grip on her car seat to bring the blade close to her ear. 'Too much. Wrong place at the wrong time she were when we had just took a delivery and one of our fellows thought as to help himself to some of the goods. Father had just sorted him out for good when your mother comes a-bustling along the street and sees it all. It were a good thing I were only half a step behind her by then.'

Kitty shuddered at the image that went through her head as Hammett described the scene. She could see it all too clearly, the man lying dead and her mother witnessing it all. She knew from a woman who had made contact with her at Christmas that Hammett had been shadowing her mother as she had walked through the city after leaving Jacky Daw's Emporium.

Her mother had gone to Exeter to see Jack, a shady friend of her father's, in an attempt to trace Edgar Underhay. There had been rumours that despite the war he had been seen in England. With Matt's help Kitty had traced her mother's foot-steps as far as Jack's shop in the city. Jack had then been the key to discovering the Hammetts' involvement and finally finding the remains of her mother's body hidden deep under the Glass Bottle public house all these years later.

'Get your speed up, wench. I can hear someone following us.' Hammett twisted in his seat to use her wing mirrors to look behind them.

Kitty took advantage of his momentary inattention to slide her hand up to her lapel, palming her mother's brooch into her jacket pocket. It was not much of a weapon against a knife, but the pin was sharp and might prove useful. It was all she had to hand that might help her escape his clutches.

'There's a motorcycle a-following us. Best we gets shot of him. I wish I had my gun on me, still, not long now and we'll be there. Drive faster, woman, for God's sake.' He waved the knife nearer to her neck and nicked her earlobe, sending a shower of scarlet drops of blood onto the shoulder of her costume.

Kitty scarcely felt the cut as she was sure she knew who must be following them so carefully at a distance on his Sunbeam. The mention of a gun alarmed her, and she guessed that Hammett must have a rendezvous spot in mind. No doubt his sister or other accomplices would have a change of clothes, a weapon and transport waiting for him.

The road ran nearer to the river, with just a steeply sloping field separating them from the water. She could definitely hear the rumble of the Sunbeam now and her spirits lifted a little. Matt must have realised that Hammett had seen him and was trying now to catch up with them.

Hammett cursed wildly now as Matt drew nearer. She risked a glance in her rear-view mirror to check that it was him. Kitty knew that Matt often carried his old service revolver with him if he thought there might be danger and she wondered if he had it with him now. She could only assume that he had decided to follow her to the prison to wait for her that morning. He had been worried about her visiting the prison alone and she should have guessed that he would try to be nearby.

The poor road surface jolted them around in their seats, the swaying and bumping made worse by Hammett's refusal to allow her to slow down. Kitty feared for her car, certain it would be fatally injured or shaken to pieces.

Up ahead she spied an opening to a field just as Hammett twisted in his seat to look over his shoulder at their pursuer. Kitty gritted her teeth and took a chance, violently twisting the wheel to send the little car off the road into the field and careering down towards the river.

'Oy, what are you doing? Turn back round.' Hammett went to grab the steering wheel to force the car back around.

Kitty pulled her mother's brooch from her pocket and stuck the pin straight into Hammett's thigh as deeply as she could. The sudden pain from the pin forced him to let go. As he released the wheel, she threw up the handbrake and flung herself in a rolling motion out of the car, desperately hoping that the tussocky grass would cushion her landing.

She rolled over and over as the car swung and bounced forwards a few feet closer towards the river, before coming to a sudden stop as the engine died. The passenger door opened and Hammett staggered out as Kitty scrambled to her knees ready to run. All the breath had been knocked out of her though in the landing. She could scarcely manage a weak totter back up the hill to where Matt was entering the field on his motorcycle.

A glance over her shoulder revealed Hammett, his face crimson and ugly with rage, starting after her. The sight of Matt's bike roaring into the field though sparked a change in his demeanour.

'Get down, Kitty!' Matt shouted as he halted the Sunbeam at the top of the field.

She gave another desperate look behind her to see that Hammett had changed his course and was now limping rapidly down the field towards the river.

'Halt or I'll shoot!'

A loud bang rang out and she lifted her head from the grass to see that Matt had produced his revolver and taken aim at the fleeing criminal.

Kitty covered her ears and flattened herself against the turf as Matt hurried towards her, keeping his gun trained on the escaping convict.

'He's heading for the river.' She wondered how close they were to Hammett's intended rendezvous point.

'Are you hurt, Kitty?' Matt asked as he fired off another shot.

'No, I'm all right. He's getting away. Be careful, Matt, I think he was planning to collect a gun and make good his escape a little further along this road.'

Matt caught up to her and extended his free hand to pull her up from the grass. He placed his arm around her to steady her for a moment as they saw Hammett reach the edge of the riverbank.

'Are you certain you are all right?' he asked, his handsome face creased with worry.

'Yes, I'm fine. Try and stop him from escaping.'

At her urging, Matt released her and ran down the field hot on Hammett's heels. Kitty followed after him as swiftly as she could over the uneven ground. Hammett was in the shrubs now that fringed the top of the bank.

'Stop or I'll fire again!' Matt shouted as Hammett started to slide down the steep nettle-covered muddy slope into the river.

Kitty heard the splash as Hammett entered the water, and muttered curses from Matt.

'What's happening? Where is he?' She panted up to Matt's side and stared at the dark stretch of deep fast-flowing water.

'He went into the river. The current looks strong here and you can't see the bottom.' Matt raised his hand to shield his eyes and scanned the swirling river.

'There!' Kitty pointed.

The current clearly had the escaped convict firmly in its grasp. They could see that Hammett was trying desperately to reach the opposite bank. The water was moving too fast, however, and they watched helplessly as he disappeared under the surface.

As of one accord they ran down the field in the direction of where they had seen him go under but there was no sign of Hammett anywhere.

'Has he drowned?' Kitty clung onto Matt's arm and tried to regain her breath.

'I don't know. I didn't see him come back up and the bank is sheer rock along that side with no place to scramble ashore.' He wrapped his arms around Kitty and she lay her head against his shirt front.

Matt had returned his gun to the deep pocket of his leather greatcoat. Her legs were shaking, and she realised that she was still holding fast to her mother's brooch. She opened her hand and saw the pin was now bent from the force she had used to stab Hammett.

Dried blood, Hammett's or hers, she wasn't sure which, caked her fingers. She suspected that the aches and pains in her arms and legs would no doubt manifest into bruises over the next day or so.

Matt stroked her cheek with a tender finger. 'Did he hurt you? There is blood all down your neck and on your jacket.'

'A small nick on my ear I think, nothing more. He had some kind of switchblade which he used to force me to drive.' She shuddered at the memory.

Her gaze was irresistibly drawn back to the river and the spot where Hammett had gone under. She didn't know what she expected to see. Matt was right, it would be difficult for a man to extricate himself from the river at that point. Unless Hammett had allowed the current to take him further along to a place where he might get out, then he must surely be dead.

Matt took her mother's brooch gently from her hand.

'The pin is damaged.' He slipped it into his pocket. 'I'll get it fixed for you.'

She nodded, incapable of speech for a moment. A tear rolled down her cheek, though whether her tears were for her mother or for herself she could not be certain. Matt placed his finger beneath her chin, so she was forced to lift her head to meet his gaze.

'Thank heaven you're safe. I swear when I heard the cry go up and saw those men drop off the end of a rope over the prison wall...' He swallowed. 'I realised it had to be Hammett's doing.' He brushed his lips against hers. 'My poor darling girl.'

'Why were you outside the prison?' Kitty sniffed and fished in her pocket for the handkerchief she had placed there just an hour or so before.

Matt sighed. 'I wanted to meet you when you came out in case you were distressed. I thought at least then I could make sure you were safe to drive back to the Dolphin.'

'You didn't tell me of your plan,' she protested weakly.

Although she was very glad that he had decided that he would follow her to the prison.

The dimple flashed in his cheek. 'I wasn't planning to interfere, just be there for you if you needed me. Anyway, you would have complained and told me you were an independent woman and that I should focus on solving Simon Travers's murder instead.'

A wry smile lifted the corners of Kitty's lips. 'You know me all too well,' she admitted. He was right, that was exactly what she would have told him.

TWENTY-ONE

He kept his arm around her waist as they started to walk back up the field to where Kitty's car stood at an awkward angle amongst the long grass. She was aware that she was trembling, and her heart was still racing from her adventure.

'I can hear the sound of sirens,' Matt said.

Kitty could hear them too, the clamour increasing as they drew nearer. The black nose of a police motor car entered the field, halting behind Matt's abandoned Sunbeam. Uniformed policemen scrambled from the car and hurried towards them.

Matt took charge of the situation once the officers had been assured of Kitty's well-being and of his good credentials. She sank down on the driver's seat of her car, glad to rest her shaking legs. Matt accompanied the policemen to the riverbank to show them where Hammett had entered the water. She presumed he would also point out where they had seen him disappear beneath the surface.

She still could not quite believe that her morning had ended in such a frightening fashion. If Matt had not decided to follow her to the prison the outcome could have been very different.

Kitty shuddered. She might have been the one disappearing under the surface of the water never to rise again.

Her mother's brooch had saved her life, buying her time to escape from the car. She hoped that Matt would be able to find a jeweller able to mend the pin. Already she felt lost without it. She knew though that her mother had been with her at that moment when she had plunged it into Hammett's leg.

She closed her eyes and gave a silent prayer of thanks for her safety. At least now she could fulfil her promise to her grandmother. Her quest for the truth of what had happened to her mother back in June 1916 was satisfied. It was over.

Matt approached her car. 'Are you ready to drive, Kitty? The police have asked us to call in at the police station in Exeter before we go back to Dartmouth. Our old friend Inspector Pinch will be there to take a statement. These constables are going to try and search lower downstream for any sign of Hammett, or anyone who may have been waiting to meet him.'

Kitty lifted her chin and steadied her nerves before nodding her agreement. The policemen returned to their car and reversed out of the entrance. They waited for Kitty to start her little red motor and to ensure she was able to guide her car back out of the field to the road.

———

Matt clambered onto his motorcycle and drew on the leather gauntlets that he had thrown to the floor on his arrival. He waved to Kitty to check that she was ready before starting his motorcycle and heading out onto the lane. Kitty followed behind him as he led the way back at a sedate pace into the city to the police station.

He was relieved to see the colour had returned to Kitty's cheeks by the time they drew to a halt near the station entrance. Of all the times Kitty had ended up in danger, this was the worst. He knew what Hammett was capable of and once he realised who was beside Kitty in her car, he knew she was in deep trouble.

The police station was a hive of activity as they entered and approached the desk. Kitty's dishevelled appearance caught the desk sergeant's attention and before long they were seated in a small back office with a cup of strong tea whilst their statements were taken.

Inspector Pinch, who had worked with Inspector Greville to capture Hammett and to restore Kitty's mother's body to them, gave his word that they would be informed if any sign of Hammett were discovered. He dispatched as many men as could be spared to search along the banks of the river looking for the escaped felon.

The police had already recaptured all of Hammett's fellow escapees and they had been returned to their cells. Matt could see that this at least had set Kitty's mind at ease for now. He knew though that she would not be at peace until she knew for certain that Hammett had either perished in the river or had somehow made it out.

While having Hammett on the loose would not be good, at least she would know to stay on her guard. The man had survived such escapades before and Matt knew they could not assume that this was the end.

Once they were given permission to leave the police station, Matt walked with Kitty back to her car.

'Your grandmother will not be happy when she learns what has happened this morning.' He looked at his fiancée's ruined jacket.

Kitty gave a small smile. 'No, she won't. She didn't want me to see Hammett so I think I can expect a lecture at the very least.'

Matt opened her car door for her, and she climbed in. 'I'll accompany you back to the hotel.' He intended to ensure she arrived safely back at the Dolphin and her grandmother's care.

'Thank you. You go on ahead and I'll follow you.' She inserted the key in the ignition.

He nodded, satisfied from her demeanour that she felt safe to drive the distance back to Dartmouth along the country roads.

On their return he went with Kitty to her office and informed her grandmother of the morning's adventures. He could see the elderly woman was both shocked and concerned at what had happened. Once he had aided Kitty in giving suitable reassurances to the elderly lady, he left his fiancée in Alice's tender care and set off for his own cottage.

The sound of Bertie's indignant howling met him as soon as he stopped the engine of the Sunbeam near his front door. He parked up and went through the side gate to the back garden where he had left Bertie snoozing happily under an apple tree a few hours earlier.

To his dismay, a scene of carnage greeted him. Every plant that had once borne a flower was now decapitated. A large hole had appeared in front of the rhododendrons and, worse still, the line of freshly washed yellow dusters his housekeeper had pegged out earlier were now trampled in the flower borders.

Bertie greeted him with a happy wagging tail and air of surprised innocence at the destruction. Matt sighed and picked up the dusters hoping he could rescue them before his housekeeper realised what had happened.

He let himself into the house to the sound of the telephone ringing in the sitting room.

'Mrs Craven.' He was somewhat surprised to be greeted by that lady when he picked up the receiver.

'My dear Captain Bryant, have you heard the news?' Mrs Craven, breathless with suppressed excitement, cut in before he could finish his greeting.

He wondered if she had heard of the prison break, although even with her connections he could not see how that would be possible for the news to have travelled from Exeter quite so quickly.

'Er...'

She rushed on before he could say anything further. 'Inspector Greville has finally made an arrest in our murder case.'

There was an expectant pause. Matt tried to gather his wits at this unexpected turn of events. He also wondered when Mrs C had joined the police force.

'Don't you wish to know who it is?' Mrs Craven demanded.

'Yes, of course, please do go on.' Matt wondered what could have happened to lead to an arrest. Perhaps Inspector Greville had uncovered the final piece of evidence that he had been seeking.

'Well, I have it on good authority that dreadful Miss Dubois is under lock and key. Now what do you think of that?'

Matt wasn't sure quite what he thought. It would make sense that Carlotta had killed Billy Ford, especially if he had discovered where the proceeds of the robbery were hidden and had passed that on. But had she also murdered Simon Travers? Or had she and Billy been working together until she had decided that Billy was expendable?

'I see. How did you learn of the arrest, Mrs Craven?' Matt asked.

'My maid – rather a silly girl in some ways, but biddable – she was in Torquay. I had sent her to collect a special order from the milliners in the town and she witnessed Inspector Greville leading Miss Dubois from the Pavilion and into the back of the police car.'

Matt suppressed a sigh and rubbed his hand across his face to dispel his irritation. 'He could have been taking Miss Dubois to the police station for further questioning.'

'Ha, that is what I said,' Mrs Craven interjected triumphantly. 'No, my girl said that Miss Dubois was behaving in a most unladylike manner. A constable had a hold of her arm, and she was wriggling like a fish on a hook and using all kinds of language. Personally, I am not at all surprised. One could see the type of person she was when we were in the waiting room.'

Matt presumed that Mrs Craven had clearly not forgotten that Carlotta had pointed the finger in Mrs C's direction after the murder.

'Hmm, a most interesting development.'

'I thought that you would be in a position to know what had happened.' Her tone was faintly accusatory. Matt guessed that she had called him hoping to find out more details about the arrest.

'I expect the inspector will be in touch to tell me of any progress in the case when it is certain that Miss Dubois is the culprit. I have been out this morning and I have no messages as yet.' He attempted to soothe Mrs Craven's feelings. 'I will, of course, pass on anything definite that I hear from the inspector.'

Mrs Craven seemed mollified by his assurances and after a few more minutes of conversation, mainly speculation from Mrs Craven about Carlotta Dubois's character, that good lady rang off.

Matt replaced the telephone receiver on its stand. It was turning out to be quite a day. Hammett's prison break, Kitty's close shave, and now this.

———

Alice was administering a lecture to Kitty as she relieved her of her damaged clothing. Alice's sister, Dolly, had gone to find Alice as soon as Kitty and Matt had returned to the hotel and gone into the office behind the reception desk to see Kitty's grandmother.

Kitty's dishevelled appearance and still pale face had shocked Dolly. When she had been dismissed from her morning's chore of taking dictation, so that Matt and Kitty could speak privately with her employer, she had gone and immediately alerted her sister.

'The state of your jacket, Miss Kitty, and another pair of stockings ruined.' Alice bustled about the bedroom tutting, while Kitty herself sat somewhat meekly in her chair with a cup of tea.

'I was not anticipating that Hammett would use my visit as an opportunity to escape from the prison,' Kitty protested.

''Twas a good thing as Captain Bryant were there to follow you. Evil that Hammett is.' Alice produced a bottle of iodine and some cotton wool.

Kitty flinched as her friend examined the cut on her ear. There was more tongue clicking and tutting as Alice cleaned the cut and applied a dab of iodine.

'Ouch,' Kitty grumbled. The cure it seemed was more painful than the injury.

'Better to be safe, miss. That's what my mother always says. You don't want to take no chances. You don't know what might have been on that knife, or if any dirt as gone in. I had a great uncle as died of tetany from a little bitty cut like this.' Alice frowned and cleared away her medical supplies.

Kitty bit her tongue. She knew her friend meant tetanus and was worried about her. She finished the cup of tea that Alice had insisted that she drink. It had been laced with a liberal nip of brandy, which her friend had administered for shock. She placed her cup back on its saucer and bent to unfasten her shoes.

Alice was right about her stockings; they were indeed beyond repair.

'I can't believe Hammett got away from us into the river.'

She rolled them down and removed them, to discover a large bruise was forming on her right knee.

'Such a wicked man.' Alice shook her head, a tendril of auburn hair escaping from under her white-frilled cap. 'Drowning is too good for him after all the wickedness as he's done. I reckon as Lucifer himself will be waiting for him when he crosses over.'

'At least I got my answer about what happened to my mother all those years ago,' Kitty said.

Alice rolled her eyes. 'And you nearly went to join her. You must have had a guardian angel a-looking after you, miss. If you was a cat you'd have used another of your lives up this morning, I reckon.'

Kitty gave a faint smile. 'Yes, I think you're right. The constables went to search the other bank and have alerted the coastguard. While we were with Inspector Pinch at Exeter Police Station, they telephoned in to say they had found a small boat hidden in the reeds. It was about half a mile further downstream from where I escaped. It contained a gun and a change of clothes for Hammett.'

Alice shuddered. 'I can't conceive of the deviousness that went into all of this, miss. I've seen a good many films, as you know, Miss Kitty, and this takes the prize for being so shocking.'

It might have been the effects of the brandy, but Kitty suddenly felt quite tearful. Her grandmother had gone quite faint when Matt had explained what had happened in Exeter. A wave of guilt washed over her, and she looked about her for a handkerchief.

Alice opened a drawer in the dressing table and passed her what she needed.

'Thank you, Alice. You are such a good friend to me.' She dabbed her eyes and blew her nose.

''Tis the shock catching up with you. Let's hope as they find that Hammett's body soon and then there will be an end to it all,' Alice said firmly.

Kitty agreed. Until she could be certain that he had met his death in the cold, deep waters of the river she would always be looking over her shoulder.

Alice took away her damaged and dirty clothes to see what she could do with them, leaving Kitty to rest for a little while on her bed. She had promised her grandmother she would join her downstairs again later when she was recovered. No doubt her beloved Grams would have plenty to say on the matter once the shock of the morning's events had worn off.

Sure enough, scarcely half an hour had passed before a young maid who had been sent from the dining room tapped at her door.

'Mrs Treadwell said as she wishes to see you in her salon in half an hour, Miss Kitty.' The girl had brought her a small trolley containing a bowl of consommé, a fillet of plaice pan-fried with summer vegetables and a slice of cherry pie with clotted cream.

Kitty thanked the girl and tucked into her late lunch. At least she was not going to have to face her grandmother on an empty stomach. The food did much to restore her equilibrium and boost her spirits once again.

Once the dishes were empty, she washed her face and brushed her hair, before applying a dab of perfume and a slick of her favourite pale pink lipstick. Suitably prepared she pushed the trolley out onto the landing for collection and walked down the stairs to her grandmother's quarters.

As she knocked on the white panelled door, she heard the murmur of voices and the clinking of china from inside.

She entered and was only slightly surprised to discover that Mrs Craven was installed in the armchair opposite her grandmother. The ladies had clearly been taking tea together. From the way they both turned their attention upon her she suspected that her earlier adventure had been the main topic of conversation.

'I'm glad that you appear to be unscathed from your ordeal this morning, Kitty dear.' Her grandmother indicated a vacant space on the sofa and Kitty obediently took a seat. 'I was just telling Millicent what happened during your visit to the prison.'

Kitty's heart sank. Now she would no doubt hear the benefit of Mrs Craven's views once more on the inadvisability of her trip. Especially since her words of foreboding about seeing Hammett had proved correct.

'You were very fortunate that villain did not kill you, Kitty.' Mrs Craven's tone subtly managed to imply that this might not have been such a bad idea.

'Yes, although fortunately Matt was at hand, and I managed to escape unharmed.' Kitty smiled cheerfully at Mrs Craven.

'I must admit I'm most surprised that dear Matthew did not tell me about all of this when I telephoned him earlier.' Mrs Craven smoothed the lightweight heather tweed of her skirt with a self-satisfied air, and smirked.

Kitty was immediately on her guard. 'You spoke to Matt?'

'Indeed. I had important news concerning our case.' Mrs Craven looked positively smug.

Kitty suppressed a sigh and wondered what had happened while she had been in Exeter.

'Millicent has informed me that Inspector Greville has arrested the culprit who murdered Mr Travers and that young brush salesman.' Her grandmother managed to convey this information, whilst Mrs Craven looked slightly annoyed at having her thunder stolen.

'Really, well, that's simply marvellous. Who was it?' Kitty had found herself changing her mind several times during the course of their enquiries as to who it might be. She still hadn't quite worked it all out in her mind yet. Although she was pleased to hear of progress, she had to admit that she would have preferred herself and Matt to have solved the case.

'It was Miss Dubois, that opera singer,' Mrs Craven rushed to answer, clearly not wishing Kitty's grandmother to beat her to the punch again.

It seemed then that Matt had been right when he had warned her not to feel too much sympathy for the girl. Still, somehow it didn't feel right to Kitty. She had thought Carlotta had been genuinely upset by Billy Ford's murder.

'The inspector must have uncovered more evidence during his enquiries. Still, you must be relieved, Mrs Craven.' She smiled pleasantly at the older woman secretly enjoying a spot of teasing at her expense.

'Whatever do you mean, Kitty?' Mrs Craven demanded.

'Well, we know you were not involved in poor Mr Travers's murder, but I suppose anyone who did not know your character may have suspected you,' Kitty said.

Her grandmother's brow creased in mild disapproval, and she gave Kitty a stern look.

'Utter nonsense. Of course, I was never a suspect,' Mrs Craven huffed indignantly, and Kitty was forced to press her lips firmly together to suppress a smile.

'I suspect that my granddaughter is teasing you, Millicent dear.' Grams gave a faint shake of her head at Kitty.

'Well, really, Kitty. I would have thought that a young woman on the cusp of marriage would be above such pranks.' Mrs Craven was not amused.

Kitty apologised and the older woman settled back in her chair. 'Speaking of your wedding, Kitty, I was telling your grandmother that you really ought to set a date soon. Autumn is a busy time at the church with harvest and so on and before you know it Christmas will be upon us. I know it's June now, but it takes time to properly organise these things.'

'And I suppose your father will definitely attend?' A cloud

settled on her grandmother's face. There was little love lost between her grandmother and Edgar Underhay.

'Father intends to walk me down the aisle,' Kitty said. She knew her grandmother had been hoping that her father would not make the crossing back from America.

Her grandmother exchanged a look with Mrs Craven.

'Has Matthew discussed any possible dates with his parents?' Mrs Treadwell asked.

Kitty knew that Matt's parents were not excited about the engagement despite their many years of friendship with her grandmother. They disapproved of Kitty's modern notions and would have preferred Matt to have married someone closer to him in age. They had even roped in Matt's Aunt Euphemia to interview her at Lucy's wedding to assess her suitability.

'I don't think so. We have scarcely had time to discuss a possible date between ourselves. There is no need for us to hurry,' Kitty said. 'I think we can talk all of this over at another time, when Matt is free.' She was anxious to escape and telephone him to discover if Mrs Craven was correct and Carlotta had indeed been arrested.

'Then, perhaps, if Matthew is available, we could arrange dinner in a few days' time. I should like to discuss several aspects of the marriage with you, Kitty. Arrangements will need to be made for the hotel and how it is to be run when you are Mrs Bryant.' Her grandmother set her empty teacup down and fixed Kitty with a steely look.

'Of course, Grams.' Kitty knew that she would have to work out where she would live once she and Matt married and how her position at the hotel would be affected.

Her grandmother was not getting any younger and the hotel was busier than ever. It had been fortunate that Dolly had come along at the right time to start her training, so Kitty had been free to take time off for Lucy's wedding and a few days of leisure. She could almost feel the weight of the ancient building wrapping itself around her and pulling her under once more.

Once she was back at work, her grandmother intended going to Scotland to stay with Livvy, her sister, for a week. That would leave Kitty with sole responsibility for running the hotel. The last occasion when that had happened had been when Kitty and Matt had first met and Kitty had become embroiled in her first mystery.

So much had happened since then. Her life now was certainly much more interesting and her relationship with Matt had definitely changed from their first, less than auspicious meeting.

TWENTY-TWO

Matt sat thinking for a moment after Mrs Craven had rung off. If what Mrs C had said was correct, and he had no reason to doubt her, then he supposed the case was solved. Yet he was still curious to discover exactly what had happened and if Inspector Greville had recovered the stolen items from the robbery.

His stomach rumbled, reminding him that in all the excitement of the morning he had missed his lunch. Bertie looked at him and wagged his tail hopefully.

'You, my boy, you are in big trouble!' Matt rubbed the top of the dog's head. 'Especially if my housekeeper discovers the insult done to her dusters.'

He drummed his fingers on his knee as he debated what he should do. Tempting though it was to telephone Kitty to apprise her of this latest development, he wanted her to rest. The incident with Hammett had been both terrifying and physically demanding. He suspected she would have more than a few bruises and abrasions from where she had flung herself free of the car in order to escape.

Bertie looked hopefully at him.

'Sorry, mate. I don't suppose there is much more damage you can do if I put you back in the garden for an hour.' Matt made his decision.

He helped himself to a chunk of cheese and an apple from the pantry to quiet his stomach, before feeding Bertie and securing him back in the garden once more.

A few minutes later he was riding his motorcycle back along the road towards Torquay.

The desk sergeant did not appear too surprised to see him when he strode into the lobby at Torquay Police Station.

'Good afternoon, Captain Bryant, I expect as you'll be wanting to see Inspector Greville, will you?'

'If he can spare me a few minutes.' Matt knew the inspector must be busy if he had made the arrest.

The sergeant nodded. 'I'll just go and find him, sir.'

Matt waited beside the desk as the man disappeared through the door at the back of the reception area. The wanted poster for Ezekiel Hammett was still in place on the notice-board and he wondered how the search was progressing for Hammett's body.

He would be surprised if even Ezekiel, with his incredible tenacity, had managed to escape the deadly undertow in that part of the river. He suppressed a shiver when he thought how close Kitty had come to ending up in the river herself that morning.

'If you'd care to follow me, sir.' The sergeant had returned and lifted the hatch to permit him through to the less public section of the station.

The inspector was in his untidy office, busy clearing paper-work from one of the chairs so that Matt could take a seat.

'Good afternoon, Inspector.'

'Good afternoon, Captain Bryant. I'm assuming that you've

heard there have been developments in the case?' Inspector Greville, having made a chair free for Matt, resumed his own seat behind the overloaded desk.

'I had a telephone call from Mrs Craven. It seems her maid witnessed you collecting Miss Dubois from the Pavilion this morning.'

The inspector's bushy brows raised in resigned surprise. 'Well, Miss Dubois certainly drew an audience.'

'May I ask if you have charged her with the murders, sir?' Matt asked.

Inspector Greville took out his cigarette case and offered one to Matt, who refused the offer, before lighting up himself. 'Not as yet. Her run at the theatre was due to come to an end and I didn't want that young lady disappearing back to London. Odds on we'd struggle to get a hold of her again if that happened. The information you gave me about her seeing Ford outside the theatre provides her with the opportunity to have killed him and Travers. She has a motive and the opportunity.'

'I take it then that you haven't found anyone yet who may have seen Ford after he was supposed to have left Miss Dubois that evening?' Matt leaned back in his seat and crossed his legs. He supposed that Miss Dubois could have killed Travers in revenge for testifying against her brother and her boyfriend. She could have killed Billy if he had recovered the jewels and didn't plan on sharing the loot.

'My men are going down there again tonight to ask questions around the green and up to the harbour. Whether anyone will say anything and how reliable they might be, well, who knows.' The inspector exhaled a small plume of smoke.

Matt was all too aware that particular part of Torquay took on a different aspect late at night once the theatre had closed and the respectable folk of the town had retired to their beds. He nodded.

'I was interviewing Miss Dubois again when you arrived. Or at least I was attempting to interview her.' The inspector's moustache drooped.

'I take it the lady is not co-operating, sir?' Matt was not surprised by this. Carlotta would be a tough nut to crack. Even when he and Kitty had talked with her, she had been reluctant to impart any information and had habitually lied to them. So much for Kitty's sympathy for the girl.

The inspector flicked his cigarette ash into the full ashtray on the corner of his desk. 'Closed up like a clam. We searched her lodgings, of course.'

Matt guessed they had probably come up empty there too. Miss Dubois was too careful to keep anything incriminating in her belongings.

'I take it that her dressing room was also searched?' He supposed she might have risked hiding something at the theatre.

'I had my men search the whole blooming playhouse from top to bottom. Not a bean.' Inspector Greville's expression grew even more glum.

'You are convinced of her guilt, sir?' Matt asked.

Inspector Greville extinguished his cigarette. 'She's top of my heap, so to speak. She's the one who knew Ford well. Whoever killed him was someone he clearly didn't see as a threat or that knife he always carried would have been at the ready. Yet Doctor Carter found it still in its sheath strapped to his leg. He turned his back on his killer.'

Matt nodded again. 'I see. Yes, he wouldn't have turned away from anyone who he thought might harm him. He was too used to looking after himself.'

The inspector shuffled forward on his chair. 'Miss Dubois was someone he knew well and trusted. He wouldn't have thought as she would injure him, especially if they was in it together.'

Inspector Greville had a point. Reverend Greenslade was an unknown quantity to Ford. He appeared a mild-mannered man of the cloth. But would Ford have let his guard down sufficiently to provide the reverend with an opportunity for murder?

Miss Briggs was so physically frail, if she had managed to somehow meet Ford then he might have not viewed her as a threat. Then there was Lady Meribel, a pretty young woman. Ford liked the ladies and fancied himself as a bit of a flirt. Would he have thought that she posed no danger?

'Hmm, I see what you mean, sir. Do you have anything else that places Miss Dubois in the frame?' Matt asked.

'Apart from her half-brother being mixed up in this robbery, and her fancy man too, apparently, so the brigadier said.' Inspector Greville looked most unhappy. 'And that she was seen in the public gallery at the start of the trial?'

'There is a lot of circumstantial evidence against her,' Matt agreed. He could see why the inspector had wanted to secure Miss Dubois in the cells for now. He also knew that unless more evidence was forthcoming then it would be difficult to make a murder charge stick.

'I heard from Inspector Pinch that Miss Underhay had a near squeak this morning at the prison?' Inspector Greville remarked. 'I hope she is recovered?'

'Yes, sir, it was quite alarming.' Matt hoped that Hammett would be found soon, and the matter finally put to rest for Kitty's sake.

'I can imagine. Slippery, vicious customer, Hammett. I heard you fired off a couple of shots. A shame you didn't get him, it would have saved everyone a great deal of trouble,' Inspector Greville observed drily.

'The river is unexpectedly deep at that point with a strong undertow and where the current has eroded the bank it's too steep for a man to scramble free.' Matt couldn't help the shiver that ran through him as he recalled Hammett disappearing beneath the water's surface.

'So, I'm led to believe. The constables have told the inspector that the farmer has lost some of his sheep in the river at that point where they've slipped down into the water.' The inspector met his gaze and Matt could see that the policeman also hoped that this was the last they would hear of Ezekiel Hammett.

————

Kitty was forced to endure another thirty minutes or so of Mrs Craven's company before she was able to plead a headache and make good her escape. She headed to her room anxious to try and telephone Matt. He was bound to have tried to ascertain the facts behind Miss Dubois's arrest. If, indeed, that was what had occurred.

To her frustration the telephone rang out for ages before finally being picked up by the flustered and breathless voice of Matt's housekeeper.

'Begging your pardon, Miss Underhay, but Captain Bryant is from home at the moment.' The woman sounded as if she had hurried from somewhere in order to pick up the receiver.

'Oh dear, I don't suppose you know where he's gone, do you?' Kitty asked.

'I'm sorry, miss, I don't, I'm afraid. He's left that dratted dog here though and his motorcycle is missing.'

Kitty wondered what fresh mischief Bertie could possibly have done. 'I see, thank you.' She would lay good money down that Matt had gone to see Inspector Greville.

She said goodbye to the housekeeper assuring her that there was no message and that she would call again later.

Kitty replaced the receiver and checked the time on her beloved Black Forest cuckoo clock, one of the few things she had left that she had inherited from her mother. It was growing late in the afternoon, and she still had a few hours before dinner. Even with the window open her room felt hot and airless.

Her mind made up, she put on her hat and decided to take a turn along the embankment. The fresh air might clear her head and the exercise would ease her restless spirit.

She left a message with Mary to say where she had gone and stepped out into the sunshine. She took her time, strolling along, nodding hello and exchanging pleasantries with people she knew. The town was busy with holidaymakers as well as the normal routine of the locals.

Out on the river, pleasure craft were passing up and down while the ferries transported vehicles, goods and passengers from Dartmouth to Kingswear and back. Sunlight danced on the waters of the river, and she couldn't help wondering if the police had discovered what had happened to Hammett yet.

Kitty walked past the boat float marina and through the park toward the other ferry station. She had no particular destination in mind. It was simply soothing to be out and away from the trouble of the morning and the vexation of Mrs Craven.

The ferry had just docked when she reached the quay and she turned ready to begin her stroll back to the Dolphin.

'Miss Underhay, Miss Underhay!' A feminine voice hailed her from the deck of the boat, and she turned to see Betty hurrying ashore towards her.

'Betty.' She was surprised to see Alice's cousin in the town at this time of day. Unless the girl had an afternoon off, of course.

'I was on my way to see you, miss.' Betty came panting up to meet her with one hand holding down her straw summer hat that had threatened to blow away in her haste.

'Has something happened at Lady Jacques's?' Kitty's instincts kicked in and she sensed the girl had something she considered important to tell her.

Betty fell into step beside her, and Kitty walked further along to a quiet corner of the park.

'That's the thing, Miss Underhay. I'm not right sure what's happening. See, the mistress has gone missing.' Betty's face looked troubled.

'Missing?' Kitty was confused.

'She had her breakfast in bed and I helped her dress for the day. Pale green shot-silk day dress and high-heeled brown patent shoes with a little bow.' Betty was clearly keen that Kitty should recognise her capabilities as a maid. 'She didn't say anything to anyone about her intention to go nowhere. Lunch is always a bit haphazard in that household as they have a cold spread in the dining room and people goes and helps themselves when they want. That's because they all go boating or swimming and suchlike,' Betty explained.

'And no one saw her at lunchtime?' Kitty asked, guessing the answer would be no.

Betty shook her head. 'No, miss. Mr Johnny, he's sweet on my lady, well he had been looking for her to play croquet. You know, that game with the hoops, miss.'

Kitty was well aware of what the game of croquet entailed. 'Yes, Betty, do go on.' She seemed to recall that Meribel had addressed the man who had opened the door for them the other day as Johnny.

'He went to all her usual places around the house and the grounds and couldn't see her nowhere. So, he got a bit edgy-like. I don't think as he liked the idea as she hadn't said what she might be doing. Well, he asked the chauffeur if he had took the mistress somewhere but he hadn't. Lady Meribel can drive though, miss. Independent she is, like you. The garage was checked though, and all the cars was there so that were a puzzle.'

'Perhaps she went for a walk?' Kitty suggested. 'The house is not too far from the village.'

Betty shook her head. 'Not in they shoes she was wearing, miss. And I checked her things to see if she had changed them, but she hadn't. Anyways, the others started searching proper but there was no note or nothing.'

'Has anyone called the police?' Kitty asked.

Again, the girl shook her head. 'Mr Johnny said as Lady Meribel wouldn't be none too happy if she had just gone someplace for a bit and the police was called. She's in enough bother with her father without causing more of a commotion. They decided to wait until dinner time to see if she come home for her dinner. Mr Johnny seemed to think as she would.'

'But you aren't so sure?' Kitty asked.

'No, miss. Well, I don't know what has happened, but you said as to tell you about anything unusual, so I thought as I'd come and see you. I didn't trust the telephone in case Mr Johnny or the others heard me like and thought as I was getting above my station.' Betty looked anxiously at Kitty.

'You must have gone to a great deal of trouble. Will you be missed?' Kitty didn't want the girl to have any problems should her mistress turn up and find her maid had gone tittle-tattling.

'Not by they, miss. The house is too disorganised for them to realise as I've slipped out. Two buses and the ferry it took me to get here but it didn't take too long,' Betty said.

Kitty opened her handbag and dug inside to find her purse. 'Here, take some money and ask Mr Potter or Robert Potter to run you back to Cockington. If Lady Meribel reappears then telephone the hotel and leave a message. Just one word or two will do. I'll know what it means.'

She gave Betty a pound note and some shillings.

'This is too much, miss.' Betty's eyes lit up at the sight of the note.

'Nonsense. Get yourself a cup of tea first as you've gone to a great deal of trouble.' Kitty was anxious to return to the Dolphin. She would try Matt once more and if she got no reply then she determined to set off for Torquay herself. She had an inkling about where Lady Meribel might have gone but she needed to make sure her guess was right and the girl was safe.

TWENTY-THREE

Matt opened his front door to discover Kitty standing on his doormat with a determined expression on her face.

'Hello, old girl.' He kissed her cheek and ushered her into the hall.

'I tried telephoning but there was no answer so I thought I would drive out and see if your motorcycle was outside the house,' Kitty explained as she walked through to the drawing room.

Bertie spotted her through the open French window and came pattering in to greet her, his tail wagging happily to and fro.

'Sorry, darling. I had a telephone call from Mrs Craven about the case, so I went to see Inspector Greville.' He suspected that she had also either received a call or a visit from the redoubtable Mrs C.

He walked over to the drinks trolley. 'Can I get you a drink? You look all in.'

Kitty did look quite pale, and he wondered if her ordeal of the morning had caught up with her.

'Thank you, a small sherry would be rather welcome. Mrs

Craven visited Grams this afternoon and they informed me that Miss Dubois had been arrested. I assume that's what took you to see the inspector?' Kitty took a seat on one of the black leather chairs near the open French window where she could feel the benefit of the light breeze that had sprung up.

Matt poured her a small schooner of Amontillado and handed it to her, before pouring one for himself.

'Yes. I wanted to find out if he had indeed made an arrest and if the proceeds of the robbery had been found.' He took a seat and told Kitty everything the inspector had said.

Kitty listened intently as she sipped her sherry. 'I have some more information for you. I went for a walk to clear my head after my interview with Grams and Mrs Craven and who should I meet but Alice's cousin, Betty. She was on her way to find me. She claims Lady Meribel has gone missing.'

Matt sat up in his seat. 'Missing? Since when?'

'Sometime after breakfast. Mid-morning, I surmise from what Betty told me. She hasn't taken a car or requested the chauffeur drive her anywhere. Betty also claims that Lady Meribel's shoes are unsuitable for walking any distance.'

'Interesting. I presume that you have a theory?' He was pretty sure that Kitty had been turning the matter over in her mind ever since she had encountered Betty.

Kitty's brow creased. 'It did occur to me that something may have happened to Lady Meribel, but since Betty said they had searched the house and grounds for her to no avail, I am much more inclined to believe that she has gone somewhere of her own accord.'

Matt agreed. 'I concur. It seems likely. How and where though, and is it connected to our case?' He waited to hear her thoughts.

'It struck me that Lady Meribel may have been thinking about Miss Briggs. It's possible that she may have decided to pay her a call and may not have wished the others to know of it.'

Matt could see the logic in Kitty's theory. 'She would not want the others to realise Miss Briggs was her mother. She might not even have decided to tell Miss Briggs herself, but may have simply wished to meet with her once more if it was playing on her mind. Is that what you mean?'

Kitty beamed at him. 'Exactly. She could have called a taxi to collect her just out of sight of the house and slipped away.'

He set down his glass and jumping up, picked up the telephone receiver.

'Hello, is that Mrs Pace? Yes, it's Captain Bryant here. I called the other day with Miss Underhay to see your sister. I'm terribly sorry to trouble you but I don't suppose you have seen Lady Meribel Jacques at all today?'

He listened to the reply and gave Kitty a quick affirmative nod.

'She was there earlier. Thank you so much, I'll try her again at her home later. I hope Miss Briggs is more rested?'

He saw some of the tension ease from Kitty's shoulders at Mrs Pace's positive response to his query.

'I see, I'm very sorry. Please pass on our regards. If there is anything we can do, Miss Briggs has our telephone numbers.' He replaced the receiver and resumed his seat.

'Well?' Kitty asked.

'Lady Meribel spent an hour or so with Miss Briggs today.'

'Then, I wonder where she was for the remainder of the day? No doubt she has headed back to the manor now. At least Betty's mind will be set at rest. I think poor Betty thought Lady Meribel may have been the murderer's next victim.'

It must have been on Kitty's mind too for all her talk of how the manor house had been searched. Now though it opened up thoughts of a different nature. Where else had Lady Meribel been, and what if she were the murderer after all and not Carlotta Dubois?

'Miss Briggs is sinking fast although her sister says that the medication means she appears not to be suffering,' Matt said.

'I wonder if Lady Meribel made Miss Briggs aware of her true identity.' Kitty's face was sad. 'It seems awful that the woman might die not knowing that she had met her daughter again.'

'We still need to see Miss Briggs to tell her that her daughter has been traced. She did commission us after all to find Dorothea,' Matt said.

'And sooner rather than later if she is deteriorating quickly.' Kitty's expression was troubled. 'At least we can tell her that her daughter is well. It may give her some peace of mind in her final days.'

'I think you are right. Shall we call in the morning, first thing?' Matt suggested. Mrs Pace's voice had sounded quietly sad when he had enquired about Miss Briggs. It must be hard for her to see her sister suffering.

Kitty finished her drink and set her glass down on the modern glass and chrome side table. 'I think it would be a good idea. At least then we shall have completed our commission.'

———

Kitty accepted Matt's offer to stay for dinner. His housekeeper had left him a large shepherd's pie in the oven, and he had merely to light the gas in order to heat it up.

'Bachelor fare,' he remarked in a laughing tone when he returned to the drawing room having turned on the oven.

'I do hope you do not expect gourmet meals from me when we are married?' Kitty grinned. 'Anything more complex than an omelette will have to be made by the hotel chef. Cooking is not something I have ever mastered.'

She could see he was amused. 'And yet you learned to play billiards.'

'Mickey was a patient teacher. There is no space in a busy professional kitchen for a small girl to play at cooking. Now sampling the food that is produced, that is quite a different matter.' She laughed out loud at his expression.

'It is a good thing then that I am not marrying you for your cooking skills.' The dimple in his cheek flashed, warming her heart.

'What about my sleuthing abilities? Do you think the inspector has made the right call, arresting Miss Dubois?' she asked.

Matt topped up her sherry glass. 'Your sleuthing capabilities are never in doubt, old thing. As for Miss Dubois, I must say I'm not entirely confident. The inspector made a good case against her as you know, but it is circumstantial unless those missing jewels are found.'

'But you do not care for her,' Kitty added.

'True,' he conceded. 'But I am trying not to allow that to cloud my analysis of the evidence.'

Kitty sipped her drink slowly and wondered how true that statement actually was. Whilst they had been talking Bertie had wandered back out into the back garden and continued to excavate his position beneath the rhododendron bush.

'Oh dear, Matt. Bertie seems to be destroying your garden.' Kitty jumped up in alarm as a large clod of red brown earth landed with a thump on the garden path.

'I swear all that dog likes to do is howl, dig or destroy things.' Matt set down his drink and they went into the garden to survey the damage. Bertie sat proudly in the centre of a now much deeper hole.

His grey and white coat was tinged with a film of red dust, and particles of dirt were lodged in his coat.

'I am afraid we shall need to bath him,' Kitty said.

Matt groaned. 'I think there are some old towels in the

cupboard. Will you give me a hand with him after supper, Kitty?'

She glanced at her nice clean dress and reluctantly agreed, hoping that Matt's housekeeper wouldn't mind her borrowing the apron she had left hanging on the back of the pantry door. Alice would have a fit if she spoiled any more of her clothes.

Matt went to the kitchen to see if their supper was ready, while Kitty set the table in the dining room. It felt rather odd but pleasant to be undertaking domestic duties in Matt's home. Soon to be their home, she supposed, when they set a date. Which reminded her that she needed to tell Matt of her grandmother's request that they dine with her to discuss the wedding.

Once supper was on the table and Bertie safely shut up in the kitchen with his dish, they sat down to dine. Kitty told Matt of her grandmother's request.

'What are your thoughts on the matter?' he asked diplomatically. 'Do you have any preference for a date?'

Kitty had given some thought to this while she had been walking on the embankment prior to meeting Betty.

'I've always thought a Christmas wedding would be nice. The hotel could close to guests, and we could host our families and have a reception and holiday, with perhaps a delayed honeymoon for the two of us in the spring?' She looked at Matt to see if he liked her suggestion.

'Your father could come over then too, I presume?' Matt asked.

She nodded. 'I think so. He wishes to give me away.'

'Then how about we telephone the vicar at St Saviour's tomorrow, after we have called on Miss Briggs, and see if he has any availability at that time of year.' Matt's eyes twinkled.

Kitty was more than agreeable to this, and they finished their meal with pleasant chatter about their future. Something which after the scare of the morning made Kitty feel much more cheerful.

After carrying their dishes to the kitchen and clearing away, Kitty donned the floral pinafore apron that she had found on a hook in the pantry. Matt grinned as he took in her appearance as it wrapped around her twice and almost reached her ankles.

'I think your dress will be quite safe. There is a tin bath outside. I propose I fill it with water if you collect the old towels and the soap.'

Bertie looked unimpressed as he watched them making preparations for his ablutions. Matt part filled the bath outside on the patio and between them they got Bertie into the tub.

'Hold his collar, Kitty.'

Matt poured water over the dog and Kitty tried to keep Bertie from shaking muddy drops of water over them both while he was soaped and rinsed. Finally Bertie's ordeal was over and he was released from the bath to shake himself dry on the patio, before Kitty and Matt started to rub him up and down with the towels.

'Shall I remove his collar now while we brush him?' Kitty asked.

Bertie looked piteously at her.

'Yes, he has some knots under his ears that I think that we need to brush out.' Matt waited with the grooming tools while Kitty undid the buckle on Bertie's red leather collar.

'This looks quite worn.' Kitty examined the collar, noticing that the silver-coloured metal disc bearing Bertie's name appeared quite shiny and new. She looked more closely and saw the back of the disc bore what she presumed was Simon Travers's address.

'I think I'll get him a new one and he'll need a new tag too.' Matt stopped brushing and looked at Kitty. 'What is it?'

'I don't know. This address seems familiar. Is it very close to Reverend Greenslade's church? I know Simon Travers lived nearby but I didn't think it was quite so close.'

Matt took the collar from her and looked at the address.

'You're right. This puts his rooms very close to the hostel where Miss Briggs was staying just across the square from the church. I have a street directory in the house from where I looked up the directions to Cairn House.'

They finished drying and brushing Bertie and went inside. Matt looked inside his bureau and pulled out the directory.

He opened it up and found the page. 'Here, it's just one door away from the Christian Ladies' Hostel.' He stabbed at the page with his forefinger. 'It explains how he was on the spot to overhear the gang.'

'Hmm, and it also means that the police and the brigadier may well be correct in their assumption that he knew where the goods were hidden. We know Miss Dubois and Mr Ford thought he did.' Kitty took off her borrowed apron and returned it to its hook while Matt made them both coffee.

'If you were Travers, where would you have stashed the goods? Assuming that you had found them?' Kitty asked as the aromatic scent of the fresh coffee began to permeate the house.

Matt shrugged. 'I don't know. Clearly they were not in his flat or the police would have found them after he died. I know the brigadier would have had his rooms searched as soon as he heard Travers had been murdered.'

Kitty frowned. The goods had been removed from their hiding place in the churchyard and were not in Travers's rooms and yet he must have stashed them locally. Or had he sent them on somewhere? Perhaps to be collected at a later date? Or was there something or someone else who had known where the goods were and had double-crossed Travers? The reverend, perhaps?

She looked at Bertie who had been rewarded with a biscuit for co-operating with his bath.

'It's a shame Bertie can't talk. He could tell us where the jewels and silver have gone.'

The spaniel wagged his tail at the mention of his name.

Matt handed Kitty an exquisite porcelain coffee cup hand-painted with a bold geometric pattern. 'Bertie has probably dug a hole somewhere and Simon has buried the goods in there.'

Kitty laughed but her mind was ticking over everything they had discovered so far about the murders and those linked to them. She spent an enjoyable further hour with Matt drinking coffee and listening to the radio before she set off back to the Dolphin.

On her return she found a message waiting for her. As they had expected, and to Kitty's relief, Betty confirmed Lady Meribel's safe return to the manor.

TWENTY-FOUR

Kitty slept badly. Her dreams were punctuated by visions of Ezekiel Hammett clambering out of the river, his clothes soaked in water. The dreams were mixed with images of Lady Meribel and Miss Dubois and the visit to the mother and baby home.

Matt and Bertie called for her shortly after breakfast. The fine weather of the previous days had finally broken, and the sky looked sullen and overcast. Rain had been predicted for later in the day. Her grandmother had gone down to the office, leaving Kitty to finish her cup of tea in the salon.

Despite her disturbed night, she greeted Matt cheerfully as he entered the drawing room. 'I telephoned the vicar, and he can see us at ten. I have also telephoned Mrs Pace and asked if we might see Miss Briggs for a few minutes before lunch.'

'Marvellous, darling.' Matt dropped a kiss on her cheek as Bertie took the opportunity to look longingly at the last triangle of toast in the silver rack.

Kitty gave in and gave the toast to Bertie while Matt took a white envelope from inside the breast pocket of his jacket.

'This arrived in this morning's post from Sister Perpetua. I thought you might care to see it.' He passed Kitty the envelope.

'What is it?' She opened it and looked inside to discover a newspaper clipping, yellow at the edges with age.

'Sister Perpetua's predecessor, Sister Michael, cut this out of the paper and kept it on file. There was no note with it, but Sister Perpetua assumed Sister Michael had placed it there should Dorothea, Lady Meribel, wish to know more about her father and what happened to him.'

Kitty read the contents of the article. 'This is a report about the fire which killed Lady Meribel's father.' She frowned. 'It sounds horrific. The poor man never stood a chance. It says the flames took hold quickly and he was unable to unlock the door of his study in time, before being overcome by smoke. The servants formed a chain with some of the neighbours with buckets of water to try and douse the flames. It says the fire was thought to have been started by the family cat knocking over an oil lantern. His wife and two sons escaped unharmed but a kitchen maid was badly burned.'

'It struck me that Sister Michael may have had another motive for keeping that cutting,' Matt said.

Kitty looked at him with a dawning sense of dismay. 'You believe the fire may have been set deliberately?'

'Why would the man lock himself in his office? And if he did do that, surely he would leave the key in the lock? It says the study was on the ground floor. He could have escaped from the window.' Matt's expression was grave.

Kitty blinked. 'You think that perhaps Miss Briggs?' The idea did not bear thinking about. Surely not. Yet the woman they had met at the church had been scathing in her opinion of the former missionary.

'I telephoned the brigadier before setting out. As you know I asked him to make some enquiries out in India using his foreign office connections. It seems there was a death at one of the compounds a few years ago. It was assumed at the time to be an accident. A male missionary who had been quite friendly with Miss Briggs was discovered to have fallen into the well and broken his neck. Miss Briggs was reported at the time to be distraught.' Matt fiddled with the teaspoon resting on Kitty's saucer.

'I sense a "but" coming?' Kitty looked at him.

'According to some reports from the servants, Miss Briggs and the man who died had argued shortly before his accident. There was some talk around the village.'

Kitty shivered. 'This could all just be conjecture.' She replaced the clipping in the envelope and gave it back to Matt for safekeeping.

'It could,' he agreed. 'However, I think we should watch Miss Briggs's reactions very carefully when we talk to her this morning.' He hesitated and Kitty sensed there was something more that he wished to say.

'Matt?'

'I also asked the brigadier to look at Reverend Greenslade's war record.'

'He seemed like a man who had suffered a great deal of trauma,' Kitty replied carefully. Matt himself still suffered greatly from the effects of his service during the war. Recurrent night terrors and a dread of enclosed spaces were just some of the things that still lingered to haunt him. It could be that the reverend also still had problems from his time on the front.

'The brigadier spoke to a major who had known Reverend Greenslade during that time. He was generally well regarded it seems. However, he did say that the reverend has a strong sense of right and wrong exacerbated by his service. His bishop says that when unwell the reverend becomes quite zealous in meting out what he feels is justice for crimes that he judges have gone unpunished. There have been a few incidents, the last one involved the verger having to extricate the reverend when he went for someone with his walking stick.'

'Oh dear.' Kitty could see that in the right circumstances the reverend might well have considered Travers or Ford sinners and decided to deliver his own brand of justice in the form of murder to one or both men.

Kitty put on her hat and a smart navy jacket over her favourite cherry print dress in preparation for their appointment with the vicar. As she walked with Matt and Bertie in the direction of St Saviour's, the ancient church in the heart of Dartmouth, she pondered this new twist in the case.

The meeting with the vicar was cordial and swift. He pronounced himself delighted to have the honour of marrying them and they determined that Monday the twenty-fourth of December, Christmas Eve morning, would be the day for their wedding.

As they walked back from the meeting to collect Kitty's car from its garage, she found herself feeling quite unsettled. She was excited at the thought of marrying Matt, but at the same time it would mean a great deal of change in her life. The mystery of who had killed Travers and Billy Ford was still niggling at her too, adding to her confusion.

The river crossing was choppy with a stiff breeze causing wavelets to slap against the side of the ferry as it clanked its way to Kingswear on its mighty chains. Grey clouds scurried overhead, and the river reflected the colour making the water dark.

Kitty wondered when they would hear from the police about the search for Hammett. The idea sent a trickle of ice along her spine and added to the feeling of foreboding she had been experiencing ever since she had seen the contents of Sister Perpetua's envelope.

She stopped her car in Kingswear to put the roof up as it increasingly appeared as if it might rain before they reached Torquay. Bertie appeared very disappointed by this decision and expressed his unhappiness by howling intermittently all the way to town.

'My ears are ringing,' Kitty said as she pulled to a stop near

Mrs Pace's guest house. 'I do hope he'll be all right in the back of the car while we are visiting with Miss Briggs.'

Matt clambered out of the passenger seat and peered at Bertie. 'I hope so too. This dog is costing me a small fortune. At least it should be a short visit, I'd rather not have to buy another leash.'

Mrs Pace's plump, pleasant face was lined with exhaustion when she opened the door to admit them to the house.

'Xanthe is quite weak this morning so has remained in her room. If you'd both care to follow me, I'll take you up.' She led the way up the stairs and onto a narrow landing. A further flight led up to another floor above their heads. They followed Mrs Pace along the corridor almost to the end. She stopped outside a brown painted door and tapped gently, before opening it to peep inside.

Once satisfied with what she saw she opened the door wider and allowed them to enter.

'She tires easily now,' Mrs Pace warned them before padding away back to her chores.

The room had a pleasant aspect overlooking the street outside with distant views of the sea in between the houses opposite. It smelled of disinfectant and of the large vase of lilies that stood on the pine dressing table. Kitty was relieved that this room at least did not have the stifling heat of the small parlour downstairs where they had previously visited Miss Briggs.

The room was simply furnished with a plain wooden wardrobe and small dresser, a bedside cabinet and two chairs set out at the side of the bed. Brown medicine bottles, tots and glasses were arranged on a brass tray on the cabinet alongside a small bell. Miss Briggs lay on her back in a neat single bed beneath a rose-coloured satin eiderdown.

The tan of her complexion had faded to be replaced with a sickly yellow tinge and the flesh seemed to have fallen away from her cheeks, leaving her bones protruding starkly under her skin. Her eyes were closed and Kitty at first was uncertain if she was asleep or unconscious.

She took her place beside Matt on one of the bentwood chairs.

'Miss Briggs?' Matt asked.

The woman's eyelids fluttered open, and it took her a moment to focus. 'Did you find her? Dorothea?' A bony hand shot suddenly from under the covers to clutch at Matt as if frightened he would escape.

'Yes, we found her,' Matt assured her.

'You've seen her?' Miss Briggs gaze was suddenly intense.

'Yes, we have. She is well and settled.'

Miss Briggs seemed to relax back slightly onto the pile of pillows supporting her head, the white linen highlighting the sickly yellow of her complexion even further.

'Dorothea.' The name was barely a whisper from between the sick woman's lips.

'Would you care for a sip of water, Miss Briggs?' Kitty asked.

She picked up the glass and supported the woman's head as she moistened her mouth.

'Thank you.' Miss Briggs looked at Kitty. 'Most kind of you.'

Kitty helped her settle back against the pillows.

'Will she see me? Will she visit?' The woman gazed directly into Kitty's eyes and Kitty noticed that even the whites of the woman's eyes had a yellow tinge.

'She may.' Kitty felt safe in giving that assurance knowing that Miss Briggs had already encountered her daughter without knowing Lady Meribel's true identity.

'She is aware that her father was killed in a fire at his home,' Matt said as Kitty watched Miss Briggs's face closely for any sign of a reaction.

'Fire. Fire and brimstone. More punishment. Beware your

sins will find you out.' Miss Briggs released her grip on Matt and her eyes closed once more.

'I think perhaps we should leave and allow you to rest,' Kitty said.

Miss Briggs's eyes remained shut so Kitty nudged Matt to signal that perhaps they should go. He took his cue and rose from his seat and waited for Kitty to collect her handbag.

They were at the bedroom door when Miss Briggs suddenly gave a cry of pain and twisted in her bed. Kitty rushed back to soothe her.

'Miss Briggs, may I get you anything?'

The older woman collapsed back, panting. 'No, nothing, it will pass. Do not be alarmed. I have sinned and must be punished.'

Kitty straightened. 'Are you quite certain you are all right? Shall I call your sister?'

Miss Briggs's eyes were closing once more. 'Nothing, my dear, nothing. Old sins cast long shadows. I must bear my suffering as Christ bore his.'

Kitty looked at Matt and he opened the bedroom door to indicate they should go. They made their way down the stairs to the hall where they were met by Mrs Pace.

'We won't stay as she needs her rest,' Kitty said.

Mrs Pace bowed her head. 'I don't think as she has much longer left now, Miss Underhay. Thank you for calling to see her. She won't tell me what's been on her mind, but she keeps asking for someone called Dorothea and muttering about India. It seemed to soothe her when I told her as you and Captain Bryant were coming this morning.'

'It's our pleasure, Mrs Pace. Has she received many visitors since she arrived?' Matt asked.

'Yourselves, the police inspector, the reverend as helped with her travelling, and Lady Jacques come yesterday with some flowers. People have been very kind,' Mrs Pace said.

'Thank you for letting us see her. You must be very busy with your guest house and with caring for your sister,' Kitty said.

'Bless you, miss, that I am. Fair run off my feet I am and my knees aren't what they used to be. It's the stairs you see, up and down. I don't mind for visitors, mind you, but those wretched salesmen are a pest. Had one here a few days ago, cheeky beggar he was, trying to sell brushes.'

Kitty looked at Matt. 'Did he have a London accent?' she asked.

'Oh yes, he was a proper cockney like you hear in a radio play. I sent him off with a flea in his ear.' Mrs Pace looked quite pleased about that.

It sounded as if Billy Ford had attempted to gain entry to the guest house before his death. He must have realised that Miss Briggs would be unlikely to receive him so had used his brush salesman persona to try to get inside. The question, Kitty wondered, was why.

They left Mrs Pace to her work and started back towards Kitty's car.

'That's strange,' Matt said. 'I can't hear Bertie.'

Kitty looked at him in bewilderment.

'Bertie always howls whenever he is left alone.' Matt hurried to Kitty's car. 'He's gone.' Matt looked around the street for the errant white and grey cocker spaniel.

'The car door is closed, and the windows are part down as I left them.' Kitty peered into the car to see if Bertie had somehow managed to slip his leash.

'Captain Bryant, Miss Underhay!' An elegantly dressed female figure was heading towards them being towed along by an energetic Bertie.

'Lady Jacques.' Matt stepped forward and relieved Meribel of the lead, while she struggled to regain her breath.

'I'm so dreadfully sorry. I recognised Miss Underhay's car

and heard this terrible noise coming from inside. I realised it must be the dog you rescued from your friend who was murdered. I tried the door thinking perhaps he was in pain or injured and he took off like a rocket.' The girl gasped to a halt and pressed her hand into her side. 'I do believe I have a stitch. I went after him straight away to try and catch him, I felt just awful. He'd seen a squirrel and was barking in someone's garden.'

Kitty thought Lady Meribel looked as if she was about to cry.

'I tried to catch him, but he kept running off and then when I did get hold of his lead, he pulled me through a hedge.'

Kitty realised that dead leaves and tiny bits of twig were stuck in Lady Meribel's tweed skirt. She immediately started to assist the girl in removing the debris.

'I'm afraid that Bertie is not the best-behaved dog. It was kind of you to try and assist him.' Matt frowned at his pet.

'I guessed that you had probably gone to visit Miss Briggs, so I had thought I'd put him back in the car and come and tell you that he was howling.' Lady Meribel's complexion was beginning to look less rosy, and her breathing was returning to normal.

'Miss Briggs has remained in her room today. She appears very unwell,' Kitty said.

Lady Meribel sighed, and Kitty saw that there were tears in the girl's eyes. 'I have decided to tell her the truth, that I am Dorothea. I have been thinking about it all night. I came to see her yesterday and left her with some flowers. I wasn't certain what to do but it seems too cruel to let her die not knowing that I came to see her.'

'We have told her that we found you but not who you were. It will, I think, give her some comfort to know you are there.' Kitty patted Lady Meribel's arm.

'Thank you.' Meribel looked at Bertie with a rueful expression. 'And I am so sorry about your dog. I can't bear to see animals unhappy or hurt. He is rather sweet.'

Matt smiled. 'You were trying to be kind and Bertie is the most undeserving of canines.'

Lady Jacques straightened her hat, which had been knocked slightly askew when Bertie had pulled her into the hedge and walked away towards Mrs Pace's guest house. Matt secured his errant pet on the back seat of Kitty's car once more and climbed into the passenger seat.

'It's all terribly sad, isn't it?' Kitty observed as she started the engine.

'Frightful,' Matt agreed.

'I wonder if there is any news yet from Exeter?' Kitty said as she pulled away and pointed the nose of her car towards the town. The longer the search went on for Hammett's body the more nervous she became. Surely he must have drowned?

'Shall we call on Inspector Greville?' Matt looked at her.

TWENTY-FIVE

'Miss Underhay!'

Kitty had not even turned off the engine of her car when Doctor Carter hailed her outside the police station.

'Good morning, both.' The doctor beamed at them as Kitty let down the window to speak to him.

'Good morning. We were just on our way to see if there was any more progress on the search for Ezekiel Hammett.' Kitty switched off her motor and applied the handbrake.

The doctor's cheery smile broadened. 'Good news, my dear. They have him. Or rather I have him, under lock and key in my morgue. I have just confirmed his identity.'

A wave of relief rushed through Kitty. 'Really? You are sure? He is dead?'

'Completely, my dear. As a doornail, to use the vernacular of the layman. You may rest easy now, he can do no more harm to anyone,' Doctor Carter assured her.

'I know one should never rejoice at hearing of the death of another human being but in Hammett's case I think we may be forgiven for our relief at this news.' Kitty wanted to kiss the cherubic little man.

Suddenly the whole day felt brighter and better. Hammett was finally gone. She had a date for her wedding, everything seemed to be looking up.

'Inspector Greville has telephoned the Dolphin and left you a message, I believe,' the doctor said. 'I rather think Inspector Pinch at Exeter has the worst end of the deal. He has had to inform Hammett's sister, Esther, of her brother's death.'

Kitty could well imagine that would not be an easy task. If Hammett was a villain, his sister was ten times worse. She was the one who called the shots and yet had somehow managed to avoid conviction. She had been behind the attempt to murder Kitty at Elm House in Torquay earlier in the year.

'It seems to be very busy out here today,' Matt observed.

There was a small knot of people standing near the entrance to the police station and a couple of cars were parked at the kerb near Kitty's motor.

'I rather think the press are here for Miss Dubois,' the doctor said.

Kitty peered through her windscreen. 'Miss Dubois? Whatever is happening now?'

'Inspector Greville is releasing her. He hasn't enough evidence to charge her at this time and, apparently, she has some powerful friend who has raised a stink. I believe her agent has invited the papers along for publicity.' The doctor looked towards the entrance to the police station. 'Here she comes now, watch this.'

Sure enough, Carlotta Dubois appeared leaning heavily on the arm of a short, stout man in his fifties. She was heavily veiled and clearly playing to the press as they paused to give a short statement, before she was escorted to a nearby Rolls Royce and driven away.

'Hmm, so where does that leave the murder case now, I wonder?' Matt frowned.

'I'm not sure. I know Greville is most unhappy about it all.

Still, unless the missing loot turns up it's going to be difficult to pin this on any of them,' the doctor said.

Matt agreed. 'I'm afraid you may be right.'

'Miss Underhay, do you agree?'

Kitty suddenly realised that both the doctor and Matt were looking at her obviously expecting a response.

It had been that statement again about the missing proceeds from the robbery that kept niggling away at her.

'I'm so sorry. I think I was wool gathering. I don't know, I have one or two ideas, but I don't think I've quite worked it all out yet, there is something that is bothering me about where the jewels might be. Somehow I feel that is the key to all of this.'

Doctor Carter smiled at her and reached into the car to pat her hand where it rested on the steering wheel. 'Then I am certain you will solve it, my dear.'

He said goodbye and walked away towards his own car. The small crowd of press people had dissipated, and the street was back to normal once more.

Kitty was aware that Matt was watching her, a quizzical expression on his face.

'Would calling somewhere for lunch assist you to think this all through?' he asked.

'I always find I do my best work on a full stomach.' She laughed and leaned across to kiss his cheek.

'Then shall we continue on down to the seafront?' he asked.

Kitty smiled at her fiancé and started her car once more. She drove down through the town and turned towards the Pavilion Theatre and the promenade. A breeze was blowing in from the sea creating white horses on the water. The green was deserted as people had clearly decided to dine inside out of the wind. A few people were still walking on the sands with their dogs and young children.

There was a vacant space a little further down so Kitty

pulled in and turned off the engine. Bertie immediately began to fidget, sensing a walk might be in the offing.

'I'd better take him out,' Matt said.

'Where shall we go?' Kitty wasn't certain which establishments would welcome a dog as unpredictable as Bertie inside their hallowed halls.

'I tell you what, I'll walk down to the hut near the ferry stop. They do marvellous fresh sandwiches. I'll bring us some back and we can eat in the car and watch the sea. It might help your thought process.' Matt grinned at her as he started to untie Bertie's leash.

'That sounds perfect,' Kitty agreed.

She sat behind the wheel looking out at the beach. On the horizon she saw a couple of boats heading in towards the harbour while the gulls wheeled overhead against the gunmetal-grey sky. The palm trees shivered and shook in the breeze and the summer flowers were losing their fight to hold on to their petals.

As she waited for Matt and Bertie to return a young woman walked by holding a boy of about five by the hand. In his other hand he carried a brightly painted red and yellow striped tin bucket and a toy spade. They were clearly heading for the beach. Kitty watched them as they walked towards the steps, her mind still idly thinking over everything they had discovered about the case.

There was a loud bang from the steps followed by the sound of crying as the small boy dropped his bucket. Kitty startled at the noise and relaxed again as the child's mother retrieved it for him. The incident reminded her of Reverend Greenslade when they had met him in Dartmouth at the castle tea rooms.

She remembered when they had been in London, the proximity of St Mark's Church to both the Christian Ladies' Hostel and Simon Travers's flat. The wilderness at the back of the graveyard and Carlotta Dubois talking about William Ford and where they had expected to find the hidden jewels.

Kitty rested her gloved fingers on the top of her steering wheel. Had Travers been murdered during the commotion caused by Miss Briggs's fainting? Or was it done before, during one of the stops at an earlier station? Travers's murder had certainly been audacious. Perhaps too audacious. Done by someone who believed that God was on their side? Or by a committed gambler, playing the odds?

Matt opened the car door, making her jump. She had been so deep in her own thoughts she hadn't seen him return. Bertie jumped onto the back seat and gave Kitty a lick at the back of her ear as Matt refastened him in place.

'Ham?' Matt handed her a parcel wrapped in greaseproof paper.

'Thank you.' She unwrapped the parcel, took out the bread roll and took a bite, scarcely aware of what she was eating. She was close to working out the murders, she knew she was.

At least she was fairly certain that she knew who could have done it, but she needed to work out why. Once she had that then she would know for certain.

———

Matt unwrapped his own sandwich and ate without disturbing Kitty's concentration. She had that faraway look in her eyes again that told him she was thinking about the murders. He knew that once she had it all worked out, she would share her thoughts with him.

He had his own idea of who might have been responsible but without something concrete it was simply a theory. He understood Inspector Greville's frustration at having to release Carlotta Dubois. The girl had admitted to expecting to profit from the robbery so there was nothing to say that she wouldn't kill to ensure that she benefitted from it, if she did have the jewels hidden away somewhere.

A woman was assisting a small boy to build a sandcastle on the beach. He watched as the child ran down to the edge of the sea scooping up some of the water from the waves in a tin bucket. The woman laughed and shrieked as the child accidentally splashed her as he poured the salt water into the moat of the castle.

'What some mothers will do for their children,' Matt mused with a wry smile.

Kitty hastily chewed and swallowed the last bite of her sandwich. 'What did you just say?' she demanded.

'The woman down there on the beach just got soaked. I said what some mothers will do for their children.' Matt stared at his fiancée.

Kitty brushed the crumbs from the front of her blouse and her skirt before crumpling up her sandwich wrapper.

'We have to go.' She started the car once more and carefully backed out of her space.

'I was enjoying my lunch.' Matt made a half-hearted protest recognising that Kitty had just received a flash of inspiration.

'Where are we going?' He gave up on trying to eat his lunch as Kitty swung her small car around the corner making Bertie grumble as he slid on the back seat of the car.

'Back to Mrs Pace's lodging house and I hope we are in time,' Kitty said.

TWENTY-SIX

Kitty halted her car outside Mrs Pace's guest house. A black car was already parked nearby at the kerb and the front door was slightly ajar.

'Kitty, what's going on?' Matt asked as she slipped out of her car and started toward the open door.

'I fear we may be too late,' she said as she pushed the door open wider and peered inside the hall.

'Miss Underhay, Captain Bryant.' Lady Jacques was coming down the stairs. Her eyes were red rimmed from crying and she clutched a sodden lace-trimmed handkerchief in one hand.

'Miss Briggs has passed?' Kitty asked. Her heart sank, it looked as if they were indeed too late.

Lady Meribel nodded. 'The doctor is with her now and Reverend Greenslade, but I was with her as she slipped away.'

'Where is Mrs Pace?' Kitty asked.

'With the doctor and the reverend, upstairs. She asked me to wait in the front drawing room and she would make tea when she came downstairs. The reverend was saying a prayer.' Lady Meribel's voice wobbled.

'Come, we shall sit with you.' Kitty supported the girl as they made their way into the room that was clearly normally used by Mrs Pace's guests.

The sitting room was quite airy and simply furnished with a chintz covered three-piece suite and side tables. A small upright piano stood in one corner and above the fireplace was a large portrait of two young women. Judging from the style of their clothes and looking carefully at their faces Kitty guessed the picture must be of Miss Briggs and Mrs Pace done in their youth.

Mrs Pace, the plainer of the girls, was still readily recognisable. Miss Briggs, however, bore a strong resemblance to Lady Meribel. Blonde haired and pretty, with a snub nose and full lips. She wondered that Mrs Pace had not noticed the likeness.

Lady Meribel took a seat beside the window and blew her nose once more. 'I'm so sorry. It was such a shock, even though I knew there wasn't much time left.'

Kitty took the seat beside her as Matt hovered by the door to the hall looking out for Mrs Pace, the reverend and the doctor.

'At least you were with her, and you were able to tell her who you were,' Kitty said soothingly.

The girl sniffed. 'Yes, that at least gives me some comfort. I thought at first she did not hear me as her eyes were closed. But then she said, my original name, "Dorothea", and gave a little smile.'

There was a murmur of voices on the landing and then the sound of feet on the stairs. Matt went out into the hall to speak to Mrs Pace and the doctor.

'Did she say anything else to you?' Kitty asked.

Lady Meribel gave a small hiccup. 'No, nothing. She looked as if she was asleep.'

Matt returned to the drawing room accompanied by Reverend Greenslade. 'The doctor has left and Mrs Pace has gone to make tea. She said her sister had left some things with her that she wished us to have after her passing.'

Reverend Greenslade took one of the spare seats. He looked tired and sad. Lady Meribel looked confused. 'What sort of things?'

Kitty sighed. 'I rather thought that might be the case. Let us wait for Mrs Pace to return.'

Matt sprang up to open the door when he heard the rattle of teacups in the hall. Mrs Pace wheeled in a small wooden trolley with a white service china tea set. Kitty assisted her to serve the tea, before taking her seat back on the sofa beside Matt. Mrs Pace took the vacant chair opposite Lady Meribel, near to the reverend.

'I'm so very sorry for your loss, Mrs Pace,' Kitty said.

The woman looked tired. Her wispy brown hair, streaked with grey, was escaping from her bun and her eyes were as red as Lady Meribel's.

'Thank you, Miss Underhay. Xanthe and I were never that close, not even when we were young, but when all's said and done she was still my sister.' Mrs Pace wiped her eyes with a cotton handkerchief.

'That's a lovely picture of you both.' Kitty indicated the portrait above the mantelpiece.

Lady Meribel looked up with a start, having clearly not noticed it until Kitty's remark. Reverend Greenslade also looked at the picture.

'That was done when I was twenty-one and Xanthe was twenty-five. She was always the pretty one of the two of us. Lovely she was when she was young, and clever too. She used to sing and play the piano. That's her instrument over there. I always thought as she would get married first. She could have took her pick.' A sobbing sigh broke from the woman's lips and she pressed her crumpled handkerchief to her mouth.

Lady Meribel was staring, fascinated at the picture. 'I

hadn't thought of what she must have looked like when she was young,' she said softly.

'I rather fancy that I see you in that portrait, Lady Meribel.' Reverend Greenslade sounded surprised as he studied the painting.

Mrs Pace frowned and looked at Lady Meribel as if seeing her properly for the first time. Her gaze travelled from the portrait back to Lady Meribel and back to the picture.

'I thought as when you first come here as there was something familiar about you. As if I'd met you somewhere before,' Mrs Pace said.

Lady Meribel looked imploringly at Matt and Kitty as if unsure if even now that she had gone she should divulge Miss Briggs's secret.

'Lady Meribel is Dorothea. She is Miss Briggs's daughter,' Matt said. His tone was kindly and gentle.

Reverend Greenslade gave a gentle cough.

Mrs Pace bowed her head for a moment before straightening again and looking directly at Lady Meribel. 'I always knew as there was something behind her deciding to go to India like that. I thought at the time it were a broken heart. Another man had let her down.'

'I take it that happened quite often? A man letting her down?' Kitty's question was as gentle in tone as Matt's had been.

Mrs Pace nodded and looked at Lady Meribel. 'Xanthe was lovely to look at and she drew men to her like a flower draws the bees but...'

'They saw a side to her that they didn't care for?' Kitty suggested when Mrs Pace hesitated.

'Yes. She could be, well, heartless at times. No proper feeling, hard like. She could turn, just like that. Then they would lose interest and go after a girl who was more kindly and soft.' Mrs Pace bit her lip as she looked at Lady Meribel.

The girl was as still as a statue. 'Was that what my father meant when he said blood would out? Am I reckless and hard?' She looked at Kitty.

'No, how can you even think that? Look at your kindness to Bertie today. If anything you allow others to take advantage of your good nature.' Kitty was thinking of all the hangers-on at Lady Meribel's holiday home.

The girl released what Kitty assumed was a sigh of relief. 'Thank you, Miss Underhay.'

Kitty turned her attention back to Mrs Pace. 'I hate to ask you this but I'm afraid it must be said. When did you first suspect that Miss Briggs had murdered Mr Travers and Mr Ford?'

A silence filled the room and Matt, Reverend Greenslade and Lady Meribel's attention was focused on Mrs Pace.

'Not at first. It was upsetting like, having that policeman come after the reverend here brought Xanthe home in a taxi and said what had happened on the train.' Mrs Pace stared into her teacup. ''Tis a terrible thing to suspect as your own flesh and blood could be capable of such a thing.'

'What made you suspect?' Kitty asked.

'It were when she was settled in her room and I was asking her about the man who was killed. She said he was a common thief, and his death was of no consequence. It were the way she said it somehow. Cold.' Mrs Pace shook her head.

'And then Mr Ford was murdered,' Kitty prompted her.

'I'd said to her as some cheeky cockney had tried to come into the house to sell some brushes and she got quite agitated. I had to go out that afternoon to get a bit of fish for our supper, so I don't know but I suspect as she got a message to him somehow to meet her. She knew as it were my bingo night and she said as she were going to bed early.' Mrs Pace looked at Kitty, her eyes wide with fear. 'I didn't know then, miss, or I should have said something, stopped her somehow.'

'I'm surprised she was strong enough to get to the harbour,' Matt said.

'I agree, she really was terribly ill.' The reverend's hand trembled and he spilled a drop of his tea.

Mrs Pace swallowed and placed her own cup and saucer back on the trolley. 'She wasn't so bad when she first arrived. Weak like, as the train journey had knocked her about. That was when I knew, well suspected. See, the day after they said as this Ford had been killed, she was very poorly. All her strength had suddenly gone. The exertion, I suppose. There was mud on the heels of her outdoor shoes, and I knew as I'd cleaned them for her before I'd put them away.'

Lady Meribel put her cup down with a clatter. She looked sick at the idea that her natural mother was a murderess. 'I can't believe it.'

'She were rambling too when the illness took her over. Kept talking about sin and the fires of hell and begging for forgiveness. Asking for Dorothea and muttering about nuns and India. Something about a well. She were seeing things too. She kept saying as they had come for her and were stood at the bottom of her bed. I kept thinking as perhaps I was wrong, mistaken, but I knew that Xanthe was capable of murder. Deep in my bones I think as I knew.' A tear rolled down Mrs Pace's cheek.

Kitty shivered and took Lady Meribel's hand in hers to give a comforting squeeze.

'May God rest her soul.' The reverend was clearly shaken by the revelations he had just heard.

'The police will have to be informed,' Matt said.

Mrs Pace emitted a low moan of despair. 'I won't be in trouble, will I?'

'I doubt it,' Kitty reassured her. 'You said your sister had left something for us?' She looked at the older woman as she dried her eyes.

Mrs Pace felt in the front pocket of her apron and took out

two envelopes. The handwriting on the front of both was shaky. One was addressed to Dorothea and one to Miss Underhay.

Lady Meribel accepted hers and held it almost as one would hold a snake, as if expecting it to bite her at any moment.

'Open it, my dear,' Kitty urged gently.

The girl seemed to gather herself and tore the letter open. Inside was a single folded sheet of notepaper and what seemed to be a left luggage ticket for Paddington Station. She looked at Kitty before opening the note and read.

'My dearest Dorothea,

Please take this ticket and reclaim the contents of the locker. They are for you to use as you wish. I would advise you to use caution if telling anyone of what you find and before disposing of the items. Be discreet and all will be well. There is a substantial reward for these items. I have nothing else to give you except to tell you that of everything that I have done in my life my only regret is that I could not keep you. If this will at least help make some kind of reparation, then it will all have been worth it.

My love always, Xanthe Briggs xx
    (Your affectionate mother)'

'I don't understand.' Lady Meribel turned a bewildered face to Kitty as Matt extracted the luggage ticket.

'I rather think that the missing proceeds from the Tower Hill Jewellers robbery may be inside this locker,' Matt said.

His statement drew a gasp from Mrs Pace, the reverend and Lady Meribel.

Kitty tore open the envelope addressed to her and read.

'Dear Miss Underhay,

I chose to write to you as I felt that as a fellow woman you would perhaps be more understanding and compassionate than a man might be. My time on this plane is growing short and soon I must meet my maker and face his judgement. I suspect that you will have already uncovered the story of the matters that occurred around the time of Dorothea's birth. I was greatly misused and injured. Cast aside like a worn-out shoe for whom the wearer has no further purpose. He knew his guilt in the matter and you must see that he had to be punished for his sin. Even as I was punished by giving up my child and moving to India.

Yet even in India I encountered snakes in human form. One such met his end in a well in our compound. Another deceiver and liar.

Travers was no better than a common thief. Perjuring himself by denying his part in the crime and double-crossing his fellow villains. He sought to deceive me by asking me to look after some items he said he had inherited. I knew where those things had come from. I was to meet him once we were both away from London and tell him where to collect the items he had stolen.

I seized my chance when the train was at a stop at the station before Exeter and we were all sorting out our bags. He was asleep and felt nothing. If that Craven woman had not stumbled upon him when she did, then he would not have been discovered until further down the line and we would have been clear.

I did not realise but Ford saw me. He said nothing but made it clear that he expected to get his hands on the items. He deserved to die. He would have been hung sooner or later for something anyway. It was clear to me that villainy was his business. This was a kindness. I had nothing to lose and at least in a small way I could do something good.

I have arranged for the valuables to go to a worthy cause.
You are free to do whatever you so wish with this note.
  Sincerely, Xanthe Briggs'

Kitty's voice was shaky by the time she finished reading the note aloud. Lady Meribel, Reverend Greenslade and Mrs Pace were silent and ashen faced.

'I rather think that Inspector Greville needs to see the note, Kitty old girl,' Matt said.

Kitty nodded. Miss Briggs had confirmed that she had murdered several people over the course of her life.

'I cannot believe I was so deceived,' the reverend said.

'I can't believe that she did all of that just so she could give me some stolen goods or so I could claim the reward.' Lady Meribel looked quite ill.

'It's clear from the note she left and from what Mrs Pace has told us that Miss Briggs had a somewhat twisted view of the world,' Matt said.

'She killed Mr Travers and Mr Ford so she could leave me some stolen jewels. That's so bizarre.' Lady Meribel looked at Kitty.

'In her mind she was making up to you for having to give you up as a baby. She clearly considered that the goods were now hers by right to do with as she wished as she deserved them, and Travers and Ford did not.' Kitty felt sorry for Lady Jacques.

'And the story of my father? I know he died in a fire. Sister Perpetua said so but... did she? I mean, do you think that is what she...?'

Kitty gave Lady Meribel's hand another gentle squeeze. 'I'm rather afraid she was responsible, yes, and also for the death of a fellow missionary out in India.'

Reverend Greenslade gasped. 'Such wickedness.'

The girl covered her face with her hands. 'Why would she

do that? How? And why would she believe that I would accept the profits of her crimes?'

'Xanthe always had a sort of warped view of the world. I have no doubt that in her head she was justified in everything she did.' Mrs Pace rose stiffly and took a couple of steps across the rug to Lady Meribel. 'My advice to you is to give that there letter to Miss Underhay and let her and this gentleman sort things out. Forget all of this. Everything. I can tell you now as beyond your looks you are nothing like your mother. Nothing at all, do you hear me? Go and live a good life and don't look back.' She placed her arm around Lady Meribel's shoulders and gave her a hug. 'Dorothea don't exist no more. Go and be happy.'

Lady Meribel lifted her head to give Mrs Pace a watery smile. 'Thank you.' She handed her note to Kitty, gathered her things and hurried out of the room. Reverend Greenslade also stood.

'I shall ensure she is all right.' He too left the room.

A few seconds later they heard the click of the latch on the front door as they both left the house.

Mrs Pace turned to Kitty. 'You'd best give them papers to that policeman.'

Matt pressed his hand on her shoulder. 'I'm so sorry, Mrs Pace. This must have been a terrible thing for you to hear.'

The woman sighed. ''Tis ended now. Xanthe has gone where mortal justice cannot reach her.'

Kitty and Matt left the house together in silence. Kitty felt completely wrung out by everything she had just read and heard, even though she had guessed most of it.

'How did you know it was Miss Briggs?' Matt asked when they reached the car.

Kitty opened the doors and slid behind the wheel. 'It had to be someone who knew Travers and was in a position to see what he had done. Since no one could find the goods, then he must have had help to hide them. It couldn't have been Miss Dubois or Billy Ford as they were busy searching for them. Reverend Greenslade was in the right place, but his nerves could not have taken the strain.'

Matt checked on Bertie who was watching them sulkily from the back seat. 'I can see that.'

'Miss Briggs wanted to do something for Dorothea. When I saw that woman today with her little boy, it just came to me. This was the only thing she could do to try and make amends for giving her up. She had so little time left it must have seemed to her like a reward almost, no matter how twisted.' Kitty shuddered.

TWENTY-SEVEN

They called back at the police station and had a lengthy interview with Inspector Greville. A telephone call to London confirmed quite quickly that the contents of the railway locker were indeed the missing jewels and silver from the robbery.

Matt used the telephone at the police station to update the brigadier. He was pleased to hear that the case was closed, and the goods recovered. However, he was less than happy that Miss Briggs had escaped justice.

Kitty was relieved once they were out of the police station and once more speeding along the road back towards Kingswear.

'Will you come back to the Dolphin with me? I dare say Mrs Craven will wish to know the outcome of the case,' Kitty said as she overtook a rather slow wagon on the hill.

'Of course. And I expect both she and your grandmother will be delighted that we have finally chosen a date for our wedding.' Matt smiled at her.

'As well as relieved that Ezekiel Hammett is no more. Although I daresay the message the inspector left for me about that will have been circulated all through the hotel by now.' Kitty's heart lightened at the thought.

Matt laughed. 'Absolutely. In fact, if anyone saw us at the vicarage or that our wedding has been entered in the vicar's diary, then Mrs C will know about that too before we have chance to tell anyone ourselves.'

Bertie joined in their laughter with a woof of agreement as they reached the ferry to cross the Dart.

They secured Kitty's car back inside its garage and strolled together along the embankment back to the Dolphin. The clouds from earlier in the day had now given way to weak late afternoon sunshine and the wind had dropped.

The old black and white half-timbered hotel building was tinged with a faint rosy glow as they approached. Overhead, the hand-painted sign creaked, and Matt held on to Bertie's lead as a couple passed by with a Pomeranian on a leash.

Mary was behind the reception desk as they entered the lobby. Her rosy, good-natured face smiling when she saw them.

'Oh, Miss Kitty, your grandmother has been asking after you. She saw the message you'd had from the inspector.'

Matt exchanged a glance and a smile with Kitty.

'Thank you, we'll go on up to her,' Kitty said and went to take the stairs to her grandmother's salon.

'Before you go on up, Miss Kitty. These flowers came for you. Proper strange they are.' Mary indicated a large bouquet of lilies with a black and red ribbon sitting in a vase at the side of the reception.

A shiver of apprehension trickled along Kitty's spine. There was something not right about the bouquet. The flowers were almost funereal.

'I wasn't expecting any flowers from anyone. Is there a card?' Kitty asked.

Mary handed her a small black sealed envelope. Kitty looked at Matt and then tore it open.

Instead of a wedding, plan for your funeral. E.H.

Matt read the card over her shoulder. He snatched the card and tore it in half. 'Esther Hammett, up to her old tricks again. Mary, get rid of these flowers.'

Mary moved to pick up the vase to take the bouquet away.

'I thought this was ended with Ezekiel's death,' Kitty whispered.

Matt placed his arm around her and gathered her to him. 'It will be, old girl, don't worry. This is just Esther lashing out. Inspector Pinch and Inspector Greville will soon put a stop on her nonsense.'

Kitty wished she could be as certain as Matt seemed to be.

'Now, come on, let's go and see your grandmother. We have a wedding to plan.'

A LETTER FROM HELENA

Thank you for choosing to read *Murder in First Class*. If you enjoyed it and want to keep up to date with all my latest releases, just sign up at the following link. Your email address will never be shared and of course you can unsubscribe at any time.

www.bookouture.com/helena-dixon

If you read the first book in the series, *Murder at The Dolphin Hotel*, you can find out how Kitty and Matt first met and began their sleuthing adventures. I always enjoy meeting characters again as a series reader, which is why I love writing this series so much. I hope you enjoy their exploits as much as I love creating them. I love an impossible murder so enjoyed creating this one, especially aboard a steam engine. There is something very atmospheric about a journey on a steam train.

I hope you loved reading *Murder in First Class* and, if you did, I would be very grateful if you could write a review. I'd love to hear what you think, and it makes such a difference helping new readers to discover one of my books for the first time.

I love hearing from all my readers – you can get in touch on my Facebook page, through Twitter, Goodreads or my website.

Thanks,

Helena Dixon

www.nelldixon.com

facebook.com/nelldixonauthor

twitter.com/NellDixon

ACKNOWLEDGEMENTS

My grateful thanks to all of the steam train enthusiasts who assisted with my research for this story. Any errors are mine alone. My thanks as always to the residents of Torbay who have all given me so much material in old photographs, memories, and advice to ensure that Kitty and Matt's world is as accurate as I can make it. My love also to the Coffee Crew with their unstinting support and advice, especially as I moved house while writing this book. Thanks to Katie Ginger for naming Bertie the dog.

Thank you to my wonderful editor, Emily Gowers, and everyone at Bookouture who work so hard to help the books come to life. Also huge thanks to my agent, Kate Nash, for her brilliant advice and support on all things literary.

Last, but not least, my family for the cups of coffee and mini bags of Maltesers.

Milton Keynes UK
Ingram Content Group UK Ltd.
UKHW040940191223
434643UK00006B/161

9 781800 195455